ON SHIPS
AT SEA

Also by Madelyn Arnold

Bird-Eyes

ON SHIPS AT SEA

MADELYN
ARNOLD

ST. MARTIN'S PRESS
NEW YORK

Design by *DAWN NILES*

Library of Congress Cataloging-in-Publication Data

Arnold, Madelyn.
On ships at sea / Madelyn M. Arnold.
p. cm.
ISBN 0-312-06463-2
1. Lesbianism—Fiction. I. Title.
PS3551.R53505 1991
813'.54—dc20
91-19939
CIP

First Edition: February 1992

10 9 8 7 6 5 4 3 2 1

*To Dee Sliney, best friend and best editor,
and to Stephanie Gerhardt, who loves stories*

CONTENTS

ON SHIPS
AT SEA

ON SHIPS AT SEA

There were red rhododendrons, white azaleas and apple trees down past the red Chinese tile, across the sculpted lawn, above the rippling iris. Past that sinking relic of a well house. The school Lee was looking down from had once been a luxury estate, and this morning it was as if Lee owned it. It was mete for her mood: except that the sunlight hurt.

And this head. Although she still felt fine, or rather, satisfied, since all she had to get through the rest of the morning was this study hall. And it was time to find out what those kids were doing in the back of the room. *O Cospiratori,* she thought, stifling a yawn. But first, aspirin.

She closed her eyes. Remembering.

You're getting old.

Lee leaned her hip on the metal pipe that was fixed to the wall like a dancer's bar, giving herself the pep talk you give the losing team. A black plastic ledge studded with iridescent glass ran two feet above and parallel to the pipe, the length of the discotheque and across each end. Lee's glass sat on it.

Smile past them. Smile at the floor. That's the way.

The entire level below where she was standing was the dance floor; tables lined the level above—reserved for the lucky or beautiful, who had dates. Heavy music pulsed through her shoes and straight out her eyes. . . . *It's true. If you can afford this place you're too old* . . . So beautiful, the graceful swing of hips . . . *For God's sake, don't stare.*

Ten steps below her undulated wonderful women she had not yet met.

In the center of a group of awkward kids was a sort of puppet, property of the new boy. One of the Very-Good-Family kind so much in evidence here.

He said: It wasn't *even mine, Miss Kuszcinski,* but his brother's (and he'd only borrowed it to show off) but his *brother didn't even know* and *Please don't take it, I tell you what? I'll just go put it in my locker and I won't get it out or play with it or anything—honest—*

His gray eyes were liar-wide. She didn't like to remember that some kids lie as a matter of policy, because she had never believed cynicism improved teaching. But unless she could make him look silly to his friends, he would keep this stuff up.

"Mr. Allen, I realize this is only your second week, but I want to make clear that the sophomore class doesn't have a show-and-tell . . ."

Adolescent giggles.

"We reserve that for the first and second grades. Now this poor, tired . . . dolly, or whatever he is, needs to take a little nap. . . . No, I'm not giving it to Mr. Fitzsimmons, not unless Dolly gives us another little visit—and I mean I don't want to see him unless he's *on my enrollment sheet.* Is that perfectly clear? You may pick it up after school and *give* it back to your brother."

You're in luck, kid, she was thinking, holding the ugly doll up. *I may be dead of a hangover but I'm also deliriously happy. . . . What is this thing?*

Over the last few weeks Lee had evolved rules of thumb about asking women to dance. Maybe they would; maybe they'd even talk.

First rule was: *Not if they were with men,* even with obvious faggots. Women with men were either straight or frightened. Second rule was *numbers:* Fewer than one white woman in five will dance; two out of that five will glare because you asked. Three out of five women of color will dance, and the fifth will swing at you, especially if she's black or Filipina.

Lee wanted to dance, or at least didn't want to leave without talking to someone. Where else to fish but in water. Some dancers liked her. . . . Actually, she wasn't bothered by explicit rejections, but the subtle ones got her. Women who murmured a ladylike no, then followed her progress across the bar with hate in their eyes. *It was impossible to tell just what the hell was the matter with them when all she had done was ask.*

The last students gone, chattering and touching and laughing, Lee pulled the ugly doll out of the top desk drawer and idly, bent on folding what could be folded, pulled its raised arm down. A little red-bulbed cock shot through the front of its trousers. As long as its leg. Some thoughtful student had written *struprio* on its little balls.

The doll was really remarkably ugly, a sort of Howdy Doody puppet, apparently some sort of slap at the school, or at her. Or at Latin. It had never crossed her mind that any one of them could read that much Latin.

Because the evening was ending, and having met the little redhead earlier, Lee shelved the Bar Rules. That is, she didn't have the time to get close, then closer, then buy drinks or dance et cetera, over a period of perhaps three hours, because they had already talked to each other—shouted, really, over the stool between them—had watched out for each other's drinks, all natural and friendly, because they sat close in the bar without anyone else to ask. She didn't have to observe the rules. She could ask for a dance, or talk. That was good luck.

The girl was in the merchant marine, had been dropped off straight from her ship, new in town and out to see the sights— you know. She had freckles as bright as the spangles in the ceiling. She laughed a great deal, and she really had an irritating laugh, but because the night was ending, Lee asked her to dance;

the girl *did* answer, but the music drowned her out. Lee shook her head and shouted over the music.

"Gee," said the girl, easily, "I don't usually dance, but okay—only I got to get another one of these." She tapped her glass. "It's been a dry week." She laughed again, maybe because it was Tuesday.

This very young sailor was short and wide, with kinky-curly carrot-colored hair; she laughed over every other word. She was beginning another rambling laugh when a breezy faggot with a thin mustache stopped next to them and shouted: "Last call, ladies." Lee was going to miss her dance. She hated nights when she didn't even dance once, although this girl had at least been friendly. That was good luck. "I know an after-hours place," Lee said. "There's the WE-3—"

"Hard liquor?"

"No—and it's guys, but—we could dance this one—I believe it's the last—"

"Not if it's my last drink—two." This to the waiter. "Bourbon, up, and bring her something. . . . I'm getting into the idea of, like, dancing. Sounds fun. Let's do it. Let's just load up and go."

Having talked herself around, the little sailor laughed and Lee took a double, paid their tab and was pleased enough with the night.

That last gin had hit her like a hammer, and the bumper in front had maneuvered too close while she was inside the bar. Everything blurred. "Don't ask *me* to drive," laughed the girl. "Nothing," she said. "I can't drive nothing at all. And anyway I'm a galley *cook!* Cooks don't navigate!"

Stopped by a red light a block away, Lee was relieved. Maybe if she sat still and breathed fresh air her head might clear. It was a nice night; a very dry night for Seattle. That was some kind of luck. Luck enough for a date, anyway.

"I'm Lee," she remembered to say. "Tracy Lee Kuszcinski, but everyone—"

"Lee's my *last* name. Isn't that something? Deedee Lee, but everybody calls me Dee L.—Deedee for Dulles-Dallas. Mom is from Dulles, Texas, got married in Big D. Mama lost two babies before she got me and I got two cities' worth: Big D–Little D. Seriously. She thought it was just a gorgeous name. She named one of my brothers Galveston Knight."

Riotous laugh. "But I'm not from Texas. I'm from Kentucky. Martinsville, near Grand Branch, Kentucky, about as far from an ocean—"

"Wait," bumbled Lee. The booze, the luck, the back-home talk and all. "Wait. Let me think." She breathed too loud. "I've got a grandmother in Grand Branch," she said. "And I used to live in Martinsville, Jefferson County, but I was just—I mean, that was *years*—"

"Go to a bar in Seattle and what do you meet but a dyke from Kentucky." Bell-like laugh. "Nobody's born here, everybody just moves in. I don't think," said the girl, leisurely, "I don't think I remember a single thing about anything back home anymore, I was too young. . . ."

"There's the, uh, Edison Speedway," suggested Lee. "It has the 'biggest high school field house in the contiguous forty-eight states.' . . . I'll bet I've *got* to know your family, or anyway, my grandma will, because she knows everybody born in Jefferson county for the last sixty—"

"I run off ten years ago, and we don't eggs-ackly talk—" Another laugh.

Baby-cheeked; smooth and unlined eyes: Ten years ago she would have been eleven. Maximum.

"Check flags, Captain!" laughed the girl—the light had changed.

Lee gunned the engine. But as the Ghia lurched into gear, her image of where they were heading cleared suddenly: the WE-3, a miserable hole, the original DIVE as a four-letter-word. It would be fun to impress this girl, but where do you go? With a certain chemical frame of mind, that place might be okay. Only one thing could make that place like a discotheque—tolerable, danceable, gaudy walls even pretty . . . What about it? she asked.

Fine. Smoking dope was absolutely fine. They'd go on to the WE-3 afterwards and dance a while. First they'd stop at Lee's and smoke some dope.

★   ★   ★

They must have been a little tipsier than either of them had been aware; they arrived home clear up onto the sidewalk of the Heartbreak Hotel, as the mid-gay-ghetto, slightly sagging apartments were called. Lee pushed some buttons in the combination lock, turned the knob, pushed more buttons, confidently turned the handle, pushed the door, and exactly nothing gave; the door stayed shut. The sailor burst into giggles. "You do need a navigator. I bet you've got the wrong building."

"Pick someplace with a view." Lee waved vaguely. "We'll move. Bay's over there . . ." Lee studied the lock, and pressed, and then it gave; then taking the much shorter woman by her loose jacket sleeve, she guided her into the foyer and began to maneuver her up the movie-star spiral staircase, exhilarated anew to be able to show it off, pleased by its faded opulence.

"Radical! This is, look at that, this is—*Really!*" said the girl.

The crimson thick-piled carpet, the cut-glass windows with leaded glass, colored reflections on the torn but gilded Depression-era walls. That chandelier—

"Look out!"

Lee grabbed the railing but the shouting girl caught her from behind, pulling her again off balance. Lee had missed a step and, losing the rail, fell backward into her laughing companion, who grabbed her shoulders as both swayed back. Lee sat hard as the sailor sat, too—and the arm around her chest tightened nicely, was lightly scented with a perfumed soap. The sleeve. No, the arm beneath. Woman and scent . . . they had perfumed soap at sea?

"Everything all *right?*"

The shout was formal. How many people could give an elegant *shout?*

Lee peered through the palings underneath the banister. One floor down, spatially arranged on the carpet like dancers, posed the manager and his handsome ox of a lover: overly polite, studiedly casual, upper-class Seattle: terrified of a noise or a laugh too loud. Businessmen. Such nervous, nervous young men. They should relax. The stuffed . . .

"Absolutely wonderful." Lee waved through the banister. "Everything's fine!"—and, starting to laugh, Lee set the girl off, too. And as they climbed the final flight of stairs, they both laughed "Wonderful!" at each other, swaying a little, holding each other up.

The key dropped to the floor, then she was turning it. The lights on; the big dog jumping and jumping on both of them, but he had already been walked. "Wow!" exclaimed the sailor. "Is that a purebred?"

The girl, Lee realized as she stood on her own, had been holding her upright. Very nice.

"I never saw but two dogs like this in my life. What kind is it? What a good old dog!" The girl had grabbed his silly small ears and was wooling his head around. "What do you call him? Can he do any tricks?"

"He's a Dobie," said Lee. "And kind of a big baby—he's supposed to be guard trained, I guess. . . . Get your ball, Siris— get your ball!"

The dog stopped dead; eyes and mouth gaped.

"Great trick," said the girl. "He know any others?"

". . . Magic. Food, sneakers, leather belts just—vanish!"

"A purebred dog," said the other, impressed. Then laughed.

The apartment was made peculiarly, so that they entered a central hall with floor-to-ceiling bookcases on both sides; it ran first by the bedroom, then to an L bend that turned right to the living room and kitchenette, with the bathroom exactly at the turn. The sailor was hard to maneuver past the books.

"Did you read all these?" she said. "We read a whole lot on the ship. I've been reading this book about this guy who got real rich selling these little toy spiders that walk up the wall? He didn't go to the ninth grade."

Lee handed her the marijuana, papers and a pipe. She didn't want to talk about books, or anything about schools. Tonight it was Scarlett O'Hara; she wouldn't think till tomorrow. "Here," she said. "You're the guest. You—"

"We just use joints on the ship." The girl was already working the leaf into heaps. Her hair was exactly orange, and her eyes were large and gray, and—every time she mentioned the ship—proud. "I could roll joints in the dark on a full tilt."

Lee had a notion of pelvic tilt, but lost it. She herself

couldn't even pack a pipe. "There's some wine. I have a Riesling, or—"

"You got any bourbon? Oh . . . Got a light? . . . Thanks . . . That sounds pretty good, though I'm not that big on . . . but wine sounds pretty good. Hey, this stuff is smooth. . . ."

The counter light was overhead, and on no particular pretext, Lee turned it low so that the bursts of light from the tip of the joint made the girl's pale skin flash angelic pink. Bathed in a holy glow and her own wild hair. A bust like a goddess—not like the virgin goddess. Her heavy nibs moved plainly under her shirt.

"I learned everything on the ship," said the not-Diana woman. "That's—ummm—your turn—I learned rolling joints, making knots, shooting stuff, working in the galley." She took a draught of wine, and, taking back the dope, drew it hard, then handed it over. And what did Lee do?

Lee walked around in front of the girl, who was seated on Lee's counter stool, a bar stool high above the only kitchen chair—a canvas thing; Lee took the joint, sucking on it heavily. "A teacher," she inbreathed, handing it back.

"You'd be ashamed to know me, then. I never even been. I mean, I'm not stupid or anything. But half the time I'm on board—" She laughed. "You'd be ashamed to know me."

"No I wouldn't. No," said Lee, warming up. "I'm the first girl in *my* whole family to finish the eighth grade, and to finish high school. And go to college. I'm not a snob to my own mother—"

"Well, I'm not the first one to *cook,*" drawled the girl. "But I'm sure the first one to get *paid* for it."

"I can't think . . . How did you get from Kentucky to—"

"Any more wine in there?"

Lee handed her the carafe and blew out a long white trail, handed the joint over butt first and drained her glass; at this point she noticed that she was very pleasantly paralyzed. She sat down quickly on the low chair. It was not good wine, but the dope had hit her hard. A pleasant slam—heightened sensation, bones feeling mutable and muscles in sort of a warble; exquisitely sensible between her legs, like a new tongue tasting . . .

The girl was talking. Had gone on talking about something Lee had obviously missed.

". . . and then this Carol knew somebody in Alaska, so we signed on. That's it."

The laugh begun about Alaska continued as Lee regrasped the joint. Smoke from between the sailor's lips enhanced her full and cupidbow mouth.

What if Lee simply touched her mouth to those lips? Placed this hand two inches below the inside of this hot left thigh? But that hadn't been the terms, of course that hadn't been the terms they'd come together on. That had only briefly crossed her mind this evening and not with this girl. But.

They were going dancing at the WE-3. Not that she could honor those terms—not that she was competent to drive anybody anywhere. Again the sharp butt of the roach was in her lips and she was sucking, the sailor watching, laughing, holding the roach clip for her. Titlike, the thin tip in her mouth, and she played it with her tongue, accidentally breathing wrong so embers shot in a spray of red and the sailor girl laughed. "That's enough, honey—better give it back!"

Lee objected.

She was sitting on the deck chair, and the girl on the stool was above her—full chest above her face, round thighs at eye level, sucking the joint, the tip redder and hotter, and the girl still seeming to laugh while she steadied herself against Lee. Lee covered that balancing hand with her own and heard her mouth say what she hadn't yet managed to think: "Listen. I invited you out, but do you want to make love? Just say no if you don't. But if you do, I would. I mean, sure I'd." Suddenly hearing herself, she shut herself up.

"Oh, I never thought about it. I mean, it makes sense, I just never thought about it, but . . . Sure." A laugh. "That sounds—"

Lee fitted her lips on the still-moving rounded ones and her kiss was heavy, the kiss back full, a thin tongue tickling her own. She concentrated on not letting any one of her senses be clearer than another, her hands under the girl's damp T-shirt onto the scented hot skin. Hands, no, fingernails curved up beneath her sweater, were undoing her bra; and her own fingers sculpted around the woman's shoulder blades, then forced themselves beneath the tight band of the blue jeans, sliding under the panties, till her palms were Braille-reading the smooth cool cheeks, and where she herself was touched, she was trembling: hot mouth and tongue on her neck, her ear, an electric tickle, shivering a laugh not from the tickle, but joy.

She dropped her head to the belt buckle come open, butted up under the shirt, which swung free, forward, rubbing her face on the hot skin under the round and somewhat cooler breasts, letting herself suck in the pungency of oil-and-woman. Intoxicating. She slid her face between the pendent breasts receiving her like hands, and the round flesh caressed her cheeks like thigh-wide palms: wide, smooth, smoking. It was happening again; again. The absolute very best of luck.

"Let's go," murmured the woman into her ear, and laughed. "Anyway, I'm fixing to fall off this stool." She said something hotter. Then laughed. And again, and laughter and promises. Or words. Make them promises.

Loath to stop even for convenience, Lee stood and, starting to fall, was caught; but they could neither together nor separately contrive to balance, clinging together and maneuvering so jerkily into the hall and toward the bedroom that the great dog lurched up to play. The mood broken.

"Hush!" hissed Lee. "Hush bad dog!" but under her ear the woman was laughing, teasing the dog—so Lee said, "Hush to you too!" digging her ballast in the ribs, making the woman fall in a heap on the floor, dragging Lee down with her onto the carpet. In this way (and with the negative help of the dog) Lee helped her shed her T-shirt, shed her shoes, the belt and jeans, and any lasting resistance as she staggered with her through the bedroom door.

There was a red swag lamp across from the bed, a light she only used on nights that had worked out better than dances. She switched it on, set it strobing, set the poster faces grinning like demons in hell; the mood returned and she was newly aware of the soles of her feet, light air on moist skin . . . the window. Amused neighbors. She pulled the drapes, handed over a robe, and when Sailor had enwrapped her full strong body Lee proceeded to peel away that robe. But slowed herself. What if the woman had told the truth, and didn't usually fool around like this? She looked timid, even sober, very young.

Lee shucked her last few things—the jeans, the panties—making a show of folding, taking her time, hoping to urge the mood . . . She looked up to find the other languidly draped on the bed, in her eyes that butterlike hardness. Lee turned away to throw on a nightshirt but a slap! on her bottom surprised her and the girl said, "Okay, honey, come on—" and Lee dropped the shirt on the floor.

When she dragged herself awake two hours later, knowing she had to be in class in one and a half hours, she was thinking, you can still feel it the next morning, the pressure in your cunt. And her sex smell clings to the skin of your face even after you shower, and the whole next day you can taste her juice in your mouth. Better than a photograph. And with this thought she kissed the wild-haired woman awake; who turned—throaty, murmuring, threading a lazy arm between Lee's breasts and under her arm and kissing her much too long till that heat came back, this time desperate. There was the drinking sickness but the flesh was too hungry to care, and neither one minded.

Lee startled awake—she'd passed out again and it was nearly seven o'clock—but then relaxed. This was the day her practice teacher—was his name Bennett?—was scheduled to teach by himself, and while she would customarily be there, she didn't actually have to teach before ten. (Scientific Derivatives: Latin and Greek for nonmajors). This day she would affirm what *great* faith she had in Bennett's grasp of Cicero. She had, at any rate, real faith in his grasp of Catullus.

They kissed again, holding surprisingly tenderly and carefully. Who would know when this might happen again? In the light of day, the sailor had the wide-nippled, blond breasts of a redhead. Unbelievable flesh. Unbelievably soft, soft lips. Lee kissed them, kissed them.

Lee was sitting in the study hall looking down over the red-tiled roof, and below that was the little manmade duck pond–cum–fountain. It was all green, the green of spring. She still had the taste in her mouth. Was Dee still on the ship being 'orientated,' as she put it? Maybe she was already back at her own place. There was an apartment she shared, a crash pad, actually, with three other people in shipping, or maybe in the merchant marine. This was home port; they used that apartment in this port, not usually at the same time. It wasn't a home.

Or maybe she wasn't there. Maybe the ship had sailed prematurely. The girl could be hours from port, unattainable on a ship at sea. Pert, funny with each new thing; soft and delicious, on a ship that was sailing away.

That taste in her mouth. Stop that. Look at her luck, so far: those coincidences. But it had been hours since signing on, and Dee L. hadn't answered an hour ago. Where was she now?

I never eat breakfast, Dee had said, and Charlie-whose-bar-and-restaurant-it-was had asked, *Who is this one?*

I don't feel like eating. I'm too nervous when I have to sign on a new ship. Dee was changing ships. Charlie staring, fascinated. Dykes who actually had sex fascinated him. Lee had to eat or she'd be hung like a goose for eons. The noise of kids, even of private-school kids, will kill you.

Charlie sucking on his ballpoint, looking at the girl: A new job? You ought to eat something, honey. . . . I went with this guy one time from the merchant marine. Wonder if you know him.

How about a shot of Drambuie and a couple of Irish coffees. A couple? *Yes!*—that laugh, the first time this morning. *I don't usually drink in the morning, but new ships are hell.* And another Drambuie. Then another. She had borrowed Charlie's pen and scrawled a number down for Lee. . . . The shower together had been nice. The girl was very affectionate. Her kiss fitted inside of Lee's own mouth so well. She had a tiny tattoo of jasmine blossoms high inside her left thigh. She loved the sea, truly loved the sea. They had so much in common. . . .

Driving along the maze that was the docks for commercial people in shipping, among the drydocked hulks and the buildings. Randomly there were dinghies, beached ships, alleylike cuts that led into water, for launching. Looking for 43. This way. No . . . Have you ever been here before? Oh? me neither. But it's 43, the mate last night told me they were hiring. Is that it? No, the numbers go down. There!

And with the car running and her head pounding, Lee waited for the girl to check the big number high up a Quonset-like building, next to the tightly tied prow of a battered ship. There were ten or eleven men and three or four women outside it, a grossly heavy woman inside the window of the building where they waited, two well-dressed men at her side. So this was sailing. Lee prim in her pink blouse, gray suit, makeup. Dee L. bounced back to the car and Lee rolled the window down, about to say something on the order of "bon voyage," when suddenly the girl reached down and, seizing Lee's cheeks, kissed her with a firm smack on the lips, to the astonishment of the officials on the dock. And of Lee. Then Dee was running up the gangplank, onto the ship next to the building and gone . . .

Lee could smell the girl on her hands and feel her mouth, but maybe that was only psychological. There'd been the shower, after all. So many things they had in common. Coincidences, the most amazing luck. Lee would try that number again in an hour. They'd see a movie, have dinner tonight. It would work.

The lights in her face making the dark shapes on the pulsing floor silver-edged and the shapes at the long bar bright-bodied, the faces shadowed by hair, brow, fear. How to make out cues. Being snubbed. Taking so long, so long even finding a dance. Why can't we even dance? Why not just say yes? Straight women do, and it doesn't mean anything but dancing.

Imagine coming in, and leaving with, a woman like that. The laughter. Imagine not having to go in that place at all. Supper, evenings like that every night of your life . . .

Her attention stopped and focused on a woman at the long bar—seemingly relaxed but tense eyes: right thumb hooked in hip pocket, left arm casually akimbo, drink half gone—Lee had earlier made for her up the ramp and stairs from the dance floor, up short twisted stairs and railings and women leaning, most of them lithe, in front of a forty-yard hip-to-seven-foot mirror—crowded, not touching. A blank stare: You misunderstand me. And the music blasting: I want to make make make sweet love to you. . . . Why can't we talk; why can't we at least dance? Making every little social thing so cheeseparingly difficult . . .

On the fourth ring someone answered and at first Lee's heart stopped; then it speeded and speeded up until she thought it would explode through her chest like shot.

The newly arrived redhead was clearly enjoying the bar hugely—the lights, the women. A redhead. Lee staring at her. Figuring chances of getting a redheaded woman to dance. Maybe. She had never worked out any equation for that. Maybe that was good luck.

Maybe she was reading the number wrong, it was such a scrawl.

"That's this number, lady, but there's no D—anybody. Just me and my brother."

Luck.

Lee walked consciously upright back to her classroom, automatically starting to check if her wallet was missing, but why? Wasn't last night good enough for whatever she paid? Why question things? God, God . . . On her way out of the study hall, on her way to her extracurricular session, on the way to the auditorium to sit through another wonderfully stupefying session of the Latin club, she almost passed the piece of notebook paper by. She knew she should just go on walking. She knew that it would be the written equivalent of the doll, and she wasn't in the mood—didn't want to recognize the handwriting, didn't think she could handle one more insult. But she had been teaching too long, and picked it up off the floor reflexively . . . a number.

Was it possible that she had had another number in her jacket pocket, was it possible that she had dropped this one at the door to the classroom, juggling her books? She remembered juggling her papers. Or that, given her intoxication, earlier in the evening she had collected the other phone number; or she'd had that number in her pocket forever, some plumber or Ghia repairman. This phone number was in red and, like the other, without a name, and hadn't Dee written in red? She seemed to remember that Charlie had written in red and had lent his pen and she wouldn't be going back to the bar tonight, or at least not alone. The kid was smart, she could give her a chance for restaurant work—or schooling or whatever she wanted. Lee could at least make a home for her when she was in port. She had left so young she'd never really had a home. Just like Lee. This girl was absolutely nothing like the other ones. Lee was lucky, and she knew this number would ring.

ONE MORE TIME, MARIE

12:30 A.M., THURSDAY

Opening the cupboard, Claire took down a can of soup, a box of crackers, and a tin of Spam. Where were the pans . . . ? Marie kept them . . . must be in the oven. She removed a skillet and saucepan and set them down on the rickety little table that served for food preparation. She found the can opener. Surprisingly, it was hanging on a nail. What to do first? No, not open a can, heat the skillet. Should she grease it? She couldn't remember. It had been too long.

Claire hauled open the refrigerator and stared at the too-many things inside: mayonnaise, milk, ketchup, sour wine, two cans of beer, bologna, cheese, wrapped things . . . (what?). Some sort of pickles. She was still perfectly capable of cooking for herself or a family (when she had been young all girls cooked) but why not wait?

She left hanging the question, *Wait for what?*, ate a cracker and drank half a beer, then lay down, suddenly sick to her gut, and was out cold.

★ ★ ★

What had happened was that they hadn't liked the movie and so had decided to have a drink, had parked in exactly the same place they always did. Their nights at the bar were infrequent. Was that incautious? People didn't know you that way. . . .

They had always stayed away from police. The times when the shop was broken into, they had always tried to avoid calling the cops, but this. They called, and the cops afterward told Claire what she herself had said, but in fact she did not remember the blows, how Marie had been—but thank God, thank God, no thanks to the goddamn SLPD—then all the questions and Marie's crying out. A heart attack. A heart. And what do the sons of bitches want to hear about but money. That's a hospital for you, like those, that piece of filthy—only without a gun!

The questions. About Claire's relationship to Marie, to that old woman in Surgery, she had snapped, "Business partner." And the ER people had written, *none*.

"None?" This to the Bright Young Man who worked in Intensive Care. This after she herself had been released from treatment. "What do they mean, *'none'* down in that looney bin? They get nothing right. I say she can't take that Lasix, her doctor says so, and I come up and if they're not about to give it to her! Said there was nothing against it on her chart. *No* relationship. Did anything else get wrote up right?"

After which the Young Man typed in *Friend* on Marie's papers for whatever. "Next of kin?"

In fact, Marie did have a next of kin, a brother in Chicago Marie hadn't seen in thirty years—a short, prognathic little thug of a man, who made you think of Mafia. Years ago he had said, stay out of his way. Which eventually had faded. He'd just got too tired to hate and gave it up; sent them a picture last Christmas of himself dressed as a silly imitation of a young buck, marrying again. The girl not quite half his age. What if he was ready to be the next of kin, decided to crowd her out, make the bad decisions? And Claire felt like hell, herself. Her face hurt.

"Next . . . ?"

"Wait, just wait, dammit!" she snarled, but he was not even mildly put out. Waited patiently, casually, helpfulness in the flesh. Of course if she didn't tell about the brother or even Leon they'd probably tell her more, but right's right, blood's thicker.

And this was the last time this could ever happen. That much she knew without being morbid, or superstitious, or boastful. St. Louis was rough—but always before they'd been lucky. Maybe they had thought by now their age would actually protect them better, but the charm had worn off; they were both too old and this was the very last time.

"Me," she snapped.

"Relationship?"

"Sister!"

"You must understand. We need a next of kin for legal matters."

How have a man in such a job? A clean job—cheat some poor girl out of a decent job. How old was he, twenty? She wouldn't explain. This was Missouri, and charity didn't mean herself and Marie.

As kin, she gave their lawyer's name and the smiling boy typed *friend* about her. *Friend.*

All that had gone on was that they hadn't liked the movie and so had decided to stop at the Karavan, had decided to have a drink. The Kar was exactly the same as it had been for years (well, with new decor), the same as back when the bar was Zenobia's and before that, the Alakazar. They had parked in exactly the same place they always did, exactly the same distance from the door (and the bouncer) and in clear sight of the bar, but statistics had caught them. Muggers, the cops had called them, but she called them filthy cocksuckers. She called them worse. Fury tore in, but its force rent only her because she was herself hurt, her nose broken and her face bruised, which was why the packed ice, and her padded wrist actually was broken. But Marie . . . Marie, Marie.

As if Claire herself didn't look like hell. Dried blood all over her face, swollen blue-black—white bandages across her nose like a bandit, the adhesive pulling loose on both sides. Except where blood glued it to her skull, her hair stood straight up. Hadn't there been a time when a hospital cleaned you up? Or maybe that was only in the movies.

She ran water into the basin and, finding the sound intensely comforting, wetted a towel and began to gently, carefully, pat the bloody night off her face. No, she had told the police, she had not seen them clearly, but not one of them had been black, or not very black at least, and she would have scratched the memory out of herself. If somebody in the bar hadn't screamed to high God—

Look at that hair. Thin and coarse like a Brillo pad, always had been thin; well, now it wasn't thin but sparse, and one day from behind her Marie had said, *I tell you what, honey. The day you turn sixty-five we're going to chop off all of that fringe and I'm going to get you a real nice Elvis wig. You always did look cute in a DA.*

In spite or maybe because of her appearance, the intensive-care young man bent the rules and, only for a minute, she was inside. Which restriction might have been pronounced even for family.

Walking into the room Claire had most been aware of a gentle sort of *shh-click, whiiii,* from a dozen sites, in random order around the room. In front of, behind curtains. With difficulty, she recognized Marie against the far wall, and frowning to clear her eyesight she could not be rid of the sense that Marie had a trunk like an elephant. Marie liked the zoo, she would think that was pretty funny. Wait till she heard—

Someone kept trying to ask Claire what she was doing. She was breathing.

12:30 P.M., THURSDAY

Claire found herself on her feet, answering the heavy banging down the hall, aware that it was now broad day—shambling to the door in an undershirt over a sundress, leaving her glasses on the back of the commode and her teeth in a jar by the bed; Claire did not realize that she was in fact awake and the knocking door would likely have somebody on the other side. She was never the one to answer. As she opened the door full out to let in the light from the hallway, she heard rather than saw the dumpy person in front of her, heard that little "oh!" delivered for nearly all occasions around Claire, knew it was her sister's girl, Janine, who blew hot and cold on saving Claire's soul. As if it helped, she usually brought her kids.

Miss Kitty Kat must have thought she brought them too, skiting past Claire's huaraches in a Great Escape. Without her glasses Claire lurched into the hall after all that she was capable of seeing, which was a black streak against a red rug.

"I'll get her, Aunt Claire," sighed Janine, and down the hall there was a squeal as her little girl spied the nice kitty and grabbed, unfortunately with real good aim.

Claire carried in the spitting Miss Kitty and dumpy, patient Janine carried in the screaming child, raked across both hands.

"I'll stick her in the back," yawned Claire, continuing down the hall. She meant Miss Kitty. "You stay with your ma," she said firmly to the boys, who, abashed, hung back a full second. About this point she realized how her own face looked, that they were horrified.

Once in the bedroom, Claire kissed the cat on the ear, squeezed her and bowled her under the bed, from which she glared as the now shoeless boys tore in and out from the hallway, sliding on Marie's waxed wood floor in stocking feet. Claire was now awake to the way she looked. No use looking jakier than your fate. Bending over the Jacobean nightstand, she fished her teeth out of their jar, and making horrible faces, thrust them into her jaws—jerked them out—shoved them in—to the horrified delight of her grandnephews.

And having done the right things as soon as she could find the tea, she demanded, "To what do I owe the honor, anyway?"

Janny wouldn't drink her tea; it was what she gestured with. "It's about last night." She sighed.

"What?" snapped Claire. "What do you mean, what do you know about it?"

"Dear. Well. The eleven o'clock news? Right after the Cardinals . . . I'm so sorry about—"

"What goddamn news? What in hell are you—"

"Please . . ."

Janny meant, of course, the little angels—two of whom had collared some of Marie's figurines, of which several hundred were arranged upon frail maple corner-brace shelves. Seeing

Claire's face, Janny made the kids put down a shepherdess and several slightly sticky lambs.

"About the mugging," she resumed, forgetting to sigh. "Channel Six said this strongarm ring that preys on . . . I called the hospital and they told me you were out. I didn't know if you needed anything. Maybe I could cook you a meal."

Claire was blowing smoke out her ears, furious.

"Hmm," sighed Janny. "I wanted you to see that you can call on your family to—"

"My family! There's cabs, they're cheaper, and there's takeout Chinese, too. Family! I don't need any help from you. I've been lower than Satan's spit to my family for forty years—" Her blood pressure. She slowed herself. "*Family* told me in 1945 to get blanked and they won't get a goddamn out of me. If you think I'm giving up and giving you the store, you got one other think coming, you hear? I've left the kids a little something and there's *nothing* for your ma and *nothing* for you and George, and you tell your ma that. It won't work, and we don't need help—" The words hooked in her throat.

Up, Marie. For God's sweet sake, get up—

3:45 P.M., THURSDAY

By the shouting, she knew it was Leon downstairs. That boy could not ask nor answer a question in a reasonable tone of voice, not once in the last forty years. It came to her that she had not been down in the shop all day, and that buyers were coming around to look at some new estate stuff. *Estate.* And for some of the auction stuff, she had a warehouse full, and here came Marie's idiot nephew. Marie, diplomatic Marie, Marie took care of the talk part. . . .

Claire shook off the robe and the Mother Hubbard and slid on some slacks and a blouse. It was almost four, but she stopped and again called the hospital—no change, no anything. She made to leave, still wearing the huaraches.

Instead of walking down the front stairs, onto the street, and hauling herself in the front doors of Marclar Antiques—as she customarily did for the simple reason that her baby-elephant entrance gave Pat and Louey the time to snap to and look intelligent—she climbed out the kitchen window onto the fire escape and stepped down onto the office window ledge, practically onto the old black Standard. She squeezed her bulk in the big window, over the ledge and onto the floor, and in the next second or so Felix, one of the movers, the part-timer, stuck his head in under the curtain and stayed to stare, bug-eyed. Not at her entrance. For a moment she entertained the notion that they were all doing something illegal or expensive out in the showroom. Then Claire remembered her face.

"What are you gawking at?" she croaked; not her usual bark.

"Hell, Claire—what the hell? You okay? You have an accident? You call the cop—"

"Say," she snapped, "you doing the news?"

She did not have to look in another mirror. But with the way her clerk and the movers kept looking at her, she finally, huffily, moved into the lavatory she and Marie had declared was for women, and surveyed the taped nose, bruised eye (it wasn't going to shut, she thought) the small bruise on the point of her chin—that shouldn't have happened. She hadn't been that easy to deck, not ever. Time was—drake's-tail, jacket, scar next to her eye (from barbed wire when she was about six)—nobody screwed with this one. Assholes at the station, ugly mugs on the street. It helps to be *ugly*. But hurts your feelings sometimes . . .

The last time anybody'd cold-cocked her was her brother, in '45; their only real argument. He had brought Marie home a few times from the Wayne Avenue USO, but she'd kept coming out to the pantry. The giggles . . . That was a fight. Before that, everybody knew Claire as just ugly, unmarriageable. . . . In 1965 he had died of cancer. No, it was later.

There was a time, back then, when you tried to explain yourself.

Actually she was never much of a fighter, she was just ugly. Nothing to be done with *this* face. But that nose. She had always hated that dough-lump German nose. Wouldn't it just be great if it healed distinguished? Marie would say—

Get up, honey. Marie . . .

Claire headed out of the small room dizzy, but straightened when she saw they were all staring at her. Mournful to make her crazy. Louey, Pat, Felix . . . the bookkeeper, Alice—behind her that ape, Leon. Hell, couldn't he learn to smile? Or get himself glasses? Not a bad businessman in his own right; owned a hardware store up north. Reasonable type, but what did he know about auctions? About styles? And what was he messing with that estate junk for?

"Well, what do you want?" This to Leon.

"Wanted to know, do you want that shellac. Got a half drum. That and I was in the area—" He was looking around; crates in the middle were opened. "Aunt Marie go out?"

The veins swelled froglike in her throat, in her temples. "Don't play dumb with me! You could have had the decency to wait. She ain't dead yet!"

His jaw dropped.

"I don't believe that innocent act! Not for one moment do I believe that innocent act! Wait—damn you, wait! You're the heir all right, but wait!"

Oh, he would inherit. They had never been able to work around the *unsound mind;* if they had anything, a will would go to court and the family would win; survivorship had seemed too far away. And you couldn't borrow money in both names—not until you already had a *business* partnership. Besides, it was Claire and her blood pressure scheduled to ship out first; and the place hadn't been supposed to do that well. Because they had bought into the building and fixed it up; then bought out the store, and before their handling it had always lost money. That part of the block would be a tax writeoff, but they worked too hard. First Marie had quit her job and filled in—her mom and dad had been in the furniture business. Marie knew all the styles, the fix-ups, the polish—then Claire had quit the railroad—did minor repairs, putty and shoe polish, built the inventory. They had so well absorbed their losses that the insurance two years in a row actually *dropped.* Marie knew markets. . . .

But auctions: Those were Claire's. Shoving through, hat over brow—she loved her effect on the thick-headed farmers. Gab and grab—*no*body elbowed Claire out. She got just about anything she had ever set her hat for.

Maybe Leon *didn't* know, and she should say. Maybe Leon

really didn't know. It was his right. And he would inherit half; maybe she should say—

No.

He can have the place, but her grief . . . No, the *hell* he could have this place!

5:30 P.M., THURSDAY

They had parked in exactly the same place they always did. Though the place had changed, Lord. The Mafia used to keep it safe. Making it legal, now *nothing* was safe. The bars were different. It used to be, at the bar you dropped your outside mental clothes and were easy in yourself. This was your home. Now bars were just a place you went when you needed to remember you were garbage. Lower-class. (Equals butch and femme—equals old.) Their old bar at the same place had had a pink neon parrot and a sign that said, *We made an agreement. The bank don't give drag shows and this bar don't cash checks.* Now these new bars with the cute ways, the ferns and loud music so you couldn't talk but you didn't need to try to. Nobody to listen, couldn't find even half the friends you had known all your life, and the men and women were strictly separated. And the ages too. Bartenders didn't see you even if they knew you had good money, not if you're no spring chicken. Better to be a pretty, young deadbeat. But it always had been better to be pretty and young. She herself had been privy-plain, while Marie—

We were so hot, then. Oh, it was bad of course, but back then they were actually afraid of us, stayed out of our places. Queers had their sections; dangerous for us down certain streets—but me and that haircut. Bull dagger, bull dyke, butch, *Les*bian . . . *Gray* Panther.

She smiled her most horrible smile at the mirror, giving up on her hair, and stepped out into the muted lighting of the unit, where the first thing she noticed was the shhhhh-click!-ing around her.

"Ms. Kohler?"

He was either from deeper south, or women's lib had made him hypocritical.

"How's she doing?" Claire mumbled. Her mouth swollen, the cheap teeth hurt her.

"No change," said a brisk nurse.

Said the Young Man, "Well, she might have been briefly conscious. It's hard to say with—"

Claire froze. "She said something?"

"She isn't able to say anything. She has a tracheal tube," corrected the nurse. "What she was probably doing was an involuntary—"

"You mean she *tried to* say something—did—"

"We were clearing the trach and Dr. Findalito said it looked a little like she was moving her eyes. That was about . . . half an hour . . . Please understand that this is not the same thing as her being conscious, of course, but there were some indications. We haven't been checking any electrical functions but cardiac—"

"Take it out. Take that tube out of her—"

Objections.

"For a minute. Just for a minute so I can ask her about—" What. What do you say. "Business. She's my— We own a store. I've got to ask her about some business—" Ask her Leon's cut. Something.

"It's not a matter of simply removing the tube." They spoke slowly, evenly. Teachers of the not-too-bright. "She cannot talk or move. She has had medicine that completely relaxes her muscles. When a patient has been intubated, the curare—"

"That's poison." She had read this in a Perry Mason novel. "Curare, that's, that's a suffocating—"

"Without relaxed breathing muscles, she might waste the strength she does have fighting the respirator. Mrs. Kohler—"

"Ain't she doing bad enough already, and now you go and *poison* her?"

"It is only given because—"

"She can't talk with it. She can't talk. Is she going to live? Is she going to get better? Is she going to get to say anything first?"

Silence.

"Take it out, then! Maybe she wants to talk!"

"Ah, with permission of the next of kin—"

"That's me! I give permission. I— That woman has just

spent the last forty-two years of her life with me, nobody but *me* in the same bank account, in the same damn bed. If there's anything she's got to say, it's to me! *No*body, *no* kin is as close, nobody in this world—take it out!"

"Well, you see," they said politely.

Which meant, Nothing. They probably understood, but what of it.

7:00 P.M., THURSDAY

She couldn't stay long.

She had guessed finally that you could visit only one at a time, so the very first relative visiting would displace her. That would be Leon. He'd get off work, go to supper, drive down to the middle of St. Louis. Down to displace her.

Wake up.

By now everybody would know what had happened; they'd be rushing forward with sentimental claims, grasping fingers.

Claire had spent the last hour and a half shaking violently through her thoroughly imperfect memory, trying to think what were the last words she had heard Marie say. About the movie? Neither of them had liked it. . . .

Head ringing with how dangerous you are. Marie was the girl in the dark piqué and Claire with her brother's massive old Dictator with the muffler that fell off in the middle of the night out in front of Marie's. So much for elopement. How dangerous they were. (And there had been others before and over the years, and for both of them, but they never except once discussed it. Claire had cried that time, cried all night. That wasn't like her.) When it had all come out, Marie had lost her ticket-selling job downtown—which was just as well. Too many rumors. When everybody'd found out, Claire was banned from her mother's house, her little sisters looking through the fence. Didn't look back. She had disciplined herself to think how she was lucky to keep her job with the railroad, growing a fine crop of ulcers wondering when it would all fall in. What attention she and Marie had commanded, for nothing much. Never thought dangerous now. Now dykes and queers gave sucker lines on sitcoms. Only one way to command much attention now.

At the store, as she was leaving, she had heard Leon asking what shape the books were in.

★ ★ ★

In and out with that elephant thing, Claire was breathing with her. Shhhh . . . click! Shhhh . . . click! —*Open your eyes. Open your eyes and show me who I am. Say my name. Only one more time.*

OUR LITTLE JUDY

It was simply that Bailey didn't come, and didn't come, and didn't come to the bar—and Jude was left alone, not something that had happened often in her seventeen years—which had made Jude smile at that woman in the first place; it was that she was left, temporarily, without a meal or a ride or a place to stay. Temporarily. She could have gone to her mom's. In theory she still did that. But for now, with a satisfying sense of ill-treatment, she was *A*-period *LONE*-period, and hungry in the neon of the Stroh's sign and the hot-pink Wurlitzer that was playing "Teddy Bear." *They,* and she meant dykes, looked at her differently; looked at her slantwise with eyes that said *Now let's see. What is this here?* And that one woman asked her to dance.

Bailey had sort of caught her on the bounce from her first. Jude's first was Christine, a girl in her high school who could never make up her mind and say what she wanted or didn't want, including Jude. Especially Jude. Then Christine went out with Salvatore Breslichi and they got drunk enough that she liked it. And that was that. So after the Suicide Attempt, and in

Muncie General's ER, Jude had met Bailey—first name, Renee—who'd just wiped out on a very rough road and needed several pecks of it removed. Bailey, colored, passed as Eye-talian, called Jude *baby* (not like in *sweetie*) and was something like thirty years old. Bailey *called all the shots,* meaning Bailey herself never took off her clothes. Jude thought with righteous opportunism that Bailey had probably run into that Susan Creetch she'd used to go with. . . .

Then that one woman asked Jude to dance, twice; and when she'd bought her a Mars bar and some drinks and ciga-rettes, and asked one more time, this time with her hand on the inside of Jude's thigh, Jude had got the idea. This was what mostly happened to the prettiest guys. Jude was *attractive.* Hot and heavy. That could mean *dough.*

It was about eleven o'clock, and this was a slow dance, and the woman, whose name was Lena, kept her arms close around Jude's arms and kept touching her backside, which was nice.

Laughing and hot against Jude's ear, the woman breathed: "What's your name, little girl?"

Jude told her.

"Well little Judy—"

"*Jude,*" said Jude. "I really hate that name." She meant Judy—like the movies and that pretty-pretty stuff. Though she knew she herself was pretty, and she liked that.

"I tell you, let's get a little more private, hon. . . . How about something to eat? I know this nice little French restau-rant. . . ."

"Okay," said Jude airily. "Only you'll have to buy. Is that okay?"

The woman laughed. So did several other people. "What kind of money do you want?" A laugh. "Or do you just want another candy bar?"

A pleasant surprise, like the valentine you wanted. Jude was offered *money,* and that was certainly better than admiration. Something else that had never happened before. Jude said, *Um, twenty-five bucks,* which was five dollars more than she had ever seen at one time, and the woman laughed. Then they were out of the bar to a big white Chrysler and Jude was self-satisfied that someone would be sure to tell Bailey everything.

★ ★ ★

This Lena kept saying how pretty, how sexy she was. . . .

Jude had never done it quite like this before. She'd been with Christine, Bailey, and a few of Bailey's friends to whom Bailey for some reason had owed favors (and who were pretty boring, but Jude was usually drunk). But not with somebody nobody knew. A stranger. And with money.

Little Jude put what would probably happen out of her head and made herself content to follow the older woman out of the car and up the apartment steps without predicting. It was more thrilling this way. She was shown down a dark hall that felt, as she walked, as if there were sharp-nosed things around her in the dark; and then she went two flights up a dusty staircase with a tatty carpet on which she could see the checked design in the light that came in through stairwell windows.

Having fussed up a key, the Lena woman threw a door back; hers was a surprisingly large apartment swept with the rustle and clicketting of delicate feet till the lighting had settled on the floor. There was an entire wall of heavy dull books, very dull. There were nice furniture and rugs upon rugs upon beautiful golden-weave rugs, some on the walls with other hangings. Jude followed Lena obediently into the back hall.

"Here, honey," said Lena, businesslike, "take that off." She only meant everything. "Put these on."

These were hose—Jude hated hose—a thin, brief silk skirt, and a tight matching blouse. Stiletto heels, black. Other things that tightened and made small bulges of thin skin.

The bed was candy-blue with a fat red pillow in the middle and the shiny comforter folded down pie-shaped, to expose the overstuffed lace pillows. "All right," said Lena, forcefully. "Now you slip into those and get more comfortable."

This was intended to be seductive, Jude guessed, for the woman turned and placed her hands on the bones below Jude's waistband as if upon a doll or figurine, and lightly kissed the crown of Jude's head. And Jude so slipped; then wandered past the window as if it were a mirror. She looked down at the black patterned hose she was supposed to wear and be sexy in, wondering if those were her legs, but then Lena's fingers were on her buttons—clumsily, jerkily—and the material was half pulled out of the skirtband as what she had just carefully done was being undone. Jude wondered if she should reach out to Lena, but the busy hands pushed her away.

"I'll be right back," Lena promised, slurring her words. She turned on a point, toward the bath; marched toward it. Little Jude kicked off her shoes, and looked at the hose; should she take them off? And she began to, but Lena came back in again. "What are you doing?" she demanded. "That's for me—I paid for it. I ought to spank you for that."

By her face, she was serious; and Little Jude felt her bottom squeezing protectively together. Lena was a good deal larger, and with the air of authority of someone much older and in an impressive profession. She was a court recorder.

"I was impatient for you," said Jude, breathless, and reached over to play with Lena's blouse, but Lena sat instead, and suddenly all Jude's view was entirely of the bedspread, and her flesh cooled into a sweat as suddenly the skirt and slip were up and the tight garter belt pulled down, leaving her flesh barely covered by the lacy black panties. She was wet with fright but with her sex welling and tender, flesh trembling. She hardly knew if she more wanted or more was afraid of what she wanted. She did not fight.

Smack! Smack! Smack! Each slap burned her bottom lightly, making her catch her breath, forcing a sound, an unfamiliar whimper in her throat. She had never known herself to make that sound before and was rather pleased with it. When it stopped, her flesh was throbbing.

"Now that was delightful," said Lena firmly. "I'm sorry I didn't think of the hairbrush first, though."

Little Jude allowed the woman to push her onto her feet and strip off the skirt, the slip, letting them ring down her thighs; then kneel, and, reaching around her waist, mouth below the garter belt and blowing warm air into the thick private hair, unsnapped the garters. Below Little Jude's eyes was the crown of Lena's head, the heavy lips working against her thigh, and again she was shocked, this time at the burning following those lips, shocked at the intensity, amazed at her own rising heat. She shifted, then squirmed. She could not be passive like she was paid to be; her breath came hard. And then came the slow skinning-down of the stockings, the fingers and tongue all over the inside of her legs—now up and hot, tapping her swollen knob. Then fingers, there seemed to be so many, the waves from one rolling over the shocks from others; shaking, she was laid back on the bed, her hot back on the cool satin sheet and Lena's cool, soft, heavy flesh fitted down over her breasts, over her aching flesh, and her arms were crushing that great burden into her, her whole body a sucking kiss.

Jude must have dozed. She awoke, looking up at the silk-paper parrots in the canopy over the bed, and tried to recapture that heat. That intensity. But she knew the woman now. Instinctively she knew that the second time would be self-conscious, that the second time Lena might expect more, perhaps want Jude to return the favor and kiss all the way down herself. Disgusting.

And Jude had made sounds; she had never heard of making any sounds before and now she was really uneasy. There were little bitchy things between them now, items that made thoughtful the unthoughtful pleasure of sex. With which she was disgruntled, anyway. No sex before had felt like much. With *that*, with a pleasure idea added to it, sex could interfere with things. She could see it cutting parts from her life she wanted concrete goods from.

Then she remembered. Lena blowing against the inside of her leg. All the way; she could like that again if she didn't know who did it. . . . She could like that from someone who offered tangible things. . . .

Passing through the silver-wallpapered living room Jude saw above the curved mantel a straight shelf with what looked like little animals, and on closer inspection saw across the shelf a red scarf with three shiny appliqued giraffes with white and silver on them and on top of this a little mother-of-pearl and wire toucan, the bill milky blue-white. She was charmed. Probably, the Lena woman would give it to her if she asked, but she might not; so Jude plucked it down and turning, there was the woman glaring at her. Genuinely angry. Jude felt a thrill, but with the sinking sensation that there wouldn't be any more play.

* * *

It was 3:35, just before closing, and Bailey's battered Dodge was outside the bar by the door. The Dodge, not her Harley. Jude didn't stop. Bailey would be thinking of her in an entirely different way: Jude didn't have to worry about details. She had learned too much.

Jude had come back to the bar in a taxi, and it was more like coming home than going to anywhere else. Thin dirty streets with thin ugly men against the brick buildings. Places where Bailey and she and the rest could strut. Across from the bar was the courthouse, no lights on the lawn and the overheads blocked by the heavy trees, with bushes along the sides. These were a "tea room," in warmer weather. There was also a wrecked house trailer along the west side, away from the entrance, which right now served as the men's toilets. The men's inside had been in the basement, which had flooded, while the women's was on the main floor of the courthouse proper. The trailer was a tea room, too. She had had to ask what a tea room was one time but now—this one night and everything hot was all her very own. Jude was the queen of the business.

Bailey was a picture. She stood brooding, surrounded by the bartender and her empties; seeing Jude, Bailey fixed her with such a drunken and enraged look that Jude stopped dead. Bailey's eyes looked bloody. Jude took in thoroughly the look on her face and the thought of the money failed . . . She didn't *have* the money! She had in fact forgotten to ask: That was what that *feeling* could do to you. And later, of course, it hadn't seemed wise to ask.

And Bailey roared: "And where the hell have *you* been all night?!"

Two old queens, a dyke couple and an old bum, the last few drunks in the bar, were prepared to enjoy this. Probably they were hoping for a really good fight.

"I get a bum carburetor and you split with some bitch in a fancy—"

The exact right sound for Wounded Love. As a usual thing Jude would have loved the attention, but her head ached. And *no money*. She would have looked so *sexy* with the money. . . .

"—treating me like shit, you hear—?"

"Oh just shut the hell up," snapped Jude. "I'm smarter

than you think and I don't want to hear another blessed word! Do you hear?"

Bailey stared, bug-eyed.

Jude screamed *"Do you hear?"* again and stopped. And thought of parrots.

ASHES, ASHES

from the pen of Myra Leah Mitzik
"Mitzi Laing"

September 11, ———

Margaret Dillon
Oceanside Theatre Project
Levy and Sullivan Productions
Attn: Props,
Box 394
Meadlin, MA

Dearest Meg—
    1) The skirt came. A 10 . . . ! Now that was sweet, really. . . .
    2) I was sorry to hear about Georgia.
    3) A letter.
    A typed letter, in fact. I do care: I got this roll of manila

towels so I wouldn't edit, just tear and send. Got the idea from this science fiction writer. I promise you I really will mail *something* before the holidays. About My Life.

Let Georgia think things out. She was never on her own before, really. If you want me to talk to her . . . Except I don't think she would listen to me.

Well. *Here* I am. Understudy for Doctor of Fine Arts. Sounds—

Well. *Here* I am. The campus is much the same, somewhat weedier. More chipped paint, and the students are all eleven or twelve or foreign. The brick is smokier, the cupolas odder, and the architecture looks somewhat sillier than I remember from when *we* ran it, but then perhaps you have a crueler memory, dear. I like the dolphins doing whatever-it-is to Venus. I think I remember you didn't, but it's only a *statue.*

There are the sort of flowers flowering that flower in the fall, and trees heavy with green persimmons—I had forgotten. I seem to remember we were all crazy about them (and you had that terrific sauce, very buttery and caramelly; or was that Annie?).

The nights are already cool. Top limbs on the highest ridges sport red-edged leaves already—it's fall, my favorite. The season when I *always* fall in love—and *yes!* Don't you know that I already *have,* dear?

(What an intro! I tell you I'm *inspired*—)

This was *exactly* the thing to do, and the place to do it— there's a game I played with myself as a little girl. I think I got it out of the comics—it goes: *This time (tomorrow / after the mail comes / next year in Israel) what will I be remembering?*

But I know. She is worth the absurdity of this whole costly escapade (except for the cast of thousands. It's still crowded here, if less so than in our teens: and at these rates). I don't know if it will work out like with Annie but . . . *I'm in love.*

About (name. rank. serial) Jean Beledin Meir, Bryn Mawr; Jesus College, Oxford; Columbia (et al.), bespectacled linguistics scholar, pianist supreme: She is everything I ever hoped to find. Wise, cool, skilled like Annie. I hate plotting, fantasizing (except *in medias res*); I suspect it distracts me from the immediate pleasures of life (my seniors are doing *Oklahoma!*—also *Murder in the Cathedral* [and *guess* who's come here to be Becket??? No. NOT ME]). But.

About Jeannie. Fantasizing in *me* of all people, the one who Acts Out.

And you see, regarding Jean, sexual attraction is knit into the romantic or the intellectual, or all intersect in such a way that I can't remember which was first, which is a drag. Because she's God knows worth presenting in all and any areas.

MONOLOGUE

A grave, black/sleek-haired 28-year-old scholar. Doesn't look as much like a woman as Annie; where she's, as you might say, Diana, I'm your Demeter. Or Venus. Or Phyllis Diller.

There are breasts: small and, I think, tender. Translucent skin, a slightly beaked, freckled nose, and large brown eyes that behind thin rims catalogue as if calling upon the world for a thorough accounting—punctuated. Thin and tall, she sometimes shows a silly sense of humor that embarrasses her so that she taps her lips with one hand. Though she moves from her hips she's slightly awkward, and has long, tapered hands, which she keeps hidden, as if something they might do could betray her. Her mouth is small, her lips are on the thin side; often, when she smiles, one side crooks—she very seldom smiles so that her dimple shows. Her earlobes seem palpable as small fruits.

Quiet, self-contained; when she has her head turned away, that's when she examines one. Comes and goes alone almost always; too modest. But when she's talking of things classical or of one of her older brothers, she has this little shoulder motion—a swagger becoming the boy in *Touch of the Poet*. The *Fancy-Somebody's-Little-Sister* look.

(I sat in on one of her scholarly seminars; she talked modestly to the podium and ironically at the aisle. . . .)

SEPTEMBER 25

A LITTLE BACKGROUND. WITH NARRATION.

We met at an Official Graduate Student Introduction Thing about the time I was telling myself things like "We were *all* that age once," telling myself that in another twenty years I'll be even older, and besides, things going the way they are, you'll need an M.A. to work *stock*—and it's not a sure thing now—when appeared to me this spirit, kindred in angst. Old, like me, was Jeannie, and a high school teacher. And we had barely exchanged anxieties when simultaneously we met an insistent Brit who recognized my last name as my first name—about whom, more later. Jeannie (who Reads Books, bless her) never could have. Jeannie was standing at the long fireplace (inlaid patterns, ruddy oak), her pale face framed perfectly as in a cameo. A long-necked beauty.

I was well done (not like I was, but the stuff is everywhere. Free. Doesn't fuck up performance.)

I was praying this sultry Diana wouldn't pop-bang-flash and disappear, and after a laugh and exchange-of-departments (yawn), asked her name and squealed, "Like the Israeli president!" (It was, wasn't it??)

Then the wind blew over our Brit friend, Sharon Blake—"Oops, now! Not like *the* Blake!"—a portly, cheerful little earful of an overeager first-year graduate who stood exactly between us. Got us babbling on teaching and cats, while from her port and starboard our "I'm one, are you?" looks sailed past her, finding no harbor.

But nothing from Jeannie. She wasn't telling. She has a comely "Are you?" look—large eyes under dropped lashes—copper-brown eyes. Wide eyes.

She comes to us fresh out of a stint as prep school English teacher. She has the most elegant *disapproving look*. The serious type.

And we did see each other in the next week—sort of. That is to say, I was in rehearsal (*Romeo* etc.: freshmen and sophomores). For the next two weeks, Jeannie and I saw each

other in the teachers' lounges and hallways, in the Poor Rela-
tions Section of the faculty club; we were always smiling, eye-
brow-raising, shrugging, waiting to talk in private.

We had rather tentatively signaled ourselves as gay, and
Sharon Not-*the*-Blake always surfaced—it was like wearing shark
bait. I think we were the only single women she has ever met, and
she wished to commiserate—dragging happily several dozen of
her very closest friends (usually male, O-T-B Germans—oh, you
know, "off the boat"). Frequently, this would happen just as
Jeannie and I had found a secluded booth in the faculty club back
bar, and then this entourage would greet, join and roost between
us: after which I would natter, chat and hold forth while Jean, at
the extreme end of the booth—and whom I could not hear in any
case—lapsed into a brooding silence. Sharon was oh-so-emphati-
cally het, you see, and was into *discussing* romance. Well, I *will*
discuss romance. It comes with the Act.

SO, finally, about mid-September, I called (preselecting a
rainy, cold, windy Friday) and we made a date, sort of, for which
I was ten minutes early and walked about up and down the side
streets until the campus chimes rang seven exactly; and on the
fifth stroke I walked up to the bench she was sitting on, with my
gold scarf doing an Isadora Duncan.

Tripped flat.

And she was up and hauling me onto my feet, somewhat
prim, with the strongest grip on the girl. She sat back down
where she had been, on the stone bench under a Budweiser sign.

Tall, stooping not to be conspicuous on that bench in those
boyish clothes, she looked like a child—the girl too tall for her
grade. Tall and wiry, nothing at *all* like me; she moves so musi-
cally.

We had a passable dinner, with the waitress originally
bringing us something like jerked viscera (Jean backed me up; it
really was not my order) and at this dinner, Jean told me all
about her philosophy of "coming out."

That's *coming out* in footnote type. I have always thought it
rated italics at least.

Stirring like a chemist this complicated brown-flecked
drink, Jeannie said she did, indeed, consider herself gay, which
assessment had been a "rational conclusion" reached as she sat

reading one evening *(WHAT do you suppose she was reading—Radclyffe Hall?)* in her booth at Oxford.

This uniquely theoretical conclusion was almost the sum of her acquaintance with what I regard as a purely empirical subject. She had never had any experience. With anybody—hetero, hip, or fuzzy—or about anything. In twenty-eight years. I thought I'd misunderstood, since it was my third carafe.

What I mean is: She is twenty-eight in '86, not '63. I thought I'd heard wrong. She was so confident. . . . You know how I admire the brainy type (opposites, etc.), but to mention one's *sexual preference* in the same sentence with the word "rational" is a clash of genres.

We then tacked down to the library to see a "forn" film (this town is *smaller* than before), *Jules et Jim,* where she marveled at Deutschified French and I, bloothered already, at its totally classic depiction of chronic male latency. We sat in the aisle, then went off to a college bar, of which all you could claim was that it was all it had to be: dim, red and gold trim—cheap drinks and a somewhat live band.

We sat in the darkest and most private booth I could find (by pretending I didn't smoke—turns out we both do) and there I confirmed what I thought she had said. That she really had had no experience, as we like to say, in relationships. A pianist Virginale. Nane tha say ha' I. It was not especially clear to me if she was proud of the fact.

Was this talk a case of gauntlet hurled or the train done gone? Was she curious? Was there a whisper of vulnerability? I tried to see through her thin, wide glasses for a sign. . . .

The light was dim; the band was loud, coarse and juvenile. Jeannie seemed a little high; I hoped perhaps she wanted to drink too much, and make one of those rational approaches to the irrational.

I blurted that if there was a thing one didn't know how to do, one could ask someone who did. And who would be raptly interested. Tender. And right handy . . .

It was at this point I noticed she was hyperventilating, frozen in position. The next thing I said (whatever it was), she misunderstood and exclaimed "No! not now, not now—" Germane to what activity, I can't say. The band was pumping out a polka with leather and chains and barking; and this, I think, and our agitation distracted us both. I had asked a question, now lost to me, about the clientele, but I got the drift of her wants. I told her I would drop the whole matter if she wanted me to.

She said nothing.

Which I take as hopeful.

But then it took me five days to find her on a zit-sized campus in a town with its high school in the basement of the armory. What do you suppose this means?

Of course she's shy, I was shy once. (Dammit, I *was*.) And I suppose I *do* know what it must be like with shall-we-say ebullient *me* in a public place—

On the fifth day we ran into each other in the student bookstore and had coffee—I think I am resigned right now to public places—and sometimes I call her. Often we have very nice talks. The last was on Proust. Who was French.

We're going to a lecture after a dinner next Tuesday—she mentioned the lecture.

Actually she did not precisely invite me, but something almost as good. She was pleasant about the idea of dinner and some social thing.

Sometimes she laughs and chatters, about, oh, England or baseball—on the latter at least, in the form of the Mets, she and her whole family are agreed. She often mentions her mother or one of her brothers and baseball. They aren't big on Education—think she's lazy—

Last Friday, I gave in to the urge to call, three times, but there was a good reason. I wasn't just being obnoxious.

She had broken a tentative engagement to go for a drive, and I was far more hurt than I had realized—I did realize I was being a drag, even to my students, calling five smoke breaks an hour just to phone her. Have to watch myself with all these Little Egos. . . .

I think she fears the car may break down *far* out of town—whether her car or mine. What a suspicious mind. Or is that my suspicious nature? God knows I dream of that sort of miracle. Would I stoop to that?

Probably.

A TOUCH OF EXPOSITION

Well.

It seems Jean has been the coddled baby of the family—and not in such a pleasant manner: the only daughter and last child of a rather religious middle-class family. She is as attached to her mother as my first was to hers—in fact there are several resemblances, none physical (unless the earlobes). I have an uncomfortable notion of her being continually, subtly, intellectually belittled—sending her into linguistics instead of, say, medicine or law, where she need be compared unkindly to her hyperverbal brothers.

She may be one of those forlorn young lovelies looking for a mother; or be male-identified. ("Thank God I'm not a woman. . . .")

Please note that Jeannie is doing a critical work on "gender assignment."

In fact, now that I write this, I have just decided to get some literature on sex changes for her. I wonder if that isn't it, frankly, that she more wants to be a little boy than a grown man or to love a woman. Except she knows so much. Reads so many pro-woman things and knows much more than the average transsexual *I've* met—remember Joanne / Joe Allen (superstitious/religious - God - is - testing - me - in - this - odious-body)?—without philosophy, insight, rational thought. And "Women belong 'Under My Thumb'—with me on the side of the thumbers." If to be "male" is what she yearns for, well, that's what you get. I guess.

But that's not Jeannie. She has many quiet, feminine ways. And such beautiful hands. And thighs . . . from such haunches sprang the Heroes' lines . . . or loins, or whichever.

But if so tended she should get started on a sex change, now, while she can still marry. I might even still be attracted to her (nah . . .). But why didn't she say just say no?

And. When I first from across that ballroom saw the way a veil drops behind her eyes when she talks to a self-effacing boy, I thought: Queer. And the way she comes on, shy and forward, both—one side of her mouth a tiny smile and her eyes shrewd—

definitely. With those tennis shoes and lavender laces, just-right jeans, and Briton Blazers with T-shirts, and That Knowledge.

I think that in part, her problem is what I call the Only-Good-Queer-in-the-World routine. It's silly, but if you're not athletic and you like your folks, you always give it a read-through.

When I was still doing many Other-People-in-the-Casts—when, in fact, I could hardly get anybody to pay attention to what I did *on*stage—I was actively paranoiac about my teensy constipated sex life. Someone Would Notice (my sex hopes). And I'd die. . . .

When you're doing the Marytr Queer, at least you're imposing. Fire would rain if only Anyone Knew. It's the most importance you'll ever have in your life.

It's only Every Other Dyke who moves her lips to breathe and thinks "lifestyle" is a deodorant—promiscuous, stupid, screams anti-Mom slogans in public—all dykes thus, except the Soon-to-be-Scorned-One (oneself) and perhaps her lover, and perhaps notable literary queers who share the enviable distinction of being irretrievably *dead*.

All easier to believe if you have a case of sociosexual myopia; but it's also true that in such a girl lurks a very Tannhauser view of *l'amour*. Someday her prince(ss) will come. Read *The Well of Loneliness*. . . .

I could hardly prove reassuring to a woman going through this. As to Tannhauser—than which I am nothing less like. But why not, and clearly, tell me NO?

Ah, Perfect Love—*perfectly unrequited.*

Even I pulled that one. My quest for perfect, virginal love stopped with my sophomore English teacher who dressed like a Medieval Handmaid—I thought. She was probably an early hippie. For her that quarter, every night I spent eight hours composing and decomposing and editing (and erasing) Death-less Prose and an occasional Awful Revelation (with the meter off) to reread before I got to class at 8:15 the next morning, when I would grasp what I had brought to be actually heard by my actual peers, and tear it up. I never turned in anything. Not a synopsis. She thought I was a moron.

One day we were all to do recitations from plays—a few

pages, at most—from a selection mostly of Arthur Miller and Eugene O'Neill, thank God not Lillian Hellman; I examined *A Touch of the Poet,* but it overawed me—instead, on the appointed day I blurted out something about my favorite play and having done stock with Uncle Max (I was a boy theorbo player) and burst suddenly into the love-by-proxy speech in *Cyrano*—

> Only let me hear sometimes, all
> alone
> The distant laughter of your joy!
> . . . I never
> Look at you, but there's some
> new virtue born
> In me, some new courage. Do
> you begin
> To understand, a little? Can
> you feel
> My soul, there in the darkness,
> breathe on you?
> —Oh, but to-night, now, I dare
> say these things—
> I . . . to you . . . and you hear
> them! . . . It is too much!
> In my most sweet unreasonable
> dreams,
> I have not hoped for this! Now
> let me die,
> Having lived. . . .

and etc.

My Hippie Love was miffed I hadn't used an assigned play, and—She Never Knew.

Unrequited Love was Marvelous Agony. (I studied it; I studied. . . .)

I took home a "D" in English and Dad swore I would never drive any car as long as there was breath in my body. But anyway.

That year, My Love married the thick-fingered, wandering-worded vice principal. He had skin like sweated lard.

* * *

The Unattainable? Frankly, my dear, I'm the hands-on type.

But of Jeannie:

Sometimes, though she's not timid in classes or group conversations, I think her reaction to me/sex is all timidity and wistfulness for that type of romance, and I am throb-throated for her, all tenderness . . . (Oh hell, what I'm not writing.)

Other times I take it as horrid prudery—the type that despises even the fact of menstruation—meaning the acts, awkward appearance, inane remarks and intimate sounds of humans in the vulnerable state of love are to her coarse and befouling. That inside, her lip is curled at me for being attracted—indeed, for being so emphatically Lesbian, knowing what you put where at the magic point of when. *She wouldn't join a club that would have me as a member.*

So at this point it's not exactly rejection I'm afraid of. Jeannie hasn't outright rejected me. It's that I could be dead wrong. It's that I am reading the features and the mind of someone who is not expressing herself, and I could be absolutely, devastatingly wrong about what she does not choose—or finds impossible—to say.

Not saying "Get lost," because I might make a scene in public. Mangle participles. Fart.

Or it's all out of misplaced kindness. Or because she is so terribly hung up about what she thinks is her social definition that the mention of the Real Thing, of the Act Itself (as opposed to abstractions *chez* Intellectuals) disgusts her. Or because she thinks if I don't get any discernible reaction I'll get bored and go away, and she won't have left anything on record in which I can assess Heideggerian subjectification or something. (Lord, I *might* pass Modern Theater Criticism. Don't ask *how*.)

Could be that, in fact, when I think I'm witty, she thinks I'm childish; when I think "interesting," she thinks "pompous"— that I misread everything. And that I'm ugly (fat at last), and one hell of an outbloomed flower. That she's disgusted at the thought, not of sex, but of me. Of me naked. Of (naked, loud, dyed-by-her-own-hand) me, lusting after Mickey Mouse T-shirts. Of course this is almost the most painful thought, being found . . . awful. And it would make her seem cruel—a terrible thought—because she's never said "Go away."

UNEXPECTED NARRATIVE BY WAY OF ILLUSTRATION

But I am also—not, I add, with any reason from her—*mortally* afraid of making a certain type of mistake at which I don't think you get two chances. This is not mere dithering. I have almost *never* propositioned a woman I was not sure identified *herself* as gay, but I did once. On this campus.

It was New Year's and I was drunk on Irish whiskey, and she was a wan, tall, very young Intellectual whom I thought just sweet. We were the only people on the very top floor of the only girls' dormitory left open for Christmas; but I was, she said politely, mistaken about her. This she told me—she firmly and pleasantly put me straight, as it were—and I apologized for perhaps making her uncomfortable. I pleaded loneliness and my obvious drunkenness.

She understood.

This directly after the first of the performances my folks refused to attend, the first holiday right after Thea (remember Thea?) saw the error of our ways and wrote them, leaving out details about herself. They refused to come—and for the first decent role of my career: *Hedda.* Now my signature role. Maybe it wasn't the Tinsel Circuit, but it was *Hedda.* And at eighteen.

That dormitory girl and I both moved, and two years later, I ran into her nursing along a smashed bicycle, bruised and rent. She had, she explained, been in training for some sort of marathon and the beast had thrown her.

I had still not placed her, only knew that she was someone I'd met, and I was genuinely sorry about the race. I cheerfully offered her my questionable ten-speed since (not being the *gears* type) I never used it—it was screwed up. I said she could fix it or ride it that way, as long as she brought it back. She was awkward (I had forgotten why), but I didn't notice. I was seriously studying for exams because I had been in love that term, so it was Deep Shit City.

She was gone a full week longer than I expected, and on a Sunday night came back.

You must remember my old rooming house (through the seasons of *Candide* and *Midsummer Night's*) four doors from the drama school, a squat frame house with one exit through the kitchen. I had a room next to the door. Convenient.

That night I was alone in the house anyway, and she showed up, banging hard; I opened the kitchen door and asked her in. Streaming hair tied back, she was blue with cold, her arms folded tightly—it was November, after all, and she had been riding a bike.

I offered her coffee and she asked for cocoa; then she asked me for tea-bag tea, and when I scrounged that up, she stood, staring, holding the cup to her chest. I offered a chair, but irrelevantly she asked which was my room—which, although I had been steadily asking her questions, was only the third thing she'd uttered in half an hour.

This gave me a peculiar feeling.

I opened the door behind her and showed her into my room, and began to chatter, nervous, about the pictures on my walls, about classes, about nothing—gestured to books, schematics, props; she kept looking at me. As I stepped back farther from the door, she crowded forward, and I kept stepping back to keep to acquaintance length. I continued easing back like this until I found myself at the wall, past my desk, chair and bed, until I was completely boxed away from the door behind her—this she abruptly turned to, locked and leaned back on, arms folded.

I said something about, something seemed to be bothering her and—out of her coat came a knife. A boning knife. I said, *Is this a joke?*, but she just began to walk toward me, exquisitely slowly. The brand was Standard. I could read the imprint.

She had this angry-fascinated look as if something horrid were inside me and she, the surgeon, was on to it. I hollowly joked that she could have the bike, but nobody laughed.

I could not defend myself without being cut, if not badly injured. All I could have done was hit her very hard with something heavy—which I did not have, and I was not feeling lucky. Squeezed back against the closet, I managed something like

Please, what's the matter? and to move, but the knife went whizz and swish and I screamed. I screamed: *Wait.*

I think what was on my face was profound hurt and disbelief. I doubt, I seriously doubt, that I looked in the least guilty of anything, and she hissed at me, *What do you want.*

Here the vividness is lost.

What I do remember is that look of profound hatred and contempt and my own gutless babbling that there was *nothing I wanted. It was just that I liked to do things for people. I would have lent my bicycle to anyone.* . . . And she told me to get down on the floor on my knees, which in their condition was not difficult.

She kept moving the knife. I was afraid if I grabbed and missed she would start and it would be all over. She said she'd been sharpening the blade all weekend and thinking about just this scene. She kept shifting the knife.

I wore glasses then. She said to throw them on the bed, and when I hesitated—from paralysis—the knife tip was under my left eye, nicking the skin. She lifted my glasses off my face, dropped them to the floor, and ground them into the carpet. Some other things happened, but somehow didn't stay with me.

She left. She just left, sometime after my thousandth repetition that I meant no harm, that I had treated her terribly wrongly, that it was not that she looked gay or anything (which she did) but that I was so degenerate and indiscriminate, and I had asked God to forgive me and reform my evil ways, and couldn't she please leave my punishment to the wisdom of God? and other such. Not convincing, possibly, but inspiration does not write as good lines as you keep hearing.

She slashed my *Midsummer Night's* gown (my only design) and left a nasty fire in the kitchen outside from my Medieval (DR435) book & notes. You remember Korg and his dates.

She was a violinist. (I have a terrible tenderness for musicians, forgetting they are mostly self-absorbed assholes.) She looked, in retrospect, a bit like J. Beledin Meir, who is a concert-grade pianist. The funny part is, I most remember shaking, crying my heart out. I had tried to help someone and in return she had honestly intended to cut out my eyes, or worse. And from this *my feelings were hurt.* . . .

Isn't that an odd reaction to deadly assault?

The Intellectual Dykes who talk and talk and TALK about sex (finally perform it like an Aztec rite, *and* rap about a Lack of Spontaneity) are probably a good deal safer. They get none of the peculiar misunderstandings that come from stating exactly what you mean. I guess I understand that, but here as in so many ways, I embody—I don't plot. Enthusiastic and on cue, but when I bleed it's Stanislavsky. It's not intellectual; I suppose I'm cerebral enough *(Boston Globe:* "Laing's Hedda is too *cerebral")* but I am *not* objective. Back to the objective Jean Meir, who withal feels (not literally, sigh) like she's well worth any risk. . . .

Except for the obvious. She's not Becky off the Farm, and has lived in the U.S., going to American public schools and colleges most years since 1963 (college in England): there is no possible way she has not been asked or demanded to screw, feel parts, drink too much and smoke a good deal of dope—plus do drugs uncountable, and probably, unaccountable. Through it all, one might say, she's been standing fast, the bastion of morality. Is this course, perfect for a perfect isolation, likely—except in the sanctified and the cowardly?

I don't mean to suggest mass addiction, only *informed* rejection. As for kids who left high school in every sense virgins, how often did that last through college? And there was Gay Lib—as we started—after she was eighteen, in every Eastern Seaboard college; if she'd wanted it. I would have. By that age and in my first bar, I would have thrown myself at Gertie Stein AND Alice.

Jean did not grow up in our paranoid time. The New Jersey of 1972 was not New York, 1962. *Why,* one must ask, this haste for chaste?

And: Jeannie. I went to watch her perform on the spinet in the Alcorn Chapel, and she was marvelous, glowing, spiritual— her smile of thanks so shy and sincere, they were ready to tie her to keep her. Technique was good but it was a certain *proscenial* innocence that charmed that house, and we were otherwise a professional—cynical—audience. So you see, Jeannie can act. But *how often?*

Why would a woman not want to be in love?

So, you see, I'm right to think that hers is a terrible if handsome nose on which to place an obsession. It comes to me that often she acts as if she's miserable about self-image (thank God, I'm not . . . etc.) and I think she's attracted only to superfemmes who are not especially smart—since she hangs around Secondary English Training strewing wisdom: easy and funny in her Oxford glow. She is a lovely thing . . . but they're all straight. Why do you think she likes being around straight girls and looking so . . . desirable?

Do you think she's into imagining and not living love? Into fantasies? You know that's hard for me. I've never explained the reason, perhaps because the reason doesn't flatter me: It's because fantasizers are immune to me. To everyone, of course, but it's I who feel it. Fantasizers think they don't need what I personally am dying to give, and in flesh, not spirit. (I'm not fantasizing about Jeannie—I'm *hoping*.) And they're probably right, of course; don't you know, age is a terrible thing to someone who loves physical love. Only when you are young can you imagine other women need you like you need them. Sometimes.

And right now all I have is fantasy. Jeannie brings up notions of the pure and noble. And shame, a condition from which, regarding lust, I do not suffer; and fantasies, in which it feels decidedly ignoble to indulge and which are almost-but-not-quite better than nothing.

PROPOSED SOLUTIONS, WITH ARGUMENT

I simply have to get more time with her, that's all, so she can see me in my best light (dim, I think, in a warm room). I prefer to jump right in bed, myself—I relax, laugh more, and stop being high-pressure—*play* more. You get to know people much quicker that way—but maybe:

A) Get someone to place J. on an important project (original Ben Jonson dialect?) & me too (nouveau direction? Star?)

Comm: Zero projects, and no money to start any.

B) Get her out fifteen miles into the Laidlaw State Park, where there is a rundown cabin (which there is), happening to bring a few things like kerosene, matches and potatoes, dawdle till dark, somehow get her to stop and whilst she's unaccountably unconscious(?), put sugar in the gas tank (did this once to an algebra teacher—total loss), and point out that it's really too dark to hike back to the main road. . . .

Comm: She'd lock herself in the trunk. And rather than spend a night alone (say under the harvest moon at the end of this month) with Someone Lecherous she'd hike through hell, barefoot. And I wouldn't trust my self-restraint in a full body cast. Remember how you met me. . . . And I would have kissed you even if you had been my understudy. I love your nose. Still.

C) Slip her a Mickey Finn while on a routine trip to Murphy's (bar) before or after a concert. Load her up and take her to her own apartment, feed her coffee, and carefully, terribly tenderly, point out my restraint.

Comm: Except knockouts give you one hell of a hangover, her entire clan is composed of lawyers, and restraint, ha.

D) Use force.

Comm: See above. Besides, she's eleven feet tall and works out in aikido(?). (I could ENJOY that, but . . .)

E) Rescue somebody from something, preferably a dramatic . . .

OCTOBER 17

I see I have not yet finished this letter. There isn't any. Finish, I mean.

A couple weeks ago *something* happened with Jeannie. I'm blessed if I understand *what.*

Opened *OK* to my Ado Annie and at the first intermission I walked off, crotch-high skirt, dripping greasepaint, having never sung better (or worse, I'm exactly the same—& it's 98 on stage—& lights *much* too bright for my hair) and there was Jeannie and our Brit friend—not stage-door Jeannies, just strolling to the smokers' john. Stage left opens onto that hall and the dears looked uncertain. A Victorian tintype: The twain are Taken Aback; makeup drips.

"Hullo, dear," chirrups Our Sharon. Jean looked cautious. They weren't exactly bowled over with the performance, though in fact, as you may remember, THE Jack Lewis drove up from Boston (loved it). For a moment I thought they were doing the "Professionals are Taking Roles Away from the Students"

(DFAs *are*—if anybody cares—students. . . .) then I thought, *It's this floozy role* (too thick a waistline; silly in the fishnet hose). They're amateurs, caught up in the Me of this Ado Annie. So, hearty as a fishwife, I go: "How do you like us? I've always liked doing Ado—this is my sixth or seventh actually—it's raunchy, but you can play it up."

"Nice," quoth our linguist.

I try: "Well, see, Ado's your original Liberated Woman. She fucks whom, but only if, she wants, and the right to say no is really the only basis for any rights. And of course she's *crazy for it*— Well.

"God, I hope it's cooler out there. It must be a hundred degrees on that stage. We were thinking of maybe doing the last act in the raw; least it would liven this place up a whoop—it's *so* much deader than when we were kids. You might have read about it—we were doing *Hair,* and would you believe it, the police came for the last matinee and the audience got up and started right in—"

"We'd best be off to the potty—intermission's almost up," said Sharon. Over her shoulder, Jeannie gave me this quirky little look. . . .

I suppose they felt awkward: me babbling about old roles. . . .

Do you suppose she loves me? Not like Annie of the Stage Door—ever there with the next sleeve extended, eyes alight (she'd still love me, I think, if we'd stayed onstage), but maybe Jeannie was abashed. I'm not ashamed to say it would be nice to be admired again. Someone who likes to audience. Though I guess you do get tired of it.

I wouldn't know. Ask Annie.

Perhaps Jeannie was shy. I remember it was hard to look at Burton onstage. (I didn't even have *one* line because when he came onstage I was an idiot. . . .) Maybe she felt . . .

Well, I had talked myself out of Jean and I seem to have talked myself back in—as I have been regularly doing, trying to expunge her image, but the only way I know to do that is with somebody else. And I just get myself past Jeannie, once and for all, and then . . . I see her. Cocking her head—playful or sly?

I suspect myself. I've come back again, after all these years, to where I met you, met Annie. I wanted, or told myself I wanted to forget anything but love and work. Is it falling in love with love in coming back here, or is it just superstition? But she's handsome, she poses. Me as Unrequited Lover.

Oh, well.

OCTOBER 21

Ring it down.

Jeannie and I went to another lecture (comparative linguistics?) in the Fine Arts Building, after a dismal cafeteria supper in which I spent most of my time trying to read her face for a cue. She smiled, her mouth without her eyes and said *OK* had been "nice." The critics certainly thought so. She said it was "interesting" to know someone who "did that"(?) That *A Thousand Clowns* looked nice, that I was nice with students—the while, she had a funny look on her face.

I said it was "hard to tell if you hate me, you want me or your feet hurt."

She didn't seem to want to talk during dinner, and after the lecture, a polysyllabic dinger by Norman Somebody, she whizzed off almost rudely—simply said good-bye, and I misunderstood, and then she repeated that she had a car, good-bye, and amazed, I snapped good-bye and headed for the exit on the side opposite J. Beledin Meir's direction. Outside, I banged my head on the wall. Quite literally. Stood looking from the steps of the Fine Arts over into the amazingly ugly fountain, the representation of a man-woman with its ponderous thighs straddling a tuna (I'm told it's Venus), and wondering why I do this to myself. Pick another who doesn't like the way the lecture limps so it's my fault, the screwups in the universe are my affair, wherein I am always responsible. Eventually I struck out for home, sort of, not remembering where I'd parked my car, wanting the house lights off and a glass-smashing onstage scream— wandering around the fountain and the gym and the Disney-like student-union building, looking for women from classes, kids from productions, strangers I could cruise; it was a black velvet night with blazing stars, their clarity through the death of local industry. This town is really failing. Depression will be lovelier than prosperity.

Everyone in the bright-lit student union was so young—one *is* at eighteen—and I felt so licentious and so conspicuous that my frustration showed because I so wanted to touch.

Boys smiled at me. I went to the venerable (fraternity and rich) hangout, Ozzie's; I went to the dive opposite; I went to all the places I had known women like us to frequent and wandered here and about thinking maybe, by some unfathomable miracle, I would see Jean. She'd come driving up this street. Be parked in this alley. Be in Murphy's place, sipping one of her stingy little beers; and when I finally gave up and went down to Wrinkle's—a loud, expensive dive full of continent queers (what hath AIDS wrought?)—and selected for myself a bottle of good wine, which turned out to have gone off, I started reviewing to myself what I have been asking for.

You can't know what this is like. You take time as time happens, which is your genius, I guess. I wait for *Where do I stand, Who do you want me to be*, because otherwise and spontaneously I never do it right; I try to stage myself—should I be smart, pretty, nice-but-foolish, strong, frightened, naïvely dependent? If this is sex am I cast as innocent or seductive? Loud or abashed or what?—taking the cues, verbal and otherwise, but I'm not really that good offstage. The older I get, the more myself I am, so I have no chance in love. I am too erratic for others to like.

Only you seemed to like me as my own bizarre self. You and Annie. I still don't understand why she prefers that boy to me. He is so *dull.*

It really wasn't that I thought you were dull. You were never dull. It was just that I was on the road. With all those others . . .

I stepped out of the bedroom scene and that's what blew it. Jeannie was so unusual—a scholar and musician and so funny, so boyish, so discreet. So like my *private self.* I hoped too much. And was myself, therefore horrified her.

It came to me forcibly that I had been going after someone who is stunned by my enthusiasm, whom I in all innocence embarrass, who would want me to walk on the other side of the street not to draw attention (with this hair not likely)—who would not talk to me in public, who blushes and goes out one faculty lounge door when I come in the other.

What have I been doing?

But why be the one to suggest the lecture?

Or was it just easier to go along? With this overwhelming . . .

Putting myself in her place, I saw this, this licentious thing. But which could hurt her, embarrass her.

That image upset me so much that, after she snubbed me twice in the hall the following day, I called her up (last night) and said I had to talk—for the first time she said to come over to her place, and I did.

It was remarkably, ridiculously virginal. I sat on the Good Chair and she sat on a sort of reclining divan about twenty feet away, her licorice-colored cat across her thighs. The phone rang twice, immediately, and she rang straight off.

She said she often thought that I was bright (here she made a Suffering Artist face), that I was extremely intense. I suppose that means intimidating. I said that that made sense, because I was trying to take cues from her about how I should be, and she didn't give any. I said that I apologized if it seemed I was throwing myself at her; she said that it was certainly a new experience(!). I said that was hard to believe; she said I was talking to some image I had and not to her; I said, What image do you think you project? And that far from intense, I had been elliptical rather than coarse, and that my perfectly honorable questions had been spoken in an exceptionally public place.

And she said, I don't know what you want from me, but I don't think I have it to give. I don't know very much about people like you. She said she needed space from me in a rather literal sense, and I got angry. I said, why on earth hadn't she told me before to back off, or that she "wanted me for a friend" or to just plain go to hell? She said she hadn't wanted to. That she did like me. It was that I was so . . . and . . . well, after all, everyone *did* know my *work*. And *respected* me. She wanted to be careful. . . .

The phone rang again, and I sat there watching her talk. I

was wearing my peasants-on-the-path-to-gather-faggots outfit: a blue Valvoline jumper, green striped socks, big hoop earrings.

She wore her all-blue jeans-and-tennies outfit, in which she attends grad classes and teaches her own, and which makes her look, in the customary way, like an undersexed boy. The Intellectual Dyke look. On the phone was Sharon Not-*the*-Blake, and after a hurry-up whispering Jeannie told me she was sorry, that she had to get ready for a seminar.

With gravity befitting a summit on world peace, she explained her embryonic paper on role choice and noun-gender assignment; and that she was . . . fond? flattered? Or bewildered? My mind blurs here. One or two months. She said, No contact between us for one or two months.

This is a small place. Among the gays here . . . how did everybody find out about this? (What does she mean, sex role *choice*? Good God, does she think people other than actors sit down some time and block out how to cross their ankles?) What am I doing here? I don't need this place for the craft. I need it for stupid teaching jobs. But I'm not that old. If I work hard enough I can critique and I'll still get the Hepburn roles. It's just harder that way. And when did you know me to take the easy way out?

—The easy way out is always too hard.

And I wanted love.

Maybe I'm envious. Maybe I want to be loved and thought wise and sexy and interesting, that I want to get as close to that scene as I can—and for this reason I enact all this from the opposite side. I court the Other—so you're not Juliet; at least you're onstage.

Can you imagine? Or perhaps it's that I fear you *can* imagine, Meg, asking someone to wait for two months. . . . I admire J.'s intelligence, obvious sensitivity, obvious sensibility, her grace, her gentleness, her wit, her noun-gender assignment, that air of the adroitly masculine within the feminine grace. But it's clear enough: "two months" means "Fuck off" in middle-class.

Afraid to *portray herself*, as the amateur.

The *easy way out*. This campus.

Touring. Killing yourself for Insurance Salesmen, for Oxford Scholars; nights of stalking home from cold rehearsals to glare at the cat. I guess I just wanted to Do It Right This Time. Come back where it started. I was tired. There was magic: I would meet another Annie.

But people only love when you amuse them.

. . . She seemed actually afraid to offend. . . .

That's the sign, isn't it?

Paint all my stuff blue; air out the dressing room.
Tell the kiddies Mama's coming home.

Myra Mitzik

P.S.: "And say to me, thy friend, oh very quietly, that she loves you not."
P.P.S.: Could I stay with you a while, dear? Just till Georgia makes up her mind. . . .

BLUE SUEDE SHOES

Anne had been peacefully involved with Therese for eight or nine weeks when one drizzly night she woke with chills, aches and a headache. It was five in the morning. Anne took the flu every spring, about the time that the weather turned wet—at least that was true in Boston, and apparently San Francisco was to be no different.

On the other side of the headboard the light was on, and Therese was looking intently at her watch.

"I suppose we both have it," Anne croaked.

Therese said "Mmmm?" And from beneath her covers she produced a glass thermometer. "Both have *what?*"

"Um, the flu," said Anne doubtfully. Therese pulled a lined form from the side-table drawer, made a dark dot, and shut the drawer on the form. Therese didn't have the flu, and Anne did, which was the end of that.

Over the course of the next few months Anne woke several times to this curious ritual, but then her lover was somewhat given to rituals. Therese was the earth-mother kind, with covens and crystals and spectral-fascinations-of-the-months.

There had been a time when this had put Anne off. Boston and schooling had left her a little old-maidish. In fact, once, thinking to explain the difference between superstition and belief, Anne had tried reading Therese a good deal of several books on the anthropology of religion. Especially a section on powerless people and sympathetic magic: a little Malinowski, a little Jung.

Yet what Therese had gleaned from this was that one could worship a "bloody Earth Mother," and she had gone about divining the proper worship.

Now Anne listened patiently to whatever Therese believed. Thus, when Therese embraced menstrual blood as plant food, or senna as mete for the spirit, Anne merely hoped the oblation didn't extend to the tomato plants on the roof—she was fond of tomatoes—and especially hoped that no one would feed her senna. Again.

Therese was sweet, fun, a good cook, stunning, hilarious—inventive, ferocious and phenomenal in bed: a country like none Anne had visited. One she'd never be a part of, but then, that was true of white-gloves Boston, where it surely wasn't due to lack of exposure.

Anne didn't want to be critical. She had been raised with critical people. Therese's ways allowed Anne reading and thinking time, and could be adjusted to. What was religion or ritual? Most people need things like that. Anne didn't mention Therese's five A.M. fever again.

It was an early evening, perhaps weeks after she had first noticed the thermometer, that Anne was told a large number of Therese's friends were about to descend. Or, actually, ascend, since theirs was the attic apartment. These Women of Power, and Anne knew several, were coming up to hold some Rituals. Anne knew in particular the Moon Lady with the ferret in her Texas-high hair, and her alarm must have shown.

"I wasn't expecting you, honey-butt," smiled Therese. "Come back at eleven."

Anne spent the evening discussing "how Thoreau's protests serve to promulgate middle-class values" with a real priest and a drag nun in a coffeehouse serving only decaf; and returned to feathers, confetti, wine bottles, candles, burnt cloths(?) and indistinguishable masses on the carpets, the table and the stove. And on her desk. Incense was a fine, perfumed powder on her desk, where feathers clung against the spines of certain books. A list of books deemed objectionable was neatly taped to a shelf. This Anne folded six times, as if it were a full sheet, and dropped in the garbage.

Therese's side of the room was an untouched totemic array of rocks, stuffed animals, books on spiritual matters and an Elvis poster. She was a little older than Anne, and a fan of The King. There were no feathers.

Anne's corner desk was a tiny place surrounded by a ladder of shelves, crammed with nonspiritual, unwitchy books like the diaries of Anaïs Nin, a good deal of untranslated Colette and Violette Leduc, and a good deal of Gide and some Jean Genet for balance. She read her books in the order of their writing, not their publishing. That was the way books were written, and she intended, when she felt ready, to do a good bit of work on the environment of Violette Leduc. Environment was much of inspiration.

So intruders at her desk tended to panic her.

"They just don't understand you like I do, honey." Therese laughed. "I didn't let them hurt anything. How about a kiss?"

That evening, feathers and all, Therese was aglow, impossible to make serious, impossible to scold. Even over books. In a red silk wrapper, black cloth shoes, her hair up inexplicably Cleopatra-like, she was stunning. Black earrings carved like grape leaves; tiny chimes twined into beadwork. She had a throaty, smoky laugh like raucous bells. Anne dropped any mention of desks or lists, and followed Therese to bed.

The next time Anne happened to wake very early, this time for a bad dream, she saw it was again five and the thermometer nowhere to be found; Therese was in deep sleep. Thus, she thought, passes Moon Phase 9572.

She cuddled up to Therese's soft back. Therese was charming. Why criticize a life that gave so much? Loving Therese; lord, did love feel *good*.

64 | *Madelyn Arnold*

It was after work on the same day Therese had buried the thermometer ritual that Anne heard more about it. It was an unusually miserable, sticky, summer-in-the-city day; and the first thing she did was vault up the stairway and drop, after patting the cat, into the claw-footed tub. She was sticky with ink, with heat; her hands were royal blue; she began to pretend that the slug-colored Goop was imported and perfumed like Chanel, and she was sinking to her chin in expensive San Francisco water when Therese waltzed in.

Therese had a way about her no other woman had. As a general thing, all she had to do was breathe to inspire Anne (unless she was reading). But this one time, Therese herself seemed abashed. And it wasn't like a ritual. It was real.

"May I join you?" she asked, very carefully.

Sometimes they bathed together. Therese liked to make a big show of undressing: unfastening this, kicking these off. Anne, chin in the water, gazed myopically upon the weird sweet goddess of her lover, now inexplicably shy.

Away went the black flat slippers. Then the wide skirt flared down around her feet, was kicked away, leaving Therese in a long-tailed silk blouse with mignonette. She took her time before the wooden buttons were free, and then tossed the flowers, too, into the corner. She was wearing a bra. That was something she didn't do. . . . Never had done. And something else.

Her breasts were larger; her belly seemed rounder, and there were pinkish marks blooming outward from the navel. But the change was not just weight. It was something indistinct, some difference, something more than Anne's short sight could interpret.

Before Anne had had time to react, Therese had tossed the bra and cupped her hands under her breasts, which sported chocolate circles around the nipples. A rosy brown. "You do see it, don't you?" insisted Therese.

"Feel," she said, grasping Anne's fingers. She placed them, hard, on the middle of her belly. "She'll be an Aquarius, darling. Someone to understand you. . . ."

★   ★   ★

Anne read. Not about stars, but pregnancies.

Children. She didn't know and didn't want any; her own mother hadn't thought much of childbearing and her two younger sisters had had their tubes tied. You might say that kids weren't a family trait, on the distaff side.

Yet Therese was mesmerizing, and the apartment wasn't that far from Berkeley and practically right over Anne's work in the print shop. In this location were three blocks filled with bookshops and a library. But throughout the pregnancy, Anne bloated, heaved, was constipated. She worked as many shifts as she could. When not around Therese, she didn't throw up as much.

And there was enough presswork; and the collective, with some loathing, agreed to pay overtime for individual jobs. This meant she could solicit jobs and get more pay. She went door to door, gas station to gas station, drag show to drag show. Which meant that the last few months, Therese could stay home and heave and bloat.

Anne's press job she owed entirely to having been thrown out of Mount Holyoke, after which, like dozens of girls bounced out of good schools at that time, she had graduated from college in the Middle West, of all places. She'd made the best of it; and when the tiny but frantic women's liberation group had liberated a radical press, she had ended up having to run it, booklet in hand.

She'd learned printing. And she'd learned about herself and her life; and along the way, that she had access to more than reading French Lesbiana or Violette Leduc. And look how far she had come, at last, from Boston. Her parents *were*. While Anne knew how to *do*.

The baby was born at home, as Anne, sipping wine in a local tavern, alternately suffered and tried to die of shame. The way they were born. The exposure. The embarrassment. Finally the mess was cleared up and she came home to wait on Therese, to find that the kid looked like a dried apple and screamed like a parrot; every time Anne held it, it screeched like a boat whistle.

Time, said Therese, exhausted, would heal all that. Therese had a genius for quieting them both.

After a week of much such bliss, Anne went back to Boston, to see Father off on another ambassadorial assignment.

They still wore white gloves to dinner. They used the proper cutlery, speaking coldly. They were still exceptionally verbally cruel. No, Anne was still not over that nonsense, and her lover looked less like Marjorie Main than like a nude of Florence, thank you *so*. She suddenly almost mentioned the baby to Mother. She suddenly almost mentioned Therese was her family. And the baby, of course; and then she sobered up.

Mother was fine, firm, aging. Her hair was almost white and her speech was more clear and precise than ever. Anne deeply shocked her by kissing both her cheeks at the airport.

And shocked Therese by kissing her mouth, on the opposite coast. In a public place. And grabbing up the baby and hugging her—gently. The little thing might break. And since the next day Anne was still off work, Therese, handing Anne the little baby, asked her to watch it. It promptly threw up on Anne's pink T-shirt.

"No," said Anne.

Therese looked surprised. As a general rule, Anne never refused her anything. She was just going to apply for a job, she said. She had a good chance to teach a yoga class three times a week, and simply needed to talk to Jeffrey about it. It was too foul to take little Star outside. Just for an hour?

No.

Since she had never in her entire life stayed an hour with anyone more than four years under her own age (her brat sister Constance) Anne was firm, panicked. What if she moved wrong? What if it turned over and fell off something? Swallowed its tongue? If she forgot it? Dropped something on it? If it was cold? Thirsty? Screamed to the welkin?

"What you do," breezed Therese, "is: you feel her hands and feet, and if they are freezing and bluish, just put her little sweater on her."

It would get into her books, her pen sets, into the cool blue inks she used for calligraphy. Anne became protectively exasperated.

"I don't know how to live with a baby. . . ." So messy, loud—so—so uncivilized.

"You are *such* an old maid, lover. Every little thing throws you off balance—honestly—you're the only person in the universe who measures the water for spaghetti. Women naturally live with children, it's programmed in to live with children—"

" 'Naturally'! It's learned behavior. *You* had ten brothers and a sister—I had a maid and a nurse and—"

"You're the oldest of five. Something had to rub off on you—didn't you ever watch your nurse *work?* Look, don't fuss. I didn't even tell you about the insemination because I thought you'd fuss. I know you naturally fuss, but you're a *woman*— Here, give her to me. I'll wrap her up. . . ."

"What about my shirt?" said Anne.

"Oh, put cold water on it." Therese tucked the package-sized baby into a shawl and opened the door to head down the stairs. "Honestly, Anne. Anyone would think you were a man."

The following day, Anne found a small, oblong package on her desk, addressed to her from the baby, Star. Unwrapping it, staring at the pair of fuzzy blue doll shoes and (a baseball card?) of The King, and the note "Don't step on me," she wasted many minutes conjuring up possible connections: Try to have childlike vision. Walk in my baby shoes. These tiny shoes (feet) are only temporarily tiny. . . . Then she saw it. Plain as the Bay. "Blue Suede Shoes." That Anne was too fussy, prissy, Elvis-Presley-out-of-date. *"Don't* you, *step* on my blue suede shoes."

About the end of April, Anne opened the door off the stairs to Therese and Star and Hound Dog bounding around in front of the door. Therese held the baby's left arm out as if they were dancing. "Oh, we're so glad you're home. Star's been waiting for you." She held the baby out, ready to be taken and watched.

Now speaker-sized, it was dressed in its booties, a diaper and a little shirt reading "Just wanna be your teddy bear" in tiny brown letters. Anne couldn't see why it wasn't cold. The room was chilly, and *she'd* be cold. But Therese would say otherwise, something about metabolism.

"No," said Anne firmly, not taking the baby.

"I'll be back about five," Therese said. "Windsong said she

doesn't want me actually doing any calisthenics. But she wants to add my name to the teaching list. It's a good draw, you know. And it's time I got a job lined up, even though I wouldn't be teaching before the middle of next month. Spring's her big time—everybody wants a reading and a better bod for the summer."

She sailed to the middle of the room, to the bassinette—a gift from Windsong—and popped the baby in; it started to scream. "Time for her nap. If she goes on crying, just walk her around."

Walk her around. As far as Anne knew, it didn't walk.

Reaching above the bassinette, Therese wound the menagerie-go-round hanging toy. The little lions pranced round and round, close on the heels of the teddies. The baby, below this thing, stopped fussing. Its large eyes fastened on the toys and the mirrors, all just out of reach, but its hands reached anyway. An instant of this and poof, Therese had gone.

Anne rewound the toy.

The intense, black eyes fastened on Anne for a time, but when the music stopped, the round eyes shut. Magical.

It stayed unconscious for nearly forty-five minutes. Anne had forgotten the kid. She was deep in *Oxherding Tale* when a peeping sound started. Soon these changed to wondering sounds. What would happen next was a full-scale howl, and so Anne sullenly dropped the book and picked up the baby.

The howl broke anyway.

"Nice baby," muttered Anne, bouncing the kid. It didn't like that either. It seemed as if it didn't like being in a prone position. She sort of sat it up, so that it looked away from her. "Look at that." She meant the scarlet pennant outside the front bay window. She walked the kid up so close they touched the glass. The red pennant was in front. The kid ceased in mid-yawp.

"Like that? Look at . . . the pretty cars or something." Anne balanced them both, kneeling on the window seat, traffic going below them up their nearly vertical street. It was a misty rainy day in San Francisco. The colors below smeared brightly across the window. Little cars crawled.

This baby, she suddenly grasped, was a native San Franciscan. She had never met a *native* San Frasciscan.

"That's your kind of street, baby," she said slowly. The baby seemed critical of something, something it was leaning forward to see. Anne was holding it with her left hand around its left side, and her right under its bottom. All four limbs and its head were splayed at angles of twenty degrees.

The kid seemed to see motion, but whatever she was looking at, she didn't like. Perhaps. She glared and concentrated, hands and feet out, toes and fingers splayed, starfishlike. The Star now had starfish hands and feet, and the toes . . . the great toe now was nearly opposed, the toes stretched as far apart as the finger. *Primate reaction,* Anne decided. Which reaction had that been? College biology courses had certainly taught her that. The splayed-out limbs?

Star began to tune up.

The little toes were blue, star-stretched and blue. So were the fingers.

Therese had always said that babies should be cool to the touch, but if they were cold and the digits were blue, wrap them up. Put on her sweater and booties and wrap her up.

First the diaper. Relieved, Anne saw that no change was needed.

"Okay," she said. "Okay, let's do this. . . ."

She plopped it in its bed. It opened to squawl. She took up its huge blue, grandma-crocheted sweater, and lifted it onto its bottom, into what was roughly a sitting position, leaning against her hand. With her right, Anne began to feed the left arm of the sweater onto the left arm of the baby.

The sweater sleeve stuck and stayed stuck, snagged on the flared little fingers. The sleeve flapped loose from about the elbow on. Abandoning the baby's left arm, Anne eased the sweater behind and somewhat under the baby and spread the sweater behind its right side. The sleeve hung free. The baby was screeching, red-faced and kicking. Anne intended to sort of sneak the baggy cloth over the hand and then pull, which did not work. Pulling didn't work. Worming the fingers into the sleeve didn't work, either.

You might say that Star had an opinion. She didn't want her sweater on. Really.

Here was this tiny scrap pitching such a fit. Maybe she'd try a real sitting-up position. Anne hauled the baby over to her reading chair, and the baby grabbed for her glasses, then for her book. Anne shook Star gently.

"No you don't—" Shake-shake. Star burst out laughing, bell-like, fairylike.

"Like that, Starfish? Well—boo!" She shook her again. Star laughed, delighted. Anne blew in her face, shook her, several times.

Anne had a vague memory of her nurse saying "Boo!" to her. Evidently babies rather liked that.

Star was to the point of staggering drunkenly about the apartment, pulling herself up on sofas and pants legs, when Anne had the bad dream. She was dreaming of being back at Mount Holyoke. Around her were bridesmaids, and the groom was her father, and the bridesmaids were only two feet tall, with very sharp teeth . . . Who were also her kids, simply herds of them. She tried to read them a book, but they wanted TV.

She came to in a sweat, grateful for a moment that the light was on. Grateful at first.

Next to her, Therese was peering at a little glass tube. . . .

There was a housing cooperative close by, where some of the collective members lived. A nice, quiet one over by the campus. There were places to go, or maybe the time for graduate school at last. She could babysit for Star, take her to the park. That would work.

Therese turned out the light and threw a sleepy arm across Anne's neck, cuddling her knees into the small of Anne's back.

Maybe it was time.

But there was no rush.

BRAKEMAN, FIREMAN, ENGINEER

She smelled cooking. Amelia was stopped out on the cement steps, thinking *what* on earth had brought her up short like that . . . the smell of bacon.

She bit off her glove to fish out her key, dropping it. Her fingers froze to the outside door but she quickened her pace; she smelled bacon, coffee, cornbread: Someone was getting supper, which was her business—Gran must be *really* mad. And Dad . . .

"Ammy! Ammy!" The door yanked back from her fingers, exploding a little boy out—he grabbed her waist, nearly knocking her flat.

"Would*ju* close that door!" squawked a girl. "It's cold!"

The moist heat wrapped around her like a Turkish towel and the half-grown pup was yapping; the TV roared and Ethan, seven, was fastened around her. She could hardly breathe, let alone move. With effort, she began to drag the storm door shut; its base always caught on the cement stoop and the stuck place squawled like nails on a blackboard; she tugged the door and closed her eyes; stepped on the pup, which squealed—

Why did she feel worn out just to come in the house anymore?

She scooped the dog up and dropped it in the little boy's arms.

"Would*ju* close that door!"

Good afternoon to you, too, Celia, she thought, grabbing for the outside door; it caught, skurled, caught again, dragging hard. Yanking on the handle, she scraped it shut, then slammed the inside door. Celia and Cleve and the babies were grouped to see the TV screen, ignoring her. She vaguely wondered where the little ones were. Ethan's nose was running.

"Wipe your nose, honey," she said automatically, judging where to throw her books. "No, not on your sleeve—"

"Lay off!" yelled Celia. "You no more been in this house maybe five seconts and you're a-bossing him around!"

"If that don't beat the Dutch! You've been sitting in the same—"

"Would*ju* shut up? I'm trying to hear teevee!" This from Cleve. He generally whined, which made his family furious. The blacked-out lens on his glasses gave him a skulking look.

Cleve was eight; Celia was eleven. Ammy figured nothing good would ever come of such: the sulking type that only *watches* life. Dad wasn't like that; Mama hadn't been that way. As for lazy . . . there were pup-worried schoolbooks right in front of the davenport. "Celia, look at that science book—"

"Now you're a-starting on me!"

"And while I'm at it, have you done your homework yet? And not go avoiding it and have Dad get more phone calls from Mr. Myers about how come you can't ever turn things in like the rest of the class, and Dad so worn out he can't see straight?"

"We got none!"

"The hell you say—"

"I'm telling! You saying 'hell'!"

"Now you said it." Ammy made for the closet, crossing in front of the TV set. "And those books. Dad's going to have to pay for—"

"WOULD*JU* SHUT UP?" Cleve exploded.

"Aw, shut up," she said, unzipping her coat.

Ethan hugged her hard, the way he had used to hug Mom;

she felt in her pockets, finding only pennies. "You got any Kleenex on you, honey?"

He shrugged, wiping his nose again on his sweater sleeve. She began a hunt through her father's jackets; with seven kids, he kept tissues in his pockets. Out from the kitchen drifted Dad's flat tenor, rising to cover the clang—crash—slam! of his mother. Gran hated to cook, which was strictly Amelia's job.

"You gone to take me, ain'tchu?" said Ethan, widening his eyes. She smoothed his hair before answering, spat on the tissue and started scrubbing the dirt streaks off his face. "Ethan—" she began.

He jerked. "You *did* say I could go! You *know* you—"

"Honey, you know Jimmy doesn't mind you coming to practice heats but"—her voice rose loud to cover his rising howl—"but at *night*—"

"*Jim*-my! He don't know anything!" Furious, his eyes were as green as Mama's. "I gone with you at night when he was racing and I gone with you last month when he was rallying and I gone with Dad to Race Day and you *promised!* You *know* you don't never lie to me!"

It was she who was racing, but she couldn't tell Ethan anything about it. "Jimmy won't do it." She shrugged, hating the look on his face. "Look." She pinched his sleeve. "You've gone and torn your—"

"*Would*ju shut up! A body can't hear with all this carrying on!" spat Celia, hands on ears.

Ammy glared at the cat-faced girl who sat with her sticklike legs beneath her in the darker, farther corner of the davenport. There was something odd, distinctly odd about her mouth.

"Celia," Ammy said pointedly, "you have been in my orange lipstick! You have gone and put on lipstick at your age!"

Celia pushed her mouth out like a kiss. "Smartass! You just prove—"

"Tell that to Dad. Just wait till *Dad* sees that!"

Dad was seated with the two-year-old on his knee, at the table, which was more or less set for supper and tonight must have been Cleve's doing: plastic forks, Welch's jelly glasses and a couple of Mom's best tumblers strewn over the milk smears from breakfast. The littlest baby was crawling by his leg, trying to pull herself up. The floor needed washing. "Real nice you could make it," said Dad.

Ammy's hands went out to the baby—conciliatory. "Hi Grammaw," she hedged. "Uh . . . they calling anybody back yet, Daddy?"

"They say maybe before Christmas. *That* would be real nice." His chin jutted out. "How come you not to pick up Kenny and the little ones? Laundry not done, your grammaw cooking supper—and that babysitter come over and dumped them kids on Celia. Where in hell have you—"

"Dumped them off on me, more like!" said Gran. "That Celia don't do nothing around here!"

Ammy dismissed the lipstick from her mind. "Daddy," she said, "don't you remember? We have National Honor Society meetings on Fridays now, and I'm vice-president so I have to open the—"

"Anything so's a body gets out of work," said Gran.

"Now I think about it I remember you a-telling me it was Tuesday nights."

"I don't see what difference it would make," said Gran, "if she was the queen of the school board—you take care of your family before you do, before you do *nothing* first—"

"You don't understand—" Ammy started to say, *It means a scholarship!*, but no use mentioning that right now. It would only start an argument she did not want tonight. Gran thought schooling made girls lazy, which, after all, was only partly false. . . . "Dad!" she said brightly. "Could I borrow the car again? I've got to go to Cherry Heights with Jimmy."

Gran's baby-bird mouth popped open—

"I can go, can't I? I mean, Daddy, it *is* Friday! I babysit and everything else all week except for just this one meeting and I don't go to choir or speech anymore, and NHS is a school thing, anyway—a lot of boring people that— I don't *go* anywhere, and don't you remember, you promised last Sunday—"

"You've got that Ethan all riled up—thinks *he's* a-going—"

"He's too little," yawned Dad, "to be a-staying up that late."

Ammy's conscience twisted; she put the baby down on the

floor, turning to speak to Gran. "You heard him tell me I could go."

"I don't know what I heard," Gran told the skillet.

"You need some help with that? I can make the gravy or—"

"Always ask when there's nothing left to do. . . ." Gran smiled, pleased to be completely in the right. "Anyway, what on earth is a grown girl a-hanging around with her sawed-off cousin for? What happened to that handsome—what was it—Frank?"

"I'm going to take a bath while there's still hot water," Ammy said, and ran upstairs.

She eased the Chevy into second, into third, conscious of the smoothness of her shifting, conscious of her spirits lifting high and light and barrierless and free—homes receding into mere pale boxes, pasted along the wide gray streets—hers this evening, only one more house. . . . Double-clutching onto 103, she kicked it down.

Flat white houses reflected the headlights, cool as graves, lit from within in toylike yellow blocks . . . everywhere houses and sheds and light—little farming and no fallow land, and the only open space was the cool black roads. In a "farming state." Summer farmers—winters, worked in the red-brick factories, sang to the piped-in music, dreamed of spring. . . .

Dreamed of the roads she dreamed on, dreamed of rolling—roving around the straggle of the black roads restlessly, as if by force of will, by simply driving long enough—some new thing might appear where shacks and factories had been. A movie house; a zoo; a man from Mars . . .

Amelia parked the little Chevy near the edge of the car-tracked field, close to some farm outbuildings. Cherry Heights was on the eastern county line: a few shacks and filling stations on abandoned farms and bottomland, now only used for racing, because farming didn't pay. Mercury lamps shone from flat tin roofs, cutting such sharp angles they were blinding her; walking, Ammy couldn't see her feet.

Though it was early, the air was cold and the grass was white with hoarfrost. Her thin shoes slid. She picked her way by irregular files of cars and trucks and Jeeps; idling cars muttered and thrummed, nickering exhaust smoke at her legs. It was so cold for October, the night was shaping blowy with the close damp smell of snow; but would it warm enough to snow? Already six thirty . . . On the far edge of the field the crowd was gathering for the race.

"Ammy Lee!" From the right; she couldn't see. . . .

"Ammy Lee! Hey Ammy *Lee!* Over here!"

White light blinded her; "Lay off," she yelled. "Jimmy! You're blinding me with that!" and the truckers' light shot promptly up to the clouds above, cutting a bright white wedge through the frigid night. Mouselike, nervous, constantly shifting his weight from foot to foot, her cousin waited for her, threw his arm around her shoulders and they headed for the bright lights of the field.

Light shone down from the arc lamps and out from the cinder track, sharply configuring features of people and things: groups of talking and drinking men; women hugging their escorts' arms or in twos and threes, dipping their heads to laugh; kids pointing at cars across the cinders—pushing each other, laughing, shouting and crying. A round-bottomed girl in a miniskirt, mufflered and fur-coated, stood shivering in their pathway; Jimmy leered. His arm was warm on Amelia's shoulder and his breath and coat were sweet with cherry tobacco.

Races were held in the open field, on a cinder track marked off with head-high palings, turns padded with loosely-wired bales of hay. Around the perimeter, twenty feet in the air, stood white-hot vapor lights. Those poles were the pampered pride of Cherry Heights—lights like the Indy racetrack had, lights like a football field. Outside their sharp white lucency, the drab world seemed to end.

"Terry's been a-looking for you—"

"He's here?"

"He is. Wants you to hunt him up and translate for him."

"I'm nervous." She hedged. "Why don't you—?"

"Shoot! He hates me talking to him, even; I mean besides the fact that he's *your* cousin."

Terry was her father's sister's son, stone deaf: he didn't work since nobody'd have him—and didn't do anything else.

"Lookit there," growled Jimmy.

Terry was posed in the center of a sniggering gang of high school kids—splay-footed, grinning, the caricature of a man blind drunk.

Ammy shrugged. "People think it's funny."

Terry was broad-backed and sandy-headed: ponderous, like a blond bear on its back feet. When he signed he looked like hell, his snub nose crinkling and smoothing, mouth stretching and folding, his gimlet eyes springing open in wide expressions.

Of course he wasn't trying to sign now—no one could have understood him—just aping a bum cadging drinks from the crowd around him. A short-haired girl offered him the mouth of a half pint, waving it back and forth, talking at him elaborately and lewdly, echoing her talk with a twist of hips. Terry was clever at reading lips, but had never been good. Whatever she had said, he took it incorrectly, and even he could not miss the effect—laughter at him, not with him. He shrugged it off by draining the bottle and sticking it in his ear—clowning and mouthing.

Why, why did he have to go and pimp himself like that? Ammy ducked down in the hope he hadn't seen her.

"Powderpuff," or women's races were held at seven o'-clock, well before the main event, and the closer that time came, the colder Amelia grew—and not with the weather alone, although it *was* unusually cold. Elbowing and ducking through the crowd, they made their way toward Jimmy's blunt-nosed Mercury, and rounding a corner of the makeshift bleachers—there, next to the Coke and cigarettes, was Frank, his arm around a girl she didn't know wearing his basketball sweater. She was cute. Bland, but cute. Obviously his fragile heart had healed.

Amelia was rather pleased to find she had really not been in love with him. So much for that. . . .

Jimmy's car shone cold.

What she first needed to do was bring the car into line at the head of the cinder track—this she kept foremost in her mind, tracing an imaginary path from its place to the flag line. The car—tonight—looked fragile.

"You'll be fine," Jimmy shouted in her ear, slamming the sprung door shut.

Light glanced off frost patches on the hood. The wheel was cold; the bucket seat was freezing; the cold bit through her stockings and her skirt, stinging her legs. No dressing down for *ladies' nights*—too bad . . .

He thrust his head in the driver's window and, pecking her on the cheek, gave her a squeeze. "You're fine, just fine, sugar. Hit the starter, hear?"

She forgot the choke.

"Ease up. You won't win nothing if you drive this thing like a woman. Now, ease up." He thumped her shoulder, hard.

Down the field, other crumpled cars were nosing into place along the flagline. The PA whined, and the engine started; it purred; Jimmy had it tuned to sweet perfection. With the soothing pulsing Ammy began to ease a little bit—but a BAM! BAM! back on the trunk jumped her nerves and she craned around in the seat.

"*Beat it*, jerk!" Jimmy yelled at the face plastered flat against her fogged rear window; Terry promptly recommenced banging his fist on the trunk. BAM! BAM! BAM!

Jarred, *See you later,* she signed at him, over the seat. He signed: *You drive that race—you? Why? You stay here—I drive that—whiz fast fancy! Wow!* He shaped each sign with a certain masculine squareness.

That woman race, she signed. *Not man race—powder face race. I race now soon* [see you] *later!*

He shook his head too cockily, drunkenly wise. *I race this smoo-ooth fancy.* His fingers fumbled—meant to slide on his thumbs for *smooth,* but signing *fingersnap.*

"He don't even know how to drive!" said Jimmy; but she shrugged; that wasn't true. . . . "Aw, Amelia, you didn't." Jimmy spat on the ground. "What's the matter with you! He can't drive a car, it's illegal for deaf-and-dumb!"

Terry banged on the car and signed, *Drunk not!* You never knew what part of what you said he would understand.

"Drunk on his behind at seven o'clock—! Aw, hell, we're losing time. I'll get him off of there."

"Heartbreak Hotel" erupted from the PA overhead, meaning the race would soon start; there'd be another Elvis song and the anthem and a few announcements. . . . In her rearview mirror, Jimmy was trying to coax Terry off the bumper. *Don't hit him, Terry,* she thought. *Just don't hit him—*

Jimmy signed laboriously and badly, and was half Terry's size. His slow moves seemed to infuriate and suddenly Terry chopped his hand through the air: *STOP. WINDOW SHUT,* and turned his broad back. He lurched off across the lot toward the stands, limping a little and drinking. She had thought he'd feel a little freer, when he'd learned to drive. Instead . . . well . . . Maybe liquor helped.

Jimmy's coupe was to start between a black car and a green; the coupe had once been solid gold but now was blotched and tiger-striped with a dull red primer that was waxed right over so that it still, Jimmy claimed, looked decent.

The black-haired driver in the black car to Amelia's left was boyish, sullen, heavily made-up, twenty at the most. To her right, in the green car with a painted "8" was a thirtyish, hard-faced woman with pink-sequined, bouffant hair. She looked to be from the regular stock-car circuit. She squinted hard at Jimmy's coupe and sneered.

The shot went off.

Ammy had trained in that car on that track, and yet with the field lights on, now muted by great opal rings of mist, the course was unfamiliar, nightmarelike.

Right hand, left foot–upshift, left foot–downshift . . . Ammy led, her mind on the preternaturally shadowed track that was silent now: crowd and all gone mute in the glassbacks' roar. In her inside lane she was flowing on, aware of the cars around and behind her, but not in the vividly tactile way she had always heard she'd be. She was only aware of the presence of cars and she wanted to look but you can't crane around to see . . .

The first curve came too quickly—she went wide, glancing against the padding bales. Wire stuck to the hood. She set her teeth and forced the coupe on course, but had lost her lead. The next curve she cut inside furiously, skated past the piled-up bales—floored it. Downshift—upshift. Ahead was green "8," to right blue "6" and the black one, close. The next curve coming, she ground down to second, skiting onto two wheels and around, the light back end in the air, while "8" went wide.

Hood to wheel with the black car, Ammy leading.

Behind her thought was a promise she had made herself, the premise upon which she'd agreed to race. It was simply that a woman could not beat her.

The third lap, two drivers oversteered and cracked up over toward the fence edge. Ammy came up leftward, forcing the "8" to more-or-less climb the fence, and took the lead again. She and the black and the "6" were close, the rest in a straggle after.

Starting the last lap slightly in the lead, the black to her left, she passed the flagman—passed Jimmy, shading the caves of his eyes—and flags, stands, gestures, friends, blurs.

A green hood cut toward her own from the right—she swerved, and her car went rocking: right, left—the wheel jerking hard as the lights jumped bright and the very air slowed down. The field was excessively bright, painfully bright; and slowly and clearly the burnished hood came at her again; slowly.

She saw a right triangle forming ahead, the green "8" coming toward her as hypotenuse. They would clinch at the angle—hard—and her grip was Jell-O.

The angles touched: BANG!

The green veered off, then back: BANG!

Panicked, out of position, sideways, heading left; *Right!* she told herself, *Toward the impact*—or completely lose control and roll the car.

Shifting, pumping the clutch, the gas, wheel wrenching almost free, Ammy jerked the car dead right, straight at the passing "8," slamming it squarely; but her car had not yet overcome the torque of the last hard knock and its too-light back end swung. And swung; she clutched at the wheel, unbelieving, dizzy—the track lights spinning as if whirled round her car on a rope.

Hauling the wheel helped nothing.

One last turn and she was leading by yards, but zigzag, out of control; she couldn't get inside the curve and the wheel wrenched, jamming her thumbs, and she crossed the path of the green and careered on right. The hay wall loomed . . . then exploded and there was the thudding and smacking of fencing and bales and her flying, light as a doll, into the wheel, into the windshield, into the mirror—bump!—in the seat. Unclear about exactly what had happened.

Except for the fact that she hadn't even finished.

The car wasn't too banged up. Worse had happened to it.

The crowd was drunker. Fights were breaking out. Jimmy bought fruit-jar moonshine, drinking it steadily—sometimes wordlessly thrusting it at her—a silent rude assertion she had more ineptness. Standing in the freezing wind that pinned them beneath the bleachers, Amelia felt it logical to try to drink. Or freeze—

It worked.

She patched the blue place on her forehead with a smear of beige; dabbed Listerine on the cut place on her ear. Her lip she didn't even worry with. The main event wasn't till nine and Jimmy, frankly sulking, wouldn't leave—instead steering her beneath the stands, where they couldn't be seen. She was literally sick. If she could just have retracted the past half hour, never have tried. All she had hoped to do was to prove she could race. That she could do things people cared about—remembered. Just since the funeral she'd been drifting away. From everyone. Even Jimmy. Even Ethan. . . . She had to be part of them, at least. And anyway, this had all been *Jimmy's* idea.

Fools' names, fools' faces, always seen in public places. *Damn,* she thought. *I have to go to school on Monday!* This they'd remember. So she made salutatorian in 1966, who'd remember that?

The 'shine was oily, coarse, and burned its way inside; she concentrated on swallowing without any obvious pain—Jimmy glaring, hoping to see her gagging, like a girl.

She wanted to leave Jimmy and head for the car, but it wasn't safe. To walk alone was a sign that you were available—or dumb; but she wouldn't have asked him to walk her back to her car to save her life.

"Would you look at that," said Jimmy to his mason jar. "Would you just lookit there."

Across the track under the brilliant lights, getting out of a bright-red stock car that was chromed and jacked, burnished to a punishing degree, was a man she thought she knew. He stalked toward the officials at the finish line. Though the man had changed his walk, still she saw a hesitation and she knew him. He was clearly here for the main event, equally clearly professional, and he stopped to talk with the Southern Circuit, who seemed to know him well. Tall and thin with a slight hitch in his carriage, a dropout from their class two years ago: Joe Kelso.

Jimmy swore, envious. Ammy took the moonshine back, unconcerned if he talked to her or not. The liquor helped.

Joe strolled purposefully up to the track officials, who were spilled out like jacks across the finish line. His limp was notable, but got up in his white and blue, a gold stripe down the side, he stood stronger than anyone, daring to flout tradition. Flashbulbs popped as he ducked his head and clapped a helmet on. And it was suddenly as if the other, bareheaded drivers were only fooling around.

He strode back toward his car with a little trail of track officials after; he stalked like God—the only driver to dare to wear a helmet. Confident; nothing like he'd used to look . . . School had always made him look suspicious and embarrassed, like a kid caught out breaking rules he didn't get.

Except for Andy Jewett, who had graduated from the second grade at sixteen and kept trying to come back, Joe had been the major diversion in the fifth and sixth grades.

Andy would break in the locked front doors of the school, stand in the hallway and scream, or pop his head in a classroom door and snort—once causing Sheba Trealy to swallow a plastic barrette. He was very retarded and somewhat dangerous. Naturally, Joe was nothing at all like that.

Joe hadn't attended Edison Elementary until Amelia was in the fifth grade, and although he was perhaps two years older, was assigned to her third-floor class. In a dull year at a dull school, Joe's appearance became most interesting. Punishment was a high point of the day and, after mid-September, featured Joe.

He was actually a cooperative boy, painfully eager to please and horribly shy, and obviously hated the attention—but he was late every single day. Never absent—late.

This infuriated Mrs. Adams; each day she pretended to overlook his absence at the start, barking "Class please rise" at exactly 8:03, and led the class at quick-march through the Pledge. Then came the Lord's Prayer (and Benny Waleskowski and the Seventh-Day Adventists stood with folded hands and examined the parking lot), then the "Battle Hymn of the Republic," and some others; she seemed to genuinely want to keep reciting up till recess—after which they recited rhyming poetry, since some kids couldn't read. You'd have thought she'd be glad if one of her fifty *stayed* away.

The classroom was at the top of the stairs, and sounds carried clearly up the stairwell. At 8:10 they could hear Joe, at the bottom, throw back the heavy-paned door with a tooth-jarring slam, the sound ringing clearly through their room. Sometimes there'd be another slam, weaker than the first, if he'd missed getting all the way through; then came a small but echoing clink at the foot of the steps—then silence. Some silences are harder on the nerves than others: This waiting for the other shoe interrupted the prayer or the hymns—whichever—while the class and the teacher strained to hear the rest.

Then, tak! his right heel-tap would hit the steps, and he'd jump one-footed, faster and faster, clicking and clacking the heel tap—sometimes he could make it up a complete flight of stairs before his left foot had to strike a step; then ka-chunk! ka-chunk! ka-chunk!

Taking forever, suspending *My Country* in the air like the Indian fakir's rope, Joe would scale the third-floor stairs. By the time he reached the top, he'd be making a slide-click-tap—kachunk! At the classroom he'd cling to the door—hangdog, gasping, his left foot skewed, bolted to the floor by the weight of its bright steel brace. He was late because he'd got tired of being shoved on the stairs and falling.

Joe looked like a matchstick set on end, with his crewcut head too large, and he walked with a ticlike hitch. But he was shed of childhood and its polio. On wheels he was someone self-possessed and vicious: ground into first place with a combination of superior skill and primitive aggression, driving two opponents into the fence, others into fiery collision—brutally wonderful to see. And successful.

How very strange.

Most of the National Honor Society would end up at GE or Dynalux or Linde, making tubes or ball bearings. Or selling insurance.

Guys, that is.

Joe went screaming by in a scarlet streak.

People becoming doctors, lawyers, television announcers—people from here did not do those things. No one she ever knew had. Except during wars. Going to college didn't seem to change that much—except there were a few librarians. . . .

Joe wasn't popular with other drivers, being hard to pin down—they were trying to run him off and burn him. Couldn't be done.

She was proud of him; she genuinely was proud of him. She really could not tell if she was envious or not.

People in twos and threes were stalking their frozen cars, stamping their feet from the cold. Engines coughed and roared as the two of them threaded among the rows. The lights on the stands were going out; the track lights would stay on all night, bright-lit as a landing strip.

"So what did you think of Joe?" ventured Ammy.

"Well he sure as shit *won*, didn't he?"

"He did," she said, enthusiasm ebbing. She hated to have to depend on his chivalry when he was pissed like that, but it wasn't safe for her to walk without him—yet.

The feeling of competence she had had before, the freedom and the confidence, was gone. The lightness, gone. But ashamed as she was of herself, she had to talk to him; she had to hear him say just one kind thing.

"You remember when Joe started the fifth grade with us?"

Jim's boots creaked across the hoarfrost.

"I was thinking about the way he'd come up the stairs. . . . He's really something now, isn't he?"

Squeak, crunch, creaking on in front of her.

"Him being late all the time, clunking that brace up the

stairs, he— You know, I can see why a cripple would want to race, can't you?"

Jimmy whirled: "Is that supposed to *mean* something? Just what the fuck is that supposed to mean, anyway? Here I give you a chance to do something good and you fuck it up and then you start screaming some goddamn thing about *cripples?* What is that supposed to—"

"I just meant Joe and his leg and—"

"Shove it, Ammy! Do you hear me good? Just shove it!"

"I lost in that pissant little tin-pile excuse for a stock car!" she screamed. "And I guess you never lost a damn thing your own self—you sawed-off little runt!"

"Least I finished," he said, sullen.

"You don't have to walk me no—any further."

"Hell, don't forget your fucking grammar!"

"Stick it up your—butt," she finished, turning.

On all sides doors squawked open and slammed shut; she began to walk quickly away toward the metal outbuildings, toward the car and refuge.

"You steer *toward* the point of impact!" Jimmy yelled.

Tears were freezing on her face.

"You drive like a *woman!*"

She didn't listen anymore.

The engine idled, and she let the windows steam completely over as she fiddled the radio dial, tracking the bands by hair-widths, picking up static and nails-on-a-blackboard squalls that welled, then faded to lonely ghosts of hollow talk, retangled in the net of airwaves. Nothing she wanted to hear came in.

Some nights she had been able to get St. Louis or San Francisco—even KDKA Los Angeles. Once a marimba band, which she hoped meant Mexico; she wanted very much to get a Chicago or Cincinnatti station, but obviously that wasn't going to work; something about the ionosphere or clouds, perhaps. All she could get was local country—not even Nashville. Local.

And for this she'd broken a promise to Ethan. Her makeup had smeared and no one could have *paid* her to fix it, since anyway she was plain as a cat.

Around her, cars were cranking, revving, leaving; lights

played across her windshield—bright, then gone, only the field lights picking out the metal on the dash. The wind had dropped, and the air smelled sweetly metallike, of snow.

Snow would be nice. Enough to deaden everything.

In English they had read this story called "Silent Snow, Secret Snow"—or something like that; she would feel just like that kid had felt in the story. Let snow bury the car. The state . . . Hunched behind the wheel, fresh tears spilled over; snow heaped over the doors, the steamed-up windows—piled up over the roof, cutting off her oxygen. . . . Imagine her father's face as they lifted her stiffened husk, pulled too late from the icy tomb of the Chevy. Daddy . . . how could he manage without her?

First, intruded her practical side, he'd make Celia learn to cook.

Someone was pounding on the driver's door.

The window was steamed, so she rolled it down; Terry's big paw groped in to pat her arm; he held his head sideways, his green eyes wide: *How feel?* he signed.

Behind him was Joe's car, door open.

Horrible-horrible, she said and mouthed, she hoped, pitifully. Gently, Terry tapped her cheek.

"I don't feel like smiling—" But she finished by smiling, shaking her head: *No.*

Not feel bad—not, he soothed. *Compete true good, whiz fast! Drive okay fine-fancy. Bitch bang-car—bah! can't help. Come with us drink-drink.* He pointed back to Joe's car, seeing her unarticulated question. *My good-friend his brother—long ago friend; meet at institution; K. sign smooth, fancy; better-than-you.*

She shrugged, hurt. Of course: Joe's older brother. She had known there was another one, but not very much about him. The Kelsos had fourteen children; the oldest one was deaf and employed somewhere—older than Terry, and *respectable.*

Terry pointed to the ignition key. *Turn off,* he grinned. *Fun! Drink, drank, drunk!*

"You sure you really want me?" she yelled at Joe.

"Come on, kid! Great to have you!" Joe opened his door and popped his head over the top of his car, cheerful and easygoing. "That one run you off was a professional—you didn't never have a chance, sugar. You done just great and don't let anybody tell you different! Come on, have a little drink and relax. You got you a chaperone right there—blood kin."

Terry opened her door with a dance-floor bow, and handed her out.

Deftly, reverently, Joe's able hands caressed the steering wheel, and motion seemed effortless past fields, copses, stands of trees knit overhead, gray tunnels in the headlights, black beyond them; Amelia luxuriated in it, confident in the car's dim light, fitted between the shift and her cousin's heat.

"Amelia Lynam," Joe said reflectively. "What, you in the senior class now?"

She made out a label by the gas-gauge light: Jim Beam.

"Who they got for president this year—Duncan States?"

The liquor was making her nose feel numb, but was smoother than rotgut corn. "Frank Gilliland," she said obediently. "You remember old . . . Frank."

"Wasn't you a-dating him last summer?"

"Wasn't what?"

"Frankie. Didn't you date him last summer?"

"How would you know that?" she said, handing the bottle to Terry. Terry was breathing stertorously, peering out the window at the lightlessness.

"Asked after you," Joe said reflectively. "Somebody said. You know . . . he's still sweet on you? Yeah, I know he's been a-working on some other girl, but you. I tell you he . . . You know he busted my nose one time? Had a lot of kids jump on me. And he done pushed me down the stairs one time at the school."

"I was just thinking about that. Funny, isn't it? Just thinking about that earlier tonight."

"Great minds track in the same run." He laughed. "Well. So now he's the president of the senior class. I'm glad I quit."

"Um, and the head of the National . . ." She stopped, clearing her eyesight. "So. Do you hate him now?"

"I don't have to, got too many things I *like* to think about. I don't have to worry about farting around with schooling. I get to be my own man. I'm 4-F."

"So am I," she said drily.

He looked away from the road, squarely at her. His face was more defined than she remembered it: wide-mouthed, sharp-nosed, light facial hair, the heavy brows meeting in the middle.

"Didn't mean that if it sounded like a *in*sult," he said slowly. "I mean, I know your mom was a teacher and I wouldn't have said a blessed thing against her, specially now. I apologize. And besides, I do know you always did like school. You was good at it—wasn't just you sucking up like them . . ." His eyes were drawn back to the blackness past the windshield, and the bottle reappeared in front of her; Ammy drank, passing to Joe, who took it, smiling with glazed eyes. "Remember you corrected Mr. Lakewood in math?"

"He was just *laying* for me to mess something up, the rest of the year."

"Don't that just show you." He wiped his mouth. "You got to suck up whatever you do. Don't matter how good you are, or how good you do, nothing you could do is as important as kissing the right—uh—*be*hind, and you know who does *that* real good. It's bastards does best. Frank Gilliland does best. That Frank was the nastiest little snot-nosed bully. Now if I run into a guy like that these days, I'd just feint one way and wrap an iron around his throat box or his—! No more problem.

"Course, the ones I got problems with *now*, they're pretty rough. . . . Well. Yeah, see the bastards don't care what fair is. Like that circuit bitch done with you; you know, you're not half bad, driving. You looked pretty good out there—when they told me that was the Amelia Lee Lynam I know, I tell you I was *im*pressed. No; you're not half bad, Ammy Lee. You got good control."

The whiskey choked her. "Guess I proved *that* all right."

"I'm not funning you, it was just you didn't have a chance. That woman's from the Louisville circuit and they're a rough bunch. It's just the bastards gets the best of things, that's all. You got to be a bastard to win in this—you seen the way I drive."

Her leg had relaxed against him, and she moved it back.

"Well," he relented, "that's not always true. There's things I just can't do. . . . Maybe that means I'm, you know, weak, or

. . . Pass me over that bottle can you get it back, okay? Well, they learn you, anyway. Down to Louisville and south."

"That where you went after you quit? Looey-ville?"

"Lou-ah-ville," he said mildly, turning her his smile. His cowlick stood straight up from his crown, like a baby's.

"I had a uncle there who use to race. Sent me on down, later, to Natchez. . . ."

She watched him talk.

She was warm and flattered, and she liked his voice; it was brash, homely, cat's-tongue-like. Sounded like home. His arm had got onto her shoulders somehow, but unlike Frank and unlike his conceit.

She seemed to have lost the thread of what he was saying. She took a drink, and sputtered: "So they bet on you? Is that what brung you—brought you—"

"You bet they do, sugar." He turned to Terry. "How's our boy?"

Terry was unresponsive, nearly unconscious.

"Honey, see can you get that other bottle back from him?" Joe frowned at the gray sweep of road. "Well, the purse ain't much—gate's not very good—I mean, it's a good percentage but a good percentage of nothing is still crap, if you see what I mean. Maybe I drop by, see my mother, see my daddy. Maybe see you. I always ask about you. Maybe I wanted to see the place again, and if it changed 'cause I changed so much. Even though most people races here hate my guts. That's always the way if you're good. . . . I don't know. Somehow it's still kind of easier here. Maybe that's what happens when you leave."

Terry was sagging against the door. She checked the lock.

"Anyway. I got a little career problem. Here, take another drink and I'll finish that. . . . Run into the mafiosa. Guess that's the end of that."

She touched his hand by accident, handing the bottle back.

"Yeah, they run it. Maybe you heard that. The gambling and all the perfessional circuits. They're . . . well, and I don't want to get my throat cut, and I never been a good asskisser, even in school. . . . Well—" He broke off. "You done a real good job tonight. I mean that."

"I could of hit her sooner."

"You could of hit her sooner." His muscled arm slipped around her shoulders. "You could of cut her off, you could of had wires and been a television set, and I coulda been a athalete. No, you didn't hit her sooner because you don't really want to treat no one that way."

There was something about his arm she didn't care for.

"You do that, and *you* see it coming, you see that crackup and the fire, and there goes your nerve. Might could be you're too smart to race—too much imagination. I seen that before. Now me, I'm not too smart for nothing; some bastard's trying to fake me out and I just put it smack out of my mind—bang! it's gone. I drive right over everything.

"Course I don't know what I'd do if this goes sour. I guess . . . I guess I just can't take a dive, and I don't know what I'm going to do if they cut me out. They're pretty mad. . . ."

He stopped.

"You ought to get right back out of it, this life," he began quietly. "Amelia, it isn't fitting."

"This was just a . . . try." To say: She wasn't too stuck up for her friends. For her family.

"Only girls get stuck in this is not normal. *Daggers,* what I mean, if you know what I mean."

She stared blankly.

"Ah," he said. "Just skip it, okay? Um." He glared at the road. "What you going to do when you get out of here?"

"College." She watched his face. "I'm going to college."

He nodded, proud. "Course you got to get out. The smarter you are, the less people like you. So you going to be a teacher like your mama?"

She hadn't really connected herself with her mother—not that way. But . . . teacher. She had no more clear idea what she was going to do than a counting-out rhyme. *Brakeman, fireman—*

Of course she wouldn't race—that wasn't decent; but . . .

How was it? She liked to know things. She did like teaching where it *showed,* like with Terry, but look where that might lead. . . . She was a little too vain to consider teaching, where the only thing noted was if she was physically there—one to a classroom, just like the clock on the wall. Like Mrs. Adams. She'd be no better. She'd be bored and discouraged.

"I'm drunk, you know," she said in the spirit of inquiry.

Maybe she was selfish but she could not stand to think of repeating herself, never progressing; so many things to know, and she didn't even know how you go about knowing them. Maybe in college. Metals. Stars. Cities. Paris. Moscow . . . What she really wanted to do was find out everything; yes. College. To be what? What was she good at? How could she know till she got to where the choices were?

Kelso was waiting patiently for her answer.

> Brakeman, fireman, engineer
> Private, sergeant-major, chief
> Robber, burglar, forger, thief . . .

Outside the wash of the headlights the world was cold, unreal and still; the night and speed made it shorter, dimmer, more manageable; or perhaps that was the booze. Terry's head bumped rhythmically against the window glass; she touched him on the right; Joe to left: disturbing against his warm, hard shoulder. It was close. Vaguely disquieting. A feeling that, under the haze of liquor, she wasn't quite sure made sense. It didn't feel right.

Yet it seemed very important that she decide how to answer him, and one way struck her as as good as any: *Brake-man,* she thought, *fire-man . . .* It struck her. It had never crossed her mind before, but was clearly the perfect answer. Absorbing, elegant, well-respected: "Engineer," she said suddenly.

"How much?"

"Engineer."

"What. Run a train?"

"Industrial de—"

"Bridges?" he laughed, squeezing her shoulder.

"Cars." In her head she added: *Steel braces.*

"Race cars?"

"Sure. Race cars, kiddie cars, boxcars. Red . . . with—"

"Fine, fine! I could say I knew this real smart girl was so smart in math she corrected the teacher—you remember when you done that?" He gave her a squeeze as she laughed; that felt wrong. Many conflicting signals at once from all over herself. From her thigh.

"Race cars." He laughed. "I'll drink to that."

"Me too," she said. "You know, that doesn't taste all that bad, really. I kind of like it. I mean I really. Kind of do." She hiccupped suddenly.

"You get used to it." He smiled, and kissed her warmly.

She pulled up in front of her father's house with one eye shut to singularize the newly plural world. There was a rock-hard, rammed-in pain in her upper stomach. What if she had been killed in the race, flamed out in glory. What if Ethan *had* come.

At least she wouldn't have been drinking, have . . .

The house was dark. Under the hulking street light, the house and yard were vivid; fat snowflakes were threading an unhurried zigzag path to the lawn and the walk, with Mama's border of trampled rosemary and the thyme bush that would not grow—so innocent with a dusting of snow on the threadbare yard as if the days to come were all good Christmases and nothing as important as death had ever twisted their lives—

Mama, she said to the walk or the snow, *that's why you didn't only teach half a year, wasn't it. I was a sooner. That's why you didn't keep it up. . . .*

The cold was hitting hard; weak and shaking, she clung to the car frame, afraid to try and stand by herself. The pain in her stomach was growing insistent.

Feeling her way around the toast-warm hood, she inched toward the passenger's side, opened the door and hung from it—hoping to vomit.

"Ammy!"

She jumped.

Jimmy fidgeted in front of her, his fists in his pockets. "Sorry, I thought you seen me."

She had other business.

"Where you been?"

"Lower your . . . voice."

"Where have you been," he hissed. "I been all over looking

for you. I found the car and I thought I'd go crazy. Where have you—"

"What's it to you? For God's sake get lost."

"You been drinking."

She hauled herself up to look squarely at him, feeling her balance shift, feeling her whole body contract. "I started drinking with you, because *you insisted!*"

"Women don't— I never let you get in a state like *that*—"

"What do you mean, not *let!*"

Then she was heaving in the gutter, hanging onto the door, vaguely aware of his maidenish fussing: "I didn't mean to lose my temper tonight . . . lost money . . . I'm real sorry you're sick, maybe I shouldn't of give you the 'shine—" Why, in the name of God's decency, didn't he go away and let her die in peace? But on he fussed. And as she was wiping her eyes he said: "Look— Ammy Lee, I chased all over this county asking about you and I come all the way over here and waited to this hour of the morning to say I'm sorry, so I'm sorry, Ammy Lee. Cain't you just say one thing about it? I don't give a hang if it's just politeness. I been here since midnight—and it's *four-thirty.*"

She wiped her face.

"I know it don't mean nothing but you should of not stayed out like that. 'Tain't safe and it isn't decent, neither. They see that car sitting there, and—you know how people can talk . . ."

She laid her head on her folded arms.

"Ammy," he murmured. "What would your mama say if she was to—"

"Nothing! She wouldn't say nothing first because she's stone dead and second because don't nobody here act no different and don't you never throw her up to me again, do you hear me?"

He stared, troubled, trying to read her. "There you go. There you go, second time tonight making fun of my talk. Ammy Lee, some people has the ability to talk like a teevee set and some—"

"We have had the same schooling and you are going to graduate in eight months—at least you could try to improve yourself—but you're lazy. All of you, lazy. Nobody in this whole damn town tries to be any goddamn thing or wants to know any goddamn thing and none of you tries, even *tries,* well you just stay a good little cracker boy but you are *not* going to *ruin my chances!*"

"I never," he said coldly, "liked no one who talked like that."

"Just leave me alone, won't you—all of you! You just stay a nice little cracker boy, but I'm going to *go* somewhere and I'm going to *be* something!"

"Well it ain't no race driver, sugar. You can bet your fanny on that."

She shut the car door and unsteadily started up the steps. Behind her his angry bootsteps squeaked on the snow then stopped, and she knew he had his eyes on her, watching her up the steps—steaming to fling at her one last furious word.

"Ammy," he exclaimed. "Ammy? Your shoe."

There was an elaborate lattice in her hose where a right shoe had been; in the street, Jimmy had the car door open and was on his knees in the snow, scrabbling under the seat. He jumped up, slamming his fist on the hood, and screamed at her: "Ammy! Amelia Lee you tell me right now!" There were tears in his voice. "You didn't—you didn't, did you? Ammy you can't get knocked up and never *get* anywhere—my God, what on earth's the matter with you?"

She was trying to quiet the scraping outside door, and didn't answer. He'd been sweet on her, and she'd truly never seen it. . . .

The gap between them had widened when she had only meant to mend their fences; and she'd done two things she could never stand to repeat again. Three things.

She looked back.

He was standing in the street light with the new snow in his hair, bawling like a baby, empty-handed.

DADDY'S GIRL

Sally had had a funny hunch, call it a premonition, before she left the restaurant. The side lot and the back of the hotel were too dark for the walk, but that wasn't it. . . . She should have gone with her first thought and had the car valeted. After all, it looked like rain—she really didn't feel that well—and the girl would have paid for it.

The surrounding buildings were blocking, or at least slowing, the rising wind, but enough moaned through to chill her completely. Or maybe it was the wine; she had drunk too much. Or was it the man near the entrance who had *looked* at them. . . . A block-built man, all ice and onyx. They had passed within a dozen feet of him and not until the sharp breath from Assina had Sally realized that this was the one she called Papa, of whom she claimed, "Papa is so *thorough*"—her inflection, as ever, placing distasteful stress. They had slipped out the back.

"He didn't see us, Sina," Sally had lied.

She wanted to get away from him. For that matter, she

wanted away from Assina. Walking quickly, she made to improve the lie.

"Didn't you see him hail a waiter? He was just getting a table," she gasped. "Maybe he's called for a phone and wants to surprise you. . . . I'll drop off and you can tell him—"

"Papa," breathed Sina.

Fifteen feet to their right, two block walls joined. It was so dark. In this corner sat Sally's Mazda, an Avis van to its left, and before the van, reinforcing its fixedness, was a blocky man in a longish dark coat. He held his head oddly, his jaw toward the side, like a foreigner. Like a foreign official.

"This is . . . Papa, this is my friend—"

"Yes?" he said sharply: he had the same peculiar accent as Assina. Somewhat thicker.

"Sally was going to give me a ride to the college with my bicycle. It's a little late, so she—"

"This is your car?" he trilled sharply. "It appears disabled."

There had been nothing wrong with the car. Before she had left it, absolutely nothing.

"The tires," he said. "There is a serving station three blocks down this street. I drove by it as I came. We will have them send someone. Get in." He was standing between Sally and the hotel. The wall was behind her. "Such"—he corrected himself—"*such* a good friend to my daughter, we must in*sist.*"

Assina had small cheeks, a sharp nose and small eyes and was perhaps contemplating Sally again, but from behind such thick lenses it was hard to guess. She watched Sally unreadably, twitching her head left–right like a bright little bug. She was a nervous kid, full of quick, erratic movements. "Do you remember when we met?" she was saying plaintively. "Oh, I *hope* you do—" Her almost-accent showed in her clipping of *t*'s.

This would be Sally's last dinner with her. The first had been a nice night, the second good, but if the girl hadn't spent money like water, there certainly wouldn't have been any others; surely Assina could not be so green she hadn't known. But perhaps she was. That could be her foreign upbringing.

"You do remember, don't you?" whined the girl.

Waiting to see if she'd spring for another drink, Sally put on her best oh-dear smile. "Of course . . ." she said vaguely.

This place impressed her: the Empress, in the heart of downtown, a place where a glass of crystal-graced water cost ten dollars. There were tiny blue phones available for every elegant white-lace table, but to Sina this place was merely passable, and only ten blocks from that small, exclusive college she attended. A college kid. A very *juvenile* college kid, and studying literature and philosophy. Or philology . . . ?

"We met at L'Amoureuse. . . ." persisted Sina. This memory seemed to give her confidence, and this confidence produced a crafty smile. "I was just going by—on my bicycle, do you remember?—and you had a Lamarc Pinot Noir on the table. A '79. That was a terrible year."

She'd looked pretty and sly, a quick little thing. Hopeful.

As she had when they had met, Sally was thinking that Sina looked like nothing so much as a mouse. A pretty little needle-toothed mouse, who said nothing interesting, but she surely was a willing little . . . Would kiss here, bend there, move that way, use this—anything to please, only murmuring: *I never tried this before, but if you like* . . . And cuddling up in your arms like a cute stuffed teddy. But an *animated* teddy—oh my lord.

And would buy you anything.

And could.

Assina Vlanda, of all the ugly handles. Thrilled and full of the awe that sparkled: *"I'm* wicked."

But this particular evening Sally had been sure the girl had called to say that they were finally agreed. That it was over between them and never should have been. And hardly had been. Yet here was Sina, with her peculiar inflections, wanting to talk beginnings—as if *nothing* would end. Sally sat drinking in the white lace alcove, awaiting any point Sina might choose to make, since she did provide the money.

Vlanda's frame crowded Sally toward the passenger side of the van. "After you," he said heavily. His hand on her shoulder, pressing her into the seat past him as Sina, on the other side, launched herself into the driver's seat. The man planted himself by the passenger door so that Sally was sandwiched between them. Vlanda placed on the dashboard a pack of American cigarettes. Too dark to read the name.

"Papa," came Assina's plaintive voice. "The door doesn't—"

"It locks over here." He leaned over Sally, blocking her light. Locks clicked on the doors, the back door, all around the van.

"It's two months. I even gave you a ring," said Sina.

They had met at L'Amoureuse, which had summer tables out along the boulevard. Sally had been sitting at one after a good dinner inside, sitting discreetly with friends—a couple, actually—drinking ouzo when this small bright-beglassed thing rested her bicycle against the flimsy wooden barrier between the street and the bar, leaned over the partition, and, resting her sharp chin on her arm, had invited, "Hey . . . I haven't seen *you* before. . . ."

Sally liked to date around. Didn't like to be tied down. but . . .

Dear, dear.

Those eyes were so wide, so dark. Little teeth flashed as she smiled, as she complained that night, as she always complained, of life, of school, of her father—which alone should have betrayed her extreme youth to Sally. With Sina, it was *Oh, Papa,* and a thrill like fear and like something else as well. A bad taste stayed in the air whenever she mentioned him.

But the girl herself. What delightful breasts. A light frame, on the small side, but a woman most definitely. And no doubt about her preference.

"I was at the bar again," Sina snapped, grabbing her attention. "I was there last Wednesday. *I paid them pretty well*—they didn't throw me out this time, you may be sure."

Wednesday? Sally thought. She had thought Sina studied on the weeknights. What happened Wednesday? "Wednesday?" she finally offered. "I was down there Wednesday night, around eleven—"

"I saw you."

Having worked late, Sally had gone out to clear her head and at the bar, met some friends: after salad and wine had run into . . . oh, yes. The dance. Assina must have seen that. Well, it was about time Sally's objections registered with Sina. Time her corrections about *things* between them implanted themselves and grew. They were, after all, just friends. Acquaintances, actually; and it would only have been one night, but the girl had spent so much.

The van lurched eagerly into traffic, Sina nearly standing on the pedals, and as they began to gain traffic speed, Sally became increasingly aware of Vlanda's stare. Studying her, dispassionate as a coroner. Maybe, she told herself, she had had too much to drink. But she was sobering very quickly.

"I saw you," said the girl pointedly. Angry. She put down the wineglass and picked up the water glass.

"Toni's a good friend."

"I would *imagine* she would *have* to be."

Sally lit a cigarette, inbreathed deeply, tapped the tip.

"You are *free*. You are one of those, those *free*, those *free* . . . You call them . . . You were with some other girl on *Thursday*."

"I did go to a movie with Stephanie. . . ." That wasn't true, but this was at least a way out. "And, you know, I still live with Gloria."

"Lived, you said *lived*, but you said you, you were not any longer—"

"I said the relationship had changed. We were dating other people."

"You," said the girl with her chin high and angry, "are a *free* woman, a—a *pleasure* seeker—"

Ordinary phrases shaped in that mouth so oddly. "You picked *me* up, dear," Sally yawned. "And not the other way around. Did you come to my bed for my beautiful soul, or because our relationship had had such time to mature?"

Sina's stare dropped. Then she shifted, and straightening, lifted her glass to the right. Like magic, a waiter arrived to fill it, overlooking Sina's obvious age. In this beautiful place, she could buy whatever she liked.

* * *

"I have been having you . . . observed," said Vlanda. Sina's head snapped right, eyes wide. "I'm pretty thoroughly angry with you." He said something in their language.

Police, Sally panicked. A confession from the girl and turn Sally in to the cops. How old was she? Seventeen, sixteen? Remind the girl they had *loved* . . .

Covertly but completely, Sina shrugged off Sally's pressing hand.

"Anyway, my father writes like he's going to be in the area again and it sounds, it sounds like he thinks something's, well, funny. He's done that once or twice before, just come. Not announced himself. He is uneasy for me. He treats me like a child."

A child *princess*, Sally gathered. But oddly; which raising could account for the unique significance she seemed to expect some words and phrases to have—simple and common words for which Sally's interpretations differed. It seemed to be a difference carried over from her language. But— Oh, hell. She had been thinking about this girl entirely too much. This must be the reason she had called Sally—not that she'd caught on that Sally wanted to break it off. . . .

"He's angry. Remember when you said I could . . . engender . . . more capital if you pretended to kidnap me? I thought it was very *funny*, but *Papa* thought—"

"You didn't tell him that!"

"Well . . ." Sina's little teeth bit her lip. "Well, he didn't be*lieve* it, of course. But he doesn't give his *approval.* . . ."

"Approval?" Sally was shocked. "What did you—?"

"Nothing. Just not a thing, really. Only he doesn't believe I'm studying very hard. . . . He comes through on business a few times a season, and—if he asks me now, where will I tell him I've been? He says he calls and calls and— He is always finding me out."

Find her out? Not likely. She had more than her share of secrets.

With ice-faced Vlanda close enough to freeze the skin of her thigh, she could not deny she held her breath. The idea of police seemed fairly agreeable. Whatever they did, they would also protect her from him. From *them*.

Sina's spectacles glinted over the elegant carafe, into Sally, prying to see her *pleasure* and her *evil*. After a moment, Sally turned away, irritated and suddenly fatigued, which was perhaps because of the wine.

The girl's stare changed, became a dull fascination. She took a sip of wine. "I guess this is over, then," she said suddenly. "You really do not want me anymore. You were just . . . *free* with me."

Sally smiled thinly. Perhaps she only meant this evening was over. Or the wine. It was too much to hope she meant the end of her "love." "You should try being a little free yourself." Her voice was too loud, people were staring, and she dropped down to a whisper. "How do you know you wouldn't like it?"

Assina was staring. "If . . . well . . . if you . . . could you just give me a ride back to the campus?"

"What about your bike?"

Sina gave her Expectant Look. She'd leave the bike locked there. So this was not to be the end of her "love." And on, and on . . .

"Sure," sighed Sally. "I'm around back."

At the top of a street, the van passed a barricade, a high street deserted through construction not far from the main intersection into Sina's college. Street lights were few or out, earthworks thrown up like a battle zone.

"Here! Stop."

Pavlovian, Sina slammed the brakes down. Her glossy head, bobbed of a piece, shined in the half light like a globe.

"There!" he snapped. "Back up, hit that large piping there!"

They were traveling backwards, Sally's head snapping back. "Why?" she said. "Why do you want to wreck the—"

"Fif-teen miles per hour," he snapped; and they slammed the pipe, killing the engine.

Wan light grayed the mounds of earth by the black ditches and the great piled ceramic pipe. Sally pulled herself off the dash, sat back in her seat. She found herself counting her heart-beats, lost count. Touched Assina . . .

"You were not true to me," whispered Sina.

Sweat was cold and slick on Sally's back.

"Not *true*, to me, and I gave you anything you—"

"We never said we were in love," blurted Sally. "I love you, but—"

The man slapped air viciously. *"That's* enough of *this filth,"* he hissed. "Out," he ordered Sina. "I'll take this up with you later."

He drew a long, calm breath. "But you"—in Sally's ear—"and *I,* we will have a short talk. . . ."

That first night, Sally had asked her *What do you do there?* about the college. Sina had said *Early entry,* which sounded vaguely obscene. *It means, I am in college early for my age.* Sally had been rocked. She was only thinking the kid looked rather athletic, which makes you *younger* looking. "Don't tell me," she had said, not really smiling. "Please don't say you're under twenty."

Giggle.

Oh, hell. "Well . . . under nineteen?"

Giggle.

"Dear God. Just don't say under eighteen. . . ."

Silence then.

Rats.

But this *early* one sure knew what she was doing.

Sina sat with one foot dangling from the van. "Run!" screamed Sally. "The cops, get—"

The blow caught at midriff. A sudden crushing; sucking for breath, she threw up her hands and bone-shattering pain hit her shoulder, her elbow—her hands numb. She strove to breathe but large fingers gripped her collar, fingering her collar, gathered the edges extremely tightly—tightly enough that she held extremely still.

Vlanda's hidden hand brought up a square whiskey bottle and an ice-liquid burned down the front of her sweater. He reached for the cigarettes. . . .

"Go!" he ordered Sina. The collar was extremely tight. "Go to your rooms and wait!"

Get help, run, thought Sally frantically, *run, run.*

The little stalls in the elaborate restroom were as formed and as fancy as rental cubicles at the airport; as Sally was arranging her clothing she was amused and puzzled to see Sina's pretty hand come down over the stall and unfasten the bolt. This was a habit with Sina. Glancing quickly and automatically around her, the girl let herself in, turned as swiftly as her eyes and fitted her sleek head under Sally's nose, confident as a purring cat, and curved herself backwards so that she fitted herself into Sally's arm. With effort, Sally pushed her back out of the stall. Just for a moment. It was always hard to talk her into some privacy. . . .

Sina continued to sit on the seat for a moment. As if Sally were something unclear . . . and *something else.* "You had better put her in the driving seat," she murmured. "A vain hope," she said to herself. "Vain hope . . ." She slid off the seat, slipped easily to the ground.

But it was not bad at all—standing, sitting or lying—not bad at all, not that it ever had been—privacy or no. Sally again wrapped around that taut, athletic body with her lips on the base of that porcelain throat. Easy to fall back into.

But as they were walking back into the foyer, the girl's tiny bright eyes turned hard. "I still hate you, though. You've been having women right along, haven't you? You didn't really love me, did you? It was *pleasure.* It was like Papa would say, it was just pleasure—and you, you've lost the ring I lent you, too. Those were real diamonds."

They had been. And lovely.

"Aren't you ever going to come out of there?" whined the girl, and finally Sally opened the stall door. Her heart was racing. She turned and traced her hand along the cool, pink marble of the wall. It had somehow been a dream, then. In the washroom. In one of the cubicles. They hadn't left—separately or together.

"Are you ill? Do you need a, a physician?"

"I think . . . maybe I drank . . ."

"At your age!" Assina laughed. "This isn't very becoming. Do you wish to lean on me?"

"No. Yes—I . . ."

"You look like someone seeing ghosts. Did they give you good advice?"

"No. That is, I . . . slept." Sally leaned on the wall in front of the exit. The rosewood furnishings seemed less real than had the nightmare. "I had a dream."

"You did drink too much. I took your keys and sent the boy for your car. Perhaps I shall drive."

Sally, woozy, sat down suddenly on a plush couch. Let the girl make the arrangements. Maybe there was something she should learn. . . .

"Lean on me," crooned Assina. "Lean on me."

And it was not far to the desk, where Assina paid the bill; and it was not far to the door, past which was Sally's little Mazda, muttering blue smoke into the mizzling rain. But her knees would not hold her. The damp air was not reviving her at all, merely chilling her.

"I'll wait. I think I want to sit for—" But Assina had opened the door. "Just lean on me." The grip was firm, Sina's arms alone holding her up. "It will only take a moment."

Past Sally's car, on the opposite, passenger side, stooped the valet. She felt in her pocket; the keys were in the car. She was dizzy. What a large man, this valet. His black coat—

"Wait," she said, but the universe turned. Hotel staff wore blue. But the door opened and as the bear-man got in the opposite side, she was shoved past the wheel by a surprisingly cool and strong little Daddy's Girl.

UNSEASONAL WEATHER

Another damned delay. But for variation this time, it wasn't the fan belt or the air-conditioning. This one came from the locals at a roadblock, and Ellen watched glumly as the driver, seated next to her, pushed up her wire-frame glasses and leaned forward intently, slowing the truck, rolling down the window toward the flagman. He was yelling something. They weren't to go any farther? It was hard to hear him, and his accent really didn't help.

"Watersup ovrda road," he bawled. "Gotta go back or down over thattaway—" Roughly north. "We're putting levees up!"

"But there's no road that way—" bleated Cameron, clutching the wheel.

"There's a temp down. Gravel, see? You get to Conner you follow that gravel. We'll open back up fast as we can. Get on offa the road!"

It smelt of broiling black earth out here. Air like a steam bath.

"You mean," said Cameron, "we can't get through to South Dakota?"

Oh, soul of logic, Ellen thought, and slid still lower in her seat.

The man began explaining various things about time and levees, the cool air began leaking out of the cab, and Ellen leaned forward and turned off the air conditioner. They needed the air conditioner, especially Ellen did, and meanwhile, as usual, Cameron chattered on.

Another delay. But at least it sounded as if this time Ellen could pick up some exercise. She had a daily goal of three miles, but would settle for two.

It seemed that the Missouri River, among others, was at flood because of the week's unseasonal rain (*Never floods this late,* claimed men at gas stations). The deluge had given way to this unseasonable heat, but engorged tributaries continued to swell the rivers, making freakish floods under a hot-white sky.

Meanwhile their laboring truck kept overheating and the air-conditioning had already failed once, necessitating a four- or five-hour delay. It was clear that something else would break, and that once again Cameron would be talked into a pocket about repairs. Ellen's pocket . . . A false economy. As Mother had foretold, this trip cross-country to Berkeley was a *false* economy.

Cameron backed, maneuvered the truck, and began to follow a less talkative driver who had been following them, had caught the drift, and had turned just short of the barrier, directly off onto the shoulder and down the dumped-gravel pro tem road that ran on bumpily next a barbed-wire fence for about fifty feet, then plunged down an embankment to join a paved two-lane road that abruptly began about a hundred yards right, directly in front of a farm lot. Cameron U-turned left, following that car, and hooked back left again under the interstate to what might have been a town, but there was no posted name.

The area seemed to be a crossroads within what was, from the bait and tackle signs, a very small fishing resort, upon an unseen tributary to the Missouri; arranged in roughly clockwise fashion stood a large fenced field, an eight-unit motel, a tavern and a grocery-restaurant. Several houses and a trailer were in easy view of the road. The announced fishing was a little way down beyond them on the roads they had reached. Any fishing was probably stalled now, like the highway.

There were large-bolled trees shading the roadside and the houses, grand but very few, and heat shimmered off the tarmac, melding a variety of greens. It was mostly open countryside, and the lately soaked landscape had cracked like an egg under the massive heat of the sky.

A few detoured cars and trucks were already stopped along the only two roads, which crossed at the tavern up ahead.

Such heat in May was incredible, especially to Ellen in her long sleeves and chinos. "Lovely," sneered Ellen. "Just where I wanted to spend—"

"Oh, it is lovely, isn't it?" mooned Cameron. "Such a nice place handy in a flood. . . . Look! A jackrabbit!"

She appeared delighted: pretty, as the saying goes, and dumb. Cameron saw, or thought she saw, bison, foxes, carrion crows . . . jackrabbits. There was no rabbit to be seen, and nothing to say.

The tiny Teepee Café, part pit stop, part grocery, had a red-and-blue OPEN sign standing out in the road. It stood on their side of the tavern, shy of the crossing road; and next the café and across a parking lot was the hot pink Smith's Motel, which had a languid pit bulldog chained along one side.

"I hope that dog has water," said Cameron.

Actually, the monster had a bucketful.

"Anyway, they have it in the shade," finished Cameron. "Let's get a Coke."

Drinking sugar, always.

One of these days she would wake up big as a barn.

Cameron straddled the little truck over a shallow ditch behind the pink motel, in direct line behind what already must be a major motor invasion of this village. This left Ellen to open her door over a ditch, and the ditch made her descent a yard longer than Cameron's. She briefly considered sliding out the driver's side, but the stick shift was blocking her way.

As Cameron was trotting toward the café, safely away from

the truck, Ellen considered that at least she could exit in peace. Irritably, she gripped her door to minimize the shock, and jumped.

Limping slightly, chafing her wrists, she followed Cameron. An air-conditioning unit was groaning and spitting from the back of the place. Air-conditioning: There was some way out of this heat. . . .

Cameron, from the back, was rather nice. She was formed rather nicely, and from the folds in her shorts to the joint with her thighs, she had a nice swing. A nice roundness . . .

Cameron turned suddenly.

"What's the matter? Did you hurt yourself? You're rubbing your hand—did you cut yourself on the door?"

Suddenly Ellen was angry. As if Cameron hadn't seen the same thing thousands of times this trip. "No," she said, clasped her hands behind her and stopped cold.

"What's the matter? Let's go!"

"I get stiff just sitting," said Ellen. "I thought I'd stretch my legs."

"You could do something about *that*. You're supposed to do half the driving."

Ellen made a parade turn, and stalked away.

It was unseasonably hot, but the dust-thick road bisecting the settlement was overarched with trees that were blocking the worst of the sun. Still the lane wasn't cool, and the once-wet earth exhaled around it heavily, though a lighter breath seemed caught in the blue of the shade. Heat waves danced on the road and on the flat land, but with the little stirring of air she found it bearable. She could walk, if not her two miles; and at least she could think in peace.

The same week she had received notice about her fellow-ship, her doctor had come up with more news—not too bad, since she was feeling giddily rich. Here was money accruing to her for no other reason than her sheer hard work; not money from Mother. Perhaps that had made her feel, well, magnani-mous. Wanting to do something that was exactly right. Not that Ellen was ordinarily extravagant, but she wanted to do, to say

. . . and there was Mother's Day and— Maybe it had been a flamboyant gesture. Ellen had seen the thing and simply bought it.

Mother—a memento . . .

As she was descending from her doctor's suite, there it was, nearly next door, in the dim window of a row-house shop.

The place was was one of those dark, old, wood-smelling antique shops that are almost like funerary sites for curios, and posed just off-center on a carved chest was a hand-figured music box: *Liebestod* a foot or so high, inlaid with many woods; the youth and the maiden pursued each other on tiny tracks with the three stern hunters, the fallow deer, the dogs . . .

It chimed out a clear and tinny "Ode to the Evening Star," Mother's favorite. It chimed other Wagner themes on the quarter hour, shifting the main theme every quarter day. This was a gift of exquisite taste; with all due consideration this was a gift that would charm even Mother.

Her husbands had never got the trick of a gift worthy. They'd received a moral pat and a shake of her head, a noble restraint at, what, taste? Expense? A lack thereof?

And then there had been this elegant, exquisite piece of workmanship.

In a sense, Ellen concluded later, the music box had been an assertion of their new relationship. Women together in a man's world.

And Mother had turned and said: "How could we have erred like this with you, Ellen?" And on came *Youngest . . . only girl. Men do so know the value of a dollar. . . . Absurd . . . an unmarried girl to spend on a trinket.*

Strange how much that hurt. A continuance of labels placed on Ellen at seven. Profligate, romantic, unrealistic. *Buying her little girlfriends at school.*

No doubt that was the reason Ellen had decided to do everything, take it all with her on her own terms. Get away. Going West—*without dying.*

But what price pride? Three hot days on the road west. What wouldn't she give to be able to stroll into a local airport, one big enough to ship freight. (Her boxes of books were a real problem. It was not easy to quit and be left at, say, a Greyhound depot with seven heavy boxes of books.)

You need how much to send them? . . . Ellie, if you need a specific book, I'll Federal Express it or you can buy another. Honestly. This is a false economy, Ellie. You act like you're emigrating. And I want you here when I marry Randal Lawson at Thanksgiving.

Ellen would not be back. The fellowship would be her independence. . . .

It might actually be possible to rent a light airplane from here. *(And Mother would say . . .)*

Cameron's ad had read:

Woman seeks same to share drive Boston to Bay
Area. Storage space, air conditioning . . .

The best-laid plans.

Yesterday they had driven 150 miles at ninety-five plus without air-conditioning. When she'd realized Cameron was going to let it go, going to—dripping—drive to Berkeley without it, she herself had paid to have the condenser replaced. Amid the squawks—

And that woman:

"You've never been West?"

"No," said Ellen.

"Why not?"

Ellen couldn't think up an answer to that.

"I lived in San Francisco for a while; there were only five or six of us then, and when I was about nineteen I moved back, went to SFS for a while. I've got some cousins and friends there; oh, yeah, I got a brother in San Diego; then we lived in Seattle when my folks worked at Boeing. Boy, was that boring. That is such a boring place, dark, and they don't have very many birds. I mean, very many kinds of birds. . . . Then Boeing went bust when I was about five, and we moved to Wichita, then we moved to Boston but then after my folks split up . . ."

Ellen stared out at the scorching grass, stupid with boredom, because reading in the jarring truck was making her carsick.

"—traveled?"

"What?" said Ellen.

"I said, Where else have you traveled?"

"Well . . . I haven't gone a lot of places. Well, I attended Oxford and picked up a junior degree, but I really didn't see much of England. I hardly got out of the libraries. I guess I'm not really one for scenery. . . ."

Ellen hadn't had enough money to protect herself in an unprotected environment. It was Mother (and her late father) who were wealthy. She had only gone where she'd had the protection to go.

"Hell, now that I think about it, I have done some traveling. I toured a little directly out of high school. You know, the trip before college. And then we used to go to Nice, autumns, but that was before Daddy died. I was rather small. It wasn't much of a place for children. So I really haven't traveled much. I used to do a little traveling with my brother Louis when we were in our teens . . . but . . ."

But Louis was bossy, and they were often tossed out of hotels, because they were brother and sister and spoke the language and knew when they were being gouged. Tourist couples bumped them. In any case youths were expected to pack into airless crowded hostels, without hot running water and with far too many aggressive boys. It was awkward and embarrassing and genuinely unclean. And she hurt. And she didn't like strangers. And she had passed as Canadian.

"Actually," she finished, "I haven't traveled much, but Mother travels a good deal."

There was silence. Watching the endless American Nothing going by, there seemed to be an echoing, unfriendly silence, and Ellen began to grasp that Cameron was not amused.

And why?

After a pregnant five minutes she'd turned . . . to a narrow-eyed Cameron. Scornful. Small. Just as she should have expected. *Petty jealousy.*

The "small truck" advertised had a sticky clutch Ellen found harder and harder to kick to the floor; and the wheel. Had she never driven a car without power steering? It must have been before her joints were so bad; she had surely not known it would hurt so much to drive it.

And the driver.

. . . Easy-going woman, nonsmoker, seeks same to share expenses. . . .

Hardly the same. They were utterly incompatible.

Things that look too good to be true, usually are (Mother would say). Quite. Right.

Mother was truly amused with graduate school, with scholarship of any kind. It had been Daddy who loved to read. How *nice*, said Mother, to be *clever*. But the main dispute had been sending all those books.

College students did this all the time, didn't they? Though this was the very first time in her life Ellen had done such a thing. She had felt protected; if things went poorly, she'd just offer more money. But . . .

Cameron talked, all the time, about nothing. To all gas station attendants. Other drivers.

Cameron saw, in rough order, woodchucks, foxes, ground squirrels, coyotes, burros and various kinds of cattle and every kind of flying thing nameable; and found all of this remarkable, and remarked, at some length, on everything and anything she saw or imagined she saw, along the roads. *Oh, a scissortail* (whatevershesaid). *Can you imagine, a scissortail* (whatevershesaid) *out here?* No. The question was rhetorical; the answer was: No. Ellen could not by any stretch have imagined the whatsit, or the foxes or hawks or any part of this last three days.

It had seemed so—American Youth. So promising: Cameron chatty, as Ellen herself was not. Irish, freckled, bespectacled, dishwater blond—homely except for a turned-up nose that lent her an elfin look. Though with really a lovely form. Young-goddess-like. In this as in everything else they were utterly different: Ellen with jet black, lightning-rod-straight hair, dark brown eyes, boyish hips, nose with a slight hook, rather like her mother's. A nose with class.

She should have shipped her things and taken a plane. Mother was right. If time was money, this was drunken profligacy.

A complete turn of the town took less than fifteen minutes, but Ellen was perspiring freely under the long sleeves, itching unmercifully. That and the intense heat drove her inside the Teepee, where the first thing she spotted was Cameron listening avidly to three women and a man and appearing to be almost on the edge of jumping in to set everyone straight. That girl was such a fool. Ellen decided to return to the truck and retrieve "Enoch Arden."

She bought an apple, found the truck locked, fretted, and took a walk only a short way down the only other road, which crossed the first. It was now far too hot, and four in the afternoon. A Coke would taste good. If she could sneak past Cameron and sit alone . . . but there was such a crowd. In fact, there was a crowd in front of the bar across from the café—perhaps there was a Coke machine outside.

The men were all talking at once.

I'll tell you I never seen it like this since . . .

A mild voice: "Well, we're going to just dump the kids. Me and Lena's going to have a nice dinner, hit the LaSalle, maybe—"

"How you getting to the LaSalle?"

"Why, Wayne—"

"When you think they're going to have that road open? You think you can get five *miles* west of here before—"

"Why, they say soon as they get the last levees shored they—"

"I'd like to see that! It's raining Hail Columbia north of here. You ought to have been at the water board meeting last month. We got a real mess. They haven't even got a dike at Lewston, and it's going to be eyeball-deep before eight o'clock, and look at here. Got six axles from every state in the union, so don't think you're going to get a decent dinner out with the Missus, either. Look around you. We got a mo-tel and not one campground and all these camp-happy tourists crapping all over the county, yapping about how the road is supposed to be open—"

A word to the wise, thought Ellen, and turned abruptly back toward the truck.

Campers and cars now lined both sides of the road and were filling up the grassy shoulders and the outermost edges of the flat, ragged lawns. Some vehicles were turning back east, going back at least fifty miles, hoping to turn north or south and take another road, though it was rather late for that. But for every impatient driver, there was one with implicit faith in the Highway Patrol. These would wait . . . and wait. And everything within fifty miles would be taken. Ellen went to Smith's Motel and produced some cash.

The crammed Teepee, its air-conditioning pointedly beginning to fail, was full enough for young kids and polite men to be sitting in the windows. Ellen was thinking about trying the tavern when she heard someone stridently shouting her name, trying to get her attention. "Ellen! Hey! Ellen, over here!"

She flinched. Why couldn't Cameron ever be civilized—

Wearing the pleasantest look she had handy, Ellen sauntered over to the booth, which Cameron was sharing with an entire family from Akron, Ohio. And seemed to fit right in. She had a gift for that. Ellen arranged her features to look interested but not invasive, good-humored but not available; and the father, a blond smiling fellow, jerked himself up and yanked a chair forward for her.

She murmured thanks, gripped the chair, and as she was sliding down into it the little boy up-dumped a glass of water. Water and ice cascaded, Ellen jumped up and the man jumped too and so collided with her; he spent the next few minutes on and off apologizing until she was thoroughly sick of him. The ice water on her jeans and shirt wasn't all that unwelcome, anyway.

"Why didn't you go the Canadian route, then?" continued Cameron over the hullaballoo.

"Well, you know . . ." apologized the man.

"We were afraid about the border. Steve checked into everything first but we were afraid we'd have trouble at the border because—"

"About Wiener!" screamed a child.

"Wiener's our dog!" screamed the spiller.

"We have a prize-winning weimaraner, and the kennel had to cancel suddenly, so there we were with a bitch about to—"

"Wiener is our dog!"

"We were afraid we'd get to the border and find out they wouldn't let—"

"You don't," launched Cameron, "mean to tell me you have a dog out in the car in this heat!"

"A weimaraner," nodded the woman. "They were going to breed her while we were gone, but . . ."

Here we go, thought Ellen, smiling inanely.

"It's too hot!" said Cameron vehemently. "You really must tie the dog out in the shade—you'll just have to watch her from the window and if she's in season, you'll just have to fix it up later—"

Ellen approved the sentiment, but why be so imperious? Full of advice. Ellen didn't approve of the dog out in this heat, but they were all, every one of them here, so exhausting. Noisy, confusing, constantly interrupting. They made her head ache. She was afraid the man would bump into her again, and hurt her elbow. At the earliest possible break, she smiled out, stopped at the cash register and wrote a note about the motel, and sent it over to Cameron in a waitress's resentful hand.

As Ellen passed the motel office, she could not help noticing irritated drivers, one in particular, standing with the rather overwhelmed Smith's owners in the parking lot. He was offering the mournful husband three and four times the ordinary weekend charge and threatening, cajoling, bullying and . . . bringing up his kids. His poor kids. His miserable wife . . .

She was genuinely sorry for him, but she had no place to go. She had to have water, and she had to have relief from the heat. Even if she had explained it, she was still a single adult, still an unattached young woman. The lowest hand one could ever play for pity.

She watched till the man had stamped off and then paid the owners three times over what they had asked. She insisted (since they had not thrown her out). And she told them the truth; she told them she was sick, which might make them feel better, at any rate.

They were very nice people and she hated to think that their kindness might be losing them money.

Ellen should have realized Cameron would be ungrateful and weird about the room, but by the time Ellen left to walk her second mile, having finished "Enoch Arden," all the shouting was over. Cameron herself was dead to the world, enjoying luxurious sleep by an air conditioner.

It was around eight o'clock, cooler, although heat like breath emanated from the ground and wrestled back and forth against the breeze from beyond the road. The wind was stronger than before, and very much more pleasant.

Everywhere there were people encamped without conveniences, though literally hundreds had scored the ground outside the asphalt of the road, turning their trucks and vans in the intersection. They appeared comfortable enough, if irritable, though Ellen felt a twinge.

Men's rough voices and the shriller ones of women came from every point of the compass but it was hard to trace them to the dim, similar owners. Night birds were still silent, but the periphery of the settlement was beginning to rattle with cicadas, with katydids, with—mosquitoes. Quite a few of those. And from a silo and a barn roof, bats rose in sharp spirals; here and there, among campfires, piled gear, pitched tents or little groups around cars, road crews had set green tanks. They said PURE IOWA WATER, PARKS DEPARTMENT. The campers, lit by the still-light sky, by makeshift fires and Coleman lamps, were dirty and stretched-looking.

If she had wanted to share with the most worthy family, how would she have decided?

Something was attracting attention farther down the road. People were walking toward, standing around a wire fence near where the highway passed above the road; there was already a strolling, standing and sweating group of men and women and kids watching something down the field.

When she came up to it, she realized there was wire only on the road edge of the lot; about a football field away, that section joined what turned out to be a white board fence edging a paddock—an overgrazed field of scorched black mud competing with patches of timothy and clover. All business was at the opposite end, where cowboys—farmers, rather—were exercising horses—to be exact, the farmers were a father and his son of six or seven, who waved his hat enthusiastically at the crowd.

A little bay colt was bouncing about, close to the heels of his dam.

Father and son had a handsome number of spectators, and the boy, bouncing a trot on a small black mare, was beaming from ear to ear. He had a sharp small nose, like a mouse's, and a pleasant face. The mare was a nice little horse, but her gait was off. Enough to be worrisome.

The man dismounted a white gelding, and elegantly, with elaborate patience, began to untangle harness. A showman. On the far side of the paddock stood a dray horse as big as a Clydesdale: gelded, handsome, doubtless the one the harness was for, since the others, mostly bays, were small. The boy slid to the ground and tethered his mare to the fence. Smiling to the crowd, strutting like a pretty little bird.

Her brother had said . . . that he and Simone owned horses . . . ? No. He had said they owned *stock* in a horse. A business. Stock in the poll, the withers. Stock in stock . . . Not in the *soul* of a horse.

The field was beginning to darken, but the bay mare and colt were kicking their heels up, bright spots in the dim light.

The mare shot by him and the boy threw a blanket across her. He was up in a flash—she was a gentle thing, unaffected by surprise.

Playing to his crowd, the boy began to trot the little mare to the far end of the field, her colt cantering awkwardly after, silhouettes tiny in the afterglow.

Trotting back, the boy slid down, hauled the saddle off the fence, fell with it, heaved it up, and hauled it up and over the mare. He cinched the strap loosely, walked her a bit till she let out air; then cinched the strap tight. The kid was really good. Really knew the tricks, though Ellen was perhaps the only one who would notice.

This was likewise true about the fence.

The owner seemed unmindful of the old insult about fences. There were many tourists mounted on it; and so, since it seemed to make no difference, Ellen threw one foot up on the lowest board and stood, not very high, so as to see better. That step hurt, so she took a fold of jeans at her right knee and pulled her foot up an additional step.

The boy was cantering toward her and, just before the place where Ellen stood, pulled down to a stiff walk, reins in one hand, hat in the other. He was starting to lift it when suddenly the colt wheeled and *bang*ed! back hooves on the fence—she laughed, delighted. So handsome! Spirited!

The colt, puffing and blowing, rolled his eyes to see if he'd frightened her. The boy slapped the reins at him, embarrassed.

Colts are colts, like children are kids. Ellen reached out to the colt and perhaps just to disobey the boy, just to show his independence, he nuzzled her hand and let her scratch his ears. Skittish, certainly, but with a sweet nature.

Now was the time to have money. Take him away from these people who'd work him to death.

"He'd really like those little fingers, ma'am," yelled the farmer, hurrying up.

She became aware of bored faces around her. And of envy perhaps. The nastiness a horse is never guilty of.

"Horses know me," she said easily. Obviously the man feared any trouble, so she slapped the colt's neck reassuringly. He tossed his head, blew, looked like mischief.

Tourists along the fence were leaning in. "How old is this little fellow, about four months?" she said. "He's going to be a good four hands higher than his dam. What was his sire?"

"Well it wasn't *him*—" He meant the nag across the field. He waited for the laughter to subside, grinning. "Three months, three weeks and one day. All in all, I'd say that's a pretty fair guess. You must have a saddle horse, ma'am."

Stables, she murmured.

"Uh, stables. You from Miss-oo-rah?" He had never heard of Cambridge, so she added "Boston."

"*Bos-ton,*" he said, making a face. "Sta-bles. You must of rode a good deal?"

"Yes," she said.

He took a long look at her, then a long look down the field. The crowd fanned out around the paddock had drawn close to hear, scraping their shoes on the whitewashed fence.

She had been careful about that fence, herself, making scrupulously sure she hadn't marked it.

"We don't have one of those little *Bos-ton* saddles out here, or I'd ask you to show us a thing or two. Don't get a chance to see much *Bos-ton* riding around here, but I'm always ready to learn a thing or two, myself." His drawl extended longer with each syllable. "I don't want to end my *life* a ig-nernt . . ."

"I would have been surprised if you'd had an English saddle. Why would you have one?"

"How's that?"

"Anyone can ride Western saddle. Not everyone can ride English, it wouldn't be very profit—"

"Not everybody can ride bareback, but I betcha you could show us a thing or two—you straddling them stallions ought to be pretty darn educational—"

Her temper ignited. "If it won't spook your horses, I'd be delighted. I've ridden bareback since I was four years old."

"The colt ain't broke, but there's old Polka." His eyes were narrow. "He's slow, but . . ." As if an idea had suddenly struck him, he said: "Why, shoot! He ain't no stallion, and he ain't very tough, but if you was to exercise him for me I'd be obliged to you. He gets real lazy when it's hot."

He was not offering any of the saddled horses.

The big horse was on the far side of the field, but even from this distance, she could see the offer was a joke—in part from the ripple of laughter around her, in part because the horse was a Percheron. He was as broad as a bed from side to enormous side. Few woman could ride any animal that size, and she started to smile No, thank you, but it stuck in her throat.

She didn't want to think how much more laughter from the tourists in jeans, business suits, shorts, cowgirl skirts would bother her. It was such a shame not to simply enjoy the horses.

"I should very much like to help," she said coolly. "Do you have a trampoline?"

The laughter was hers.

"You get up on the top of that fence, ma'am; I'll get him over." The man whistled. The big horse trotted over like a dog.

She deliberately did not catch at her jeans to pull each leg up, but forced her joints to move. But when she let herself down onto the smooth warm back and her knees stretched to grip, road-wide, it struck her how serious a mistake she had made. Even before achieving a seat, she was in torture.

The horse moved uneasily beneath her and began to shift his weight; her knee grip was loose. Laxness would tell him she was a novice.

There was an arc of sunset left, against which floodlights were coming to life. The light caught the glint in the farmer's eye, and she knew she would stick this out; her knees gripped; the horse attended.

Exactly right. Except the pain; God, it hurt. But with the grip, she raised the reins and began to walk him; to trot; she rose to a canter down the field, rising from off her own grip. Stop. Start. Head up for the crowd, it hurt; back him up (only a little, he wasn't used to backing, he was not much of a saddle horse, and his moves were crude.) But she took him forward full-tilt and around at a sharp turn and stop, far down the field from the crowd, of which all she could make out were white light shirts and light faces, floating in the dark at the the far, motel end of the field, lights behind them.

The little figures were nearly handsome that way.

From around the big stars a cool wind had sprung up; the breeze was in her face, mussing her hair, and she was riding again. She hadn't known it was possible. Down here, away by herself with the horse, she could enjoy the evening and the mammoth sky—more constellations now than at midnight at home. There was a pale blue glow most of the way around the sky and only the very top of the bowl was a dark blue, its innermost point blue-black against stars. Down the field, down the field a thousand miles away were little lights and little people, and the pain.

She made him bow.

The gelding danced to the side and she tried to stand from her knees and wave, but she could not. Instead she dug her knees in, which hurt, and so did the joints at her thighs by now, but she knew that from afar she looked good. She would have liked to lift off him the eight or so inches that strength and skill would have granted a year before. But she was riding.

She trotted up toward the fence. The field lights would pick out her blouse and face. When she cantered back away she knew they hoped he was out of control and she let the packed earth pound beneath her, shutting her eyes in the almost-wind, cool

at last, happier than she had been in months. She had him
wheel, hooves deep in a paddock still muck beneath dried mud.
She turned him round and gave him his head, racing back toward the pasty impressions of faces, stopping him easily. Wishing she had a hat to wave.

But she could not see the ruts and gouges; she was posting
a painful trot directly in front of most of the crowd when the big
horse stumbled, throwing her forward. He jerked his head back
so it slammed against her teeth. He panicked. He shrugged her
off and she went sideways and somersaulted forward, into the
crust-and-muck surface of the field. Fortunately there was mud.
It broke her fall, she told herself; the dark sky, watery with stars.
Or were they internal?

Her mouth was only painful. . . . She rolled and began to
stand as the impatient farmer approached, stooped, and more
snatched than helped her to her feet; she could not move. Every
joint was screaming, the knees, the thighs, the elbows . . . and
as soon as her left foot touched she immediately jerked it back
up. Everything hurt. All of the joints, especially the left ankle.
"Hurt y'self?" he said, with real hostility.

"Twisted my ankle," she lied brightly.

Her head down, keeping her hand over her bleeding
mouth—onlookers still laughing—she took the five long, shock-
ingly painful steps toward the gate, grabbed and opened it,
shifted her weight onto a board at waist height and concentrated
on walking, unaided, three paces. She then made two strides to
the hood of a truck parked almost nose to the fence, and was
hidden from the crowd.

During the last few moments, it seemed, the natural light
had failed, and it was pocket-dark. Forcibly, she straightened
both knees and, favoring her apparently injured left foot, hopped
low and covertly, touching the hood and under cover of the
truck. From a quarter mile past it light poured from the Smith's
Motel sign, toward which she had to somehow feel her way
without limping.

Someone blocked her light.

She touched down her foot and straightened to force herself

to walk but it was Cameron's voice, anxious, almost a whisper, "Listen, I saw that. Can you walk?"

"Please!" Ellen hushed her.

Wordless, Cameron took her arm and half lifted her. Ellen hopped forward. Twenty feet past the end of the truck they met their first lot of refugees camping on the ground and Ellen shoved her arm off Cameron's shoulders. Yet here, in spite of their fires' glare, it was for all purposes completely dark. Ellen took a step and the pain forced her to stop.

"What can I—?" She heard herself whining, and stopped.

"Your hand?" Cameron whispered. "Where's your—"

Taking Ellen's left hand, Cameron touched the fingers to her own belt and said, "Hook your thumb inside and lean. It's so dark and they're so crowded in, no one can see us. Just make some talk, make it look natural, okay?

"What a day," began Cameron unsteadily. "Imagine, one thing after another for seventy-two hours, and then—"

A group of standees parted from in front of them, another group just behind. Ellen was giddy with it all. Cameron laughed as if she had told a joke, and began chatting. Clever. You never thought of this woman as very clever.

When the groups were behind them, Cameron asked about the ankle.

"I can favor it—I mean I can hop if your jeans don't give out. . . ."

"They're too tight," said Cameron. "At least the belt's too tight—you're cutting me in half."

"Hey," said a man from a group to their right. All they really could see of him was his cigarette tip. And voice. "Hey, girlies. You want a real good time?"

"Leaning . . . leaning, safe and secure from all harms," sang Cameron.

Ellen was shocked.

Cameron laughed, and they were almost into the circle of motel light when they were suddenly accosted by an impatient man in a suit, who offered them money for their room. He must have seen them go in. *Three times what you've paid for it, and I mean the price you actually paid. . . .* He called them whores, and then as if for balance, called them dykes. People were curious.

They had collected quite a following before they reached the motel.

Long after Ellen had ceased to touch her, her arm held a flawless impression of Cameron.

The ankle wasn't broken or even sprained, but its usual swelling was alarming, lively with pain; still, it was only a bruise or twist, unpleasantness added to the usual pain. Ellen was becoming very good at simply not thinking about it. She tended her hope that this would make it all go away. On the other hand, it would probably be impossible to walk on this ankle before long. She resolved to walk while she was still able to, and asked for the keys.

Cameron was sprawled, poring over the map of Iowa. "You're leaving again? You're nuts!"

"I'll settle for getting something out of the truck, thank you."

"Your wrist is hurt, too—"

"It's fine. That's the way it always looks." Ellen rolled her left sleeve up for comparison. "See? Matched set."

Cameron stared.

"Don't look, then." Ellen rolled down both sleeves and began to pull the Velcro very tight. "I'm going to go out for a moment while I can still walk. In half an hour, the swelling will be too much."

"You need a doctor. In fact, if you walk on *that* sprain, you need a doctor for your *brains.*"

"Quite; it's all in my head. That's my theory."

"But why? Why do you want to go out there again? Am I supposed to protect you?"

Ellen looked at the ankle. Maybe a bandage . . .

"You're calling your mother. Am I right?"

"And what do you mean by that?"

"On that ankle. If I called my mother twice in a week, she would want to know what the ransom was. And a third time she'd—"

"Perhaps if I had your mother, I wouldn't call either, thank you very much!"

* * *

Ellen was mad at herself. Certainly, she told herself, one should not criticize another's parents. Especially someone who had helped and supported one. And she didn't want Cameron mad at her right now.

Ellen stumbled and hopped on her right foot across the lot, hopped briskly around the side of the restaurant and then made herself appear to walk, gingerly, to the phone booth in front. It was clear from the pain that she would not be able to put much stress on that foot in the morning—but at least she would have an excellent reason not to drive the truck.

Behind her and to left and right along the main road were campers bedding down for the night, probably trying to sleep, while country music and red light poured out of the tavern across the road. A radio blared from the cab of a truck. A man and woman in line for the phone waved her past, possibly because of her foot. She was grateful.

Cameron, ready to shower, was stewing over the television screen with the room at about fifty degrees; Ellen sneezed. But at least the place wasn't packed like the road outside.

"You hear what they say about this flood?" said Cameron. She was wearing a towel across her round behind, pleasant.

"I forgot something—" Ellen managed.

She speed-limped around the lot and café and across the road to the Dave's Haven tavern and stood by the bar while the bartender fished out the last six-pack of beer, and would only sell three, though she offered him lots of money. Thank God she had some Tanqueray in the truck. As he fished in his cooler, she stood, aware of the curious or hostile stares of the (nearly all male) patrons around the corral-style wooden tavern; she put on her mother's best Boston Pleasantness and when grasping the sack, smiled her "Hello, boys" smile. But with her mouth so swollen it probably came out odd.

The now sallow moon was large and the people in the room next door had filled the little space between a poplar windbreak and the back of the motel with guests and some kind of music system, and they were dancing. They were loud enough to hear over the air conditioner. Loud enough to hear over Cameron's lengthy shower.

Ellen, sipping her gin, again heard the bird song she had heard outside. Cameron would like that. Cameron who was always seeing the natural thing. . . . this bird song was almost but not entirely masked by all the noise. She was prepared to ask Cameron what it was, but when Cameron had finished her shower and emerged in the short towel, peering around for her glasses, Ellen forgot.

"What is the matter with *you?*" said Cameron. "Cat got your tongue?"

Ellen recovered: "Listen. Do you know what that is? The one singing?"

"You mean Tammy Wynette?" Nipples like kisses.

"That—that, right there. That sound—"

"*Sing*ing?" Cameron listened. "That's not singing. That's an owl."

"What do you mean?"

"What do you mean, what do I mean? It's an owl. A screech owl. You've heard of owls." She picked up her glasses and dropped them across her nose. Her eyes were enormous.

"I thought owls *hooted.*"

"Maybe they do at Harvard." Cameron was irritable. "How much are you going to drink? All underprivileged owls ever do is *screech.*"

Cameron was wrapped in a white towel printed SMITH'S. Looking Irish.

"That," said Ellen coolly, "is an unnecessary, unfriendly, critical re—"

"Critical! You dare to say critical to me? You criticize my conversation. You're bored all the time, but you *will* not look outside. You don't like to sit but you don't like to drive and you buy everybody off—including me!"

"Buy you!" Ellen was stung. "You mean to have that lunatic truck—"

"How much did you pay him to let you pull that stunt?"

"Who? What? That . . . stablehand? Nothing! I paid him nothing! He saw I knew horses and he must have intended to have a little fun at a tourist's expense. He assumed, possibly rightly, that nobody would have the nerve to ride a—a plow horse without a saddle, but I did ride him—"

"Did you ever."

Ellen poured herself a drink.

"What did that prove? You fall off a horse no sane person would get up on and what did that prove?"

Ellen swallowed.

"I know he tripped, but what did you *prove?* There's something wrong and you won't discuss it. You do everything ass-backwards and the hard way, and what does it *prove?*"

The anger had drained out of Ellen. She didn't want to argue.

Cameron got up from the bed, came to the window. At the window, Ellen could feel her heat. "Screech owl," Cameron murmured, gestureless. Tight, wet curls were clinging around her forehead. She smelled clean, like good soap. She radiated heat.

"Uh," said Ellen to the atmosphere. "What do you want to do about sleeping?"

"Sounds pretty good."

It was beautiful in this place. Cameron was right. The stereoptic sky. Birds(?) singing. A huge, orange moon hung over the fields, framed by the black sheet spattered with diamonds. A constellation shape hung above; she didn't remember the name but it looked like *something.*

"What I mean is, do you want to put our sleeping bags on top of the covers? I don't think it'll be too hot, if we leave on the air conditioner."

"You know," said Cameron. "I was talking to the waitress—she's really overworked right now. They're not even sure the road will be clear before Monday. You paid them off, didn't you?"

"I didn't pay much. Not nearly what it could have got them. They could have got four times what I paid them."

"The sign says twenty-five bucks a night. Is that what you paid?"

Ellen shrugged.

"Seventy-five? Look, tonight at supper somebody offered

me two hundred dollars, but this wasn't mine to sell. Nobody believed me. I still don't see why we couldn't let people—"

"Then I'll tell you. It's because A, I need the air-conditioning and the water; and B, in any competition for comfort, single people lose privilege. It doesn't have very much to do with who needs help. One just isn't as important as a set. All society revolves around twos, couples, sets. I could—

"Without cash. If we let people in here, we'd find ourselves out in the road. They'd take a vote." She poured herself a drink. Then poured it back. She might want something later. For the pain.

"Okay, so you're lucky. Enough money, no vote."

"Yes, lucky!" exploded Ellen. "Lucky—and rich, of course—except for the fact it's Mother's. I'd think you'd be relieved to have a—an air conditioner, and a clutch plate—and a place to sleep! Don't worry about the room, that's my affair. I paid for it!"

"You don't understand." Cameron touched her. "Maybe I'm just upset because—what could I have done? I couldn't have paid and there's no room to sleep in the truck—"

"Well, you don't have to worry about it, do you? Tonight we're here and tomorrow we'll be gone." Ellen stopped. She didn't want to be angry. She could feel the airy burn where Cameron had touched her.

"You know," Cameron said, careless of Ellen—lucky, talkative, barely covered Cameron was standing at the window. Ellen wondered if anyone could see. "You remember the guy who screamed at us?"

"Yes . . ."

"They always guess. It's a funny thing. I *am* gay. And you don't strike me as exactly the marrying kind.

"And I'll bet something else, too . . . I'll bet you're not going to answer me. You'll . . . duck your head. And rub your wrists, and keep your eyes down."

The towel almost reached her thigh. There were worse things than keeping one's eyes down.

"When you want to avoid something, you . . . start chafing your wrists."

So observant.

"I can see they hurt you. I can see"—she reached over, took the drink out of Ellen's hand—"there's really something . . . and I talk about luck . . . ! I always talk too much and manage to say something stupid." She touched Ellen's arm. Wherever she touched, the impression persisted like a light flame. Cameron had an unusually beautiful throat. Mesmerizing. "You don't have to tell me about it—"

"Arthritis," she said coolly. "It's a kind of arthritis."

After a moment Cameron sighed, stretching, standing back. "Well," she said briskly, seizing Ellen's shoulders, "look at you! You really ought to be soaking that foot—you stand like a cop. You are the most tense person. . . . Here," she said, businesslike. "Let me rub your shoulders."

She began, pushing Ellen down on the chair, to press and rub Ellen's shoulder; each place she massaged was lonely when she stopped.

Ellen had to tell herself: *Breathe.*

"Let me give you a back rub. Here—don't jump. . . . At least," said Cameron, quietly, "you could let me do your neck. Really. You just sit down, soak your ankle, and I'll massage your neck. It's good for you. Maybe it would unstiffen you."

Ellen doubted it. She watched without comment as Cameron filled the ice bucket. She took a breath, raised her foot as if to touch the water—but one smooth, cool hand touched her neck and Ellen jumped straight up, sloshing the water out, one foot in the ice. "Wait, wait!" she said. "Just wait, all right?"

She turned to Cameron. "Yes I am!" she exclaimed. "It was an intellectual decision!"

"You," Cameron said, "are *what?*"

"Gay. It was an obvious decision."

She held her breath. When she managed to look, she found Cameron squinting as if at a specimen on a needle. "So you're queer. *What* was ever rational about that?"

It was terribly important that Cameron understand. It had something to do with the paddock, with the money.

What she herself had never understood. Friends she had at camp. She began to explain. School chums she had given expensive parties for. Her brothers' girlfriends' cigarettes; riding students she'd given tack and money. Teacher friends . . . She managed to mention her brothers' arrogance. It was all something she had to make her understand. . . .

"You just," interrupted Cameron, "dreamed it up, you mean?"

Ellen stared.

"Maybe you need a good course in sociology or something. What on earth gave you the idea that any of this was intellectual? 'Social and sexual awkwardness may translate among the very rich into sexual perversion,' or some drivel." Cameron had arranged herself cross-legged. Towel on shoulders. Dark below, dizzying.

"You left out a few important facts. Like attraction. Sexual love. The love of women. And sexiness and sexuality, how a woman feels. And that when you, the hyperintellectual type, don't feel any sexual pressure and you get with someone who does, someone who is strongly attracted to you, someone like me, you make me *miserable.* I'll tell you what, you make some nice girl happy and never come out, okay?"

To place hands on that waist.

"Imagine two together like *you*—like a shrink conference, don't you think? Don't you *have* any strong feelings? About women? About *any*thing? Other than horses—"

Ellen was stung. "I—I'm just trying to say—"

"Stop saying it." Cameron's neck was perfect. "Sit here. Next to me. Here." She patted the bed.

Ellen dropped numbly, twisting away as she sat. She couldn't tell if she'd fallen a little on purpose. She reached for the glass; stopped.

She had almost missed it.

"It's like horseback riding. There's just so much you can learn from books."

She had just been propositioned and had almost missed it.

"Here," said Cameron. "Come *closer,* you silly. Here."

LET ME SEE

Every time I walked into her cafe, Lela would tell me about plastic.

"We're gonna get rid of all this here," she'd tell me, working widening circles with her dishcloth on the chipped linoleum counter. "Set down, honey. You're the onliest one understands this." She'd pass me the single-sheet menu and fool with the ammonia water in the sink. "One of these days, you know what? We're gonna get some nice chairs, the plastic kind, 'stead of these here wooden things."

"You want coffee?" she'd ask as she slopped molten liquid into a buff china cup. "Let me see . . . and we're gonna get some disposable stuff that I don't got to wash fifteen hundred million times. . . ."

"I don't need any water," I would say. "Save the glass."

"I bet I washed a set a dishes for every man, woman and child in the U.S.A!"

I'd always look at the menu, just because that's the way I am, picking out words among the creases—taped and retaped—

and the splashes of coffee and catsup. I knew it by heart, but every now and again I'd have to make up my mind to order something different, would take a breath to say so and—

"How do you want your eggs?" she'd continue; and something like: "We don't have no sausage today. You want some fresh pie? Rhubarb"—or whatever it was, if there was a change from the day and the week before.

She liked to talk to someone who liked to listen, or anyway, didn't mind it. Her voice was like that old song on the radio that you like because you know the words. I'd reach for the cream and—

"When you going to start that diet, honey?" And she'd fix her eyes on me critically. Generally I'd take cream anyway.

"Fried," I'd try sometimes about the eggs, just as she poured them out, beaten into water.

"This place is driving me nuts," she'd say. "We're gonna get a nice counter too, not like this here. Lookit this. It's splintered all to the devil on the one side and one of these days some hill jack is gonna run a piece through his hand and we're gonna be up seeing your boss in front of the judge. And these kids—" She'd gesture toward the booths and the handful of tables. "Lookit what they do to them chairs! Crash them around like pool balls. And carve their ignorant names—I bet every idiot over the age of five got his initials somewhere on my tables. And them girls, in the potty. Yeah, one of these days we'll get the Melamite kind that don't stain. It's gonna be real nice."

The stains did take your attention. They almost made a pattern everywhere, like calico overlaid on a checkerboard design. The floor was of tired, mottled fir, and nearest the door it was bowed down. Behind the counter the walls were spattered with grill grease, and everywhere else messy fingerprints, notices and pieces of yellowed notices gone by. All the wall space was covered within high reach. The chairs were shaky and unsightly, no two of them close kin.

Folks would come in and show their kids where they'd carved their initials in something. Chair backs, usually. I'm not sure how she handled that.

"You know," she'd sigh, scrubbing the pattern off the counter, "I think I'll paint it all yella, nice and cheerful. This color is pukacious. I'll put up some of them pictures of kids, the kind with the big eyes, like you see at K Mart?"

The color came closest to olive drab, and it wasn't very attractive. I'd lift my saucer as her grinding hand rounded the catsup, creeping up on my plate. "Let me see, here. . . . And flowers. I'll put nice flowers out. Oh, I know you got to wash them every so often, but all you need to do is dip them in a little ammonia water and there you are! Fresh as a daisy!"

She'd be so pleased when she said that. She'd stand up and stretch her cramped-up back and wipe her hands on her apron. "Well, how is everything this morning?" She meant my food.

I never did have the heart to tell her I didn't always want my eggs scrambled, or even want eggs at all. Maybe I liked having something taken completely out of my hands, something done by a powerful force that didn't change like the rest of life. It was the closest thing I've known to a religious experience.

My fate was eggs because the first time I came into the diner some twenty years before, back when she wore her hair up and she looked very good that way, I had been so confused. That was after my one employer, Julius Meredith, had passed away, and there aren't many places around here for a legal secretary. I was so nervous about learning to work for Mr. Sams that I couldn't make any kind of a decision, and Lela's place was close to my new employment. That morning the café was crowded and I had to sit at the counter, which I was not raised to do.

The menu was discouraging, and I simply ordered the first thing I saw, sausage and eggs. Now, I actually don't care for sausage, and that sausage, Lela's own, gave me the most amazing heartburn, but mornings after I ordered the same thing because at least I knew what it was like. I just can't cook in the mornings, and there you are.

After a time, I really didn't have a choice anymore, because she knew me. She would have been mortified if I'd told her otherwise. She prided herself on knowing people's minds.

It seems to me that I only once tried somewhere else in all those years, and that was because of my sister's third. She wasn't well, and I was the unmarried one; so one time when I went over and fixed a little something for Forrest and the boys, I found myself running late. I had to take a taxicab. I couldn't see me stopping for breakfast out of a taxi (with Lela's questions and me running late as it was), so I just went on; and then later I went over to the new restaurant at the Stratford for an early lunch. Just go where it was quiet, I thought.

It was made inside of pink stone, pink like the inside of a Virginia ham, and after being stuck behind a pillar without even coffee for forty-five minutes, you might say I just didn't go back. That is, I didn't go back except when Harrison Sams actually *won* a case and took everyone out to dinner. But that wasn't often. Down here, the defense attorney is what you might call a formality.

I never went anywhere aside from Lela's where you could get a decent conversation. And she was always there.

I need things like that in my life, that don't blow away with the next elections or with some stranger buying up the woods next door . . . and you grieve. You and the birds.

That's why one already-sticky summer Saturday, I was surprised to see her clean, grim young nephew punishing the grill with a dishrag, alone in the café. Years before, he had worked summers with Lela. It hit me as an impossible thing to see, as if he had been scrubbing along the ceiling. He looked up at me, all business, and was surprised to see me take a seat at the counter. That's not the thing a lady here will do.

"Why, where's Lela today?" I said first.

"Well . . ." he began, real polite. He was most always and truly polite. "Well, I'm a-going to be watching things for a while."

This alarmed me, and I said positively that I was a personal friend, and was she all right?

"Hmm . . ." he said, concerned. It was plain how much he liked her. Lela had introduced him as "my jewel" the first time I saw him. "Well, she has been a-working too hard, you know how she does . . . needs a little rest. . . ."

Which she was getting at Sacred Heart, in the state capital. A little trouble with her heart, they said.

Of course, the place changed. I had to steel myself.

Junior was an industrious young man who worked like some people play. He must have had her genes, but couldn't handle them. He painted the place, threw out the chairs and the carvers as well, with the selfsame energy and attitude.

He was polite to me, even nice in his way, because I was fond of his aunt and he was fond of her; he liked having me tell him about her letters. But he was impatient, even though he never complained about anything, and I hate to be hurried, especially about a meal. He'd stand and wait and twist his toothpick, and after a time he'd kind of twist himself. And day after day I ordered eggs and toast and grits (a #1); and he never once remembered what I wanted.

It was just barely before Christmastime when he got in a lot of little counters to line the walls and got rid of the booths and the tables. The walls were lemon yellow; the wooden floor had fake-brick linoleum all over it. It was all bright as an operating room, light reflecting off the shiny counters with the chrome stools in front, very nice for anyone who likes to eat facing a wall. But to each his own. Each section had paper napkins in a large dispenser and pastel chrysanthemums tucked into a new square plastic box. There wasn't any catsup or sugar, you had to ask for that; and sugar was extra that year.

"You want coffee, Miz Heilmann?" he asked that morning with an automatic smile. That was the one thing I didn't really care for in him. Lela never smiled unless she felt like smiling; Junior's smile was fixed to his office, not his pleasure. Like the smile you see on the guest of honor at a funeral.

Well, I always did want coffee, and while he coaxed it out of a big new machine into a white foam cup, what was the principal difference in the café sort of came to me. It was so cleanable.

"You going to get the pictures, Junior?" I asked.

"Ma'am?" He looked surprised. "Say, pictures? What pictures you mean? I got a tree up."

And he did. With the morning crowd, I hadn't even seen it, but there it was. Over behind one of our high school teachers was a small metal tree with little winking lights.

I don't usually draw such attention to myself, but now that I'd started I'd finish. . . . I hailed his attention. "Well, you know, for decoration's sake. Just, well, pictures. Lela always said she was going to have flowers around and, well, pictures on the walls."

This was clearly something she hadn't told him, and he frowned a bit.

I was just finishing my coffee and thinking, *What should I get my sister's new girl, poor thing with all those brothers,* when what should pop in but Lela herself, and radiant.

"Junior!" she exclaimed. Her cheeks were pink and friendly with the cold. "Merry Christmas, honey! And to everybody! Why, Martha Ann! How in the world are you! Them cards was so nice!" she said to me. "And to come all the way up there. . . .

"And the flowers. Junior, she sent me vi'lets. Real ones. I got one as a bookmark," she confided. Junior grinned and recommenced bruising the counter. "And Merry Christmas. And it *is* one, for me—you been losing weight?" she asked me. "You look . . . Why, just look at this place. . . . Just lookit what he's doing here. My . . ." She stopped, peering around her at the walls and floor, up to the grill with its new aluminum hood. "My," she said. "Just look."

Not that it was all a complete shock, of course. They had told her Junior was making some of her changes. Still. You think of all those initials, and you have to wonder.

"Why, Junior, look what you've done. I declare, this boy is gonna work himself to death! It's just—beautiful!" she said finally, shaking her head. "He always was that way, even before they took him into the army."

He smiled a real smile, like hers. It took off years.

He looked around for a word and found himself a cup, a real china one. "Here, honey," he said shyly, placing it in front of her. "You want you some cream in your coffee?"

She took the cup without looking, shaking her head. She couldn't take her mind off the counters, off the flowers.

"Merry Christmas," I said, finally. Now that she was back, that was all of the old place I needed.

"It's just like, just like the Stratford, only cheerier," she said. "Oh, and look at this," she said, floating over to the tree. "Let me see. . . . Now, isn't that cute. Needs a little red to it, though."

"They's ribbons. I put them around back," said Junior.

"Oh, good," she said. "Onliest thing," she said to me alone, "I do love a real tree. The plastic's nice, only the real thing's so pretty, don't you think?"

WISH ME LUCK

Dear Jackie. You rat.   December 1, 1976

Well, here I am. I am looking out the window and it is certainly raining, yes indeed. I am looking out the window over the gray roof out into the yard or whatever you call it which is mostly made of yellow muck and is wet, very very wet. Merry Christmas, this was a wonderful surprise, little brother.

I can't look out this window without thinking about climbing out, and I have this image in my head of dangling off the roof like tinsel. I rather like it.

It is so *wet*. It leaks in here.

This room is Group Therapy. And I would certainly say that as a group, we certainly do need therapy. I believe I am the youngest person in the building. The man to my right is gray all over. He has his finger in his nose. He is about fifty-six and appears to be pregnant (hallelujah!). The woman to my left is a monotone. That is like a metronome that talks and talks and talks. She is talking about her relationship with either Jesus or a brand new cleanser (new! drink Drano) which is what she has talked about for the previous three sessions. Group therapy is remarkably predictable in here. I could write you a script that we enact here every day. I'll send it to you and you can follow it every afternoon at three o'clock exactly:

A says A.

B says B.

C says C.

D says D.

I says X—

—and the green grass grows all around hi-ho with a rowley, powley, gammon and spinach, hey-ho! says I want a *drink*.

There are Things You Say and Things Which You Do Not Say, and if there's anything you want to say including "I want to go to the bathroom" it has to be in acceptable form. I'm still figuring *what*. You can follow the script at three o'clock and be with me in spirit which is safer because if I had you here I'd kill you.

Rat.

I'm probably going to mail this in the morning.

Helen R.

Jackie: Dec. 3, 1976

How do you like the snazzy stationery? I thought it added that Bergen-Belsen touch that anyone who would stick his own sister in a place like this dump would certainly appreciate. Notice the position of the name, which is off-center. It is my opinion they are very *mingy* here (hey nonny *look it up*). The layout was done by an inmate, and we're generally seeing double in here and that calls for a little drink.

Do not worry about me starving (you should worry?). Or even losing any weight.

For breakfast we have grits and toast and eggs. It's a kind of ritual.

For lunch we have macaroni and chuck steak, rice and grits.

Guess what we have for supper. No it's mashed potatoes. It's amazing what you can save by serving grits. I wouldn't eat them if they soaked them in champagne. They scrape them off and sling em out the next delightful meal. Do please come for dinner sometime.

I am in the Group Therapy room again and waiting for us to get started on another thrilling session. I am not certain why it is we have this; I think it is to prevent communication. There are several things that one is supposed to say. You say them or for all I know they never let you out. You have to come up with a new way in which to say you are a drunk.

You have to admit that

Never mind I think we're going to start. . . .

Little Brother: 2:55 PM Dec. 6, 1976

Yes of course I receive your letters. I even read them. I suppose you are wondering why I never answer (and yes, Ed did write me. To which I respond with a rousing So what?) It is because my fingers shake and I cannot hold a pencil. It is because I hate you and Mom and I never will forgive you. It is also because I do not have a stamp. You can't mail letters here until you have been here three weeks and I have only been here not counting the two nights and a day in jail for eleven days seven hours and fifty-six minutes and that calls for a little drink.

For the weather report, it is raining. It is nice to know the weather feels like I do. For atmosphere, in here the walls are puce. I am not sure what you would call the ceiling (know why my therapist Jane says that I am hostile? Because I said the walls were babyshit brown. She may from the looks of her never have met one. Baby, not wall.) The ceiling has these big brown rust blotches all over it and this certainly adds a lot to the

We're starting . . . .

        * @ ?!! & & & & & & ?!!!!!!
      #*@&@ ^ @@@!!!!! ##. . .

         . . . .

Well wasn't that interesting?

I hope you pay attention to the script I wrote you (oh hell, I guess you don't have it, do you?) Well in case you have forgotten (in case I've lost it by the sixteenth which seems likely) it goes:

A says A.

B says B.

C says C.

D says A, B or C.

I says X.

—and X, X, *X!* **X!**

And everyone who is not in a coma like Bill the drunk who is pregnant stares at me and passes it off like God she's off again what weirdness is it *this* time.

Let me tell you about Jane. Jane is Our Leader here in Therapy Land. I see her in the morning for half an hour and we Discuss Strategy. She is the only human being in the universe who talks entirely in italics and caps. And if I talk in caps and introduce any topic which actually interests me she knits her blessed masculine fuzzy little eyebrows and says, Helen, I am concerned about your progress. I don't believe you take this very seriously.

Au contraire (that's French for *merde*), I take this very seriously, I take booze morning noon and night and any way I can get it, so put that up the spout and tuck it, lady.

O yes. They are not going to let me do any painting, as that's what I use for masking my emotions. Jackie get me out of here.

Helen

Ho, ho, ho!   Dec. 8, 1976

And what do *you* want for Christmas little brother?

Well, here I am in my nice green room watching the rain rust out the wire mesh.

Are you planning to take me out of here for Xmas? I can be checked right out like a library book. I am very tall and can reach the tops of (small) trees and I have an enormous reach like an orangutan and I am *friendly* (don't believe what you hear), am I *friendly*. I make a nice rum torte and a hell of an eggnog. Very trainable, good with kids, returnable for deposit. When you catch me. . . . Yes, you can tell its Christmas. There are these lovely dust-fraught plastic holly boughs decking the Receiving Area (drunk tank) and the blank, painted-over windows in the hallway. Never mind the fact that these (alleged) grounds include something like 114 holly trees; it's not Christmassy if you don't go out and buy it—kosmic kapitalism. It made me think of Aunt Evangeline—I don't suppose you'd remember. She was my favorite, except she gave me rotten presents. Candy she *made*, fruitcake with lime peel she had *dried*. I loved that fondant she gave me almost every year until I caught her actually *making it*, how *icky*—here I was, her favorite niece who invested three and a half dollars in a bottle of Eau Sauvage and she only slaps cheap sugar and cheap eggs together and tries to fool me into thinking it's a present. You know she lived on something like sixty bucks a month.

That's life, isn't it?

Mostly I know it's Christmas because of Jane (ol' Here Today). I was sitting in the cafeteria rearranging grits and she told me (this out of a clear sky, I don't remember asking) that I could help with the creche and the Santa soap-painting in the bay windows tomorrow. I said wahoo.

You can imagine how much I adore slopping cold water on a freezing window, with the charming bars outside framing my form.

Seriously—you know I don't mind helping out. I'm not a lazy, antisocial asshole (well?)—but I don't think this place is working out for me exactly. I mean, I *get it* (quote Jane). I'll buy that some people are just born alcoholics (like Dad) and I think if you drink enough you can award *yourself* that honor. I'll even buy that I'm that kind of loser.

And what of it? I don't believe that by seeing people as nothing but alcoholics—as nothing but a part of what they are—you make them feel more integrated, more functional, less isolated. Drinkers drink to make their skin fit.

Here "fit" has no metaphorical meaning—if they had Einstein in here he'd be doing the office inventory—and that's funny until you realize that to them there's no such thing as an Einstein. In this world there are only drunks and human beings.

Maybe we deserve it. Maybe it doesn't make any goddamn difference. Maybe I *am* "avoiding the impact" of something-or-other.

Right now I'm avoiding the impact of Christmas—though of course I shouldn't bitch. There are two times (not necessarily re-occuring) when people remember you're supposed to be artistic (um, *autistic?*)—when you're showing at the Met Museum or they need a "little design" and could you help? I wish I had a nickel for every poster, picture, leaflet I've designed *(can you handle this, I know you'll help us out)*—I could bribe my way straight out of here so fast *(design, schmezign—put the lettering right* **there**). I could buy back my husband. And how *is* Eduardo?

Maybe everyone always has been right: To draw is to indulge oneself in a morbid new excretion. (And *anyone could paint if he just didn't have to work—unlike,* they chime in, *yours truly.*)

Oh bitch, bitch, bitch. Right? The hell with it.

Good night. Helen R.

Jack, old sock: Dec. 9, 1976

Somebody else knows "Who Threw the Overalls in Mrs. Murphy's Chowder." ("Won't you bring back / Won't you bring back / Mrs. Murphy's chowder!") As a matter of fact, the Treatment Director. We rarely see him since he's usually out there drumming up cash & routing the Demon, Rum.

He sang it with me in the hallway outside the drunk tank. I was talking to Yvonne (from Group); I was trying to tell her about you and Dad and the year Dad decided we were the von Trapps, and I got stuck on the line about "da-da, da-da, dadadada, da-da / string beans, blue jeans, swimming all around" and here comes Ferdinand (that's his *name*) down the hallway. He couldn't remember either, so I asked him if he knew "Does Your Chewing Gum Lose Its Flavor," which he did. We sang that and a couple of others and then I asked him if he knew " 'Twas Only an Old Beer Bottle," and either he was embarrassed that he knew it or that he didn't, which was odd since we had just been singing "Sweet Violets." The booze thing, I guess. These people are very odd about the life outside.

Anyway I'd been telling her about Dad and his pillowcase full of little orange pills and his bribes to the drugstore, but I didn't tell her about your being a lawyer. I mean *some* things we should keep *deep* in the bosom of the family.

Hah.
Helen.

Dear Diary: The 10th, I think . . .

Know what I want for Christmas? Just a nail file. A modest, solitary nail file will do nicely. If it goes through wire mesh.

Today we made these little Christmas doggies (and therein hangs). Originally we were slated for Recreation but there's something gone wrong with the van, so with two hours to kill, the staff thought up projects and I ended up with a group making cookies. Well, I like cookies as much as anybody.

There were two cutters and one was a broken Santa Claus carrying a geodesic cactus and the other read "Christ is risen." I said, "Why don't we cut out gingerbread boys? All you need is a pattern." Everyone stares (which is Hedda and Yvonne and Axel). I said, "You draw a pattern on cardboard and cut it out. Then you place it on the dough and cut around it."

"That sounds *dirty,*" says Hedda. We got some clean cardboard (I mean you do *bake* them), and I drew a lollipop-headed doll, and we made cookies. Of course they weren't gingerbread and they could have been ladies in pantsuits, but they looked like gingerbread boys to *me*. Even Axel got into it, pushing in raisins like a man killing bugs, saying "See this guy? I'm givin' 'im a fat lip, see. See this guy—"

Hedda made row after row of identical cookies, stupefyingly un-unique, and Yvonne designed all these Christian Dior confections—checks and pinstripes of dough-and-dents, paisley whorls of allspice—and I cut out cookies and cookies and cookies with all the panache of which I seem to have so much.

About our third batch Jane comes in and says *"What* are you *doing?"* I thought it was obvious. They were, it seems, too big (not to mention *germy*). We were supposed to have got four dozen from the mix. She told us to cut them in half. They look like a toddler's rendition of a dog. Of many dogs. Speaking of which, how are yours?

Toddlers, that is. Unless of course by now they are in college. 'Tis the season for remembering my nephews. Please Jack, buy Stacy that little Mattel train he wanted and sign the card *Aunt Helen.*

And get Peter something loud and gimmicky, like a slide trombone. Yes I know he doesn't need it—do it for *me.*

Group Therapy was almost interesting today. Everyone is awake now and even Hedda (who used to ramble and ramble) seems to notice that everyone else is here. Today Fred (who wears the old green baseball cap) was talking about the time that he and his father sat down to celebrate Fred's manhood. He was fourteen.

They were drinking themselves into a stupor and Fred goes out through the kitchen to get to the backhouse and finds his mother sitting at the kitchen table, crying her eyes out. This annoys Fred since he's having a good time. So she tells him he's going to be just like his dad, that she hates to see him this way—it occurred to him that by "this way" she meant happy— his mother was always moping, always miserable—so Fred laughed. He goes out to the privy, laughing. So he comes back and she's cut her throat and there's blood all over the table, all over the floor, all over the walls. Fred was telling this story and he started laughing all over again, very nervous.

He laughed like an idiot until I finally said What the hell are you laughing about, for God's sake? And he said, I never cried about it, and he started to. And then Yvonne cried. And then Jane chimes in with: Yes, we are subject to the Loss of Important Others, we can relate to the context of this kind of loss—and I said, Dammit, this guy's mother kills herself because he laughed at her and to you it's Psychology 101. What have you got in your chest—vermiculite?

And Fred said *Shut up,* so I did.

Love, Helen

Snickelfritz: Dec. 11, 1976

Here is a lovely transcript to pass on to your successor. I'm firing you and getting a better lawyer. A deal with the judge that includes this place is a crummy little deal.

A: I came in here to get my life in order.

B *(synopsis of plot):*   I came in here to get my life under control.

C: I came in here 'cause I'm fifty-three and I wanted to make it an even fifty-four haw haw haw haw.

D: Oh like they say I came in to get my head together hee-hee.

H: I came in here in a straitjacket.

J (eyes to heaven):   *Helen.*

H: I *did* come here in a straitjacket. That's the only way they could get me in the patrol car.

C: Hoo, haw, haw!

A: My *word.*

H: You're offended, I can tell. You're offended because that seems undignified, I'll bet. I'll bet *you're* dignified passed out on the kitchen floor, aren't you, dear?

J: How is your wife responding about your recovery, Bill?

C: Huh?

(—And drawing a veil over sheets and sheets of drivel, skip to . . .)

B: Well if you hate it so much that you have to drink, why do you paint?

H: It's my life. It clears up and transmits how I feel about things.

All: ?????

H: It's like, sometimes what I care about is especially unclear to me; like I don't quite understand the way I feel about a thing and so I paint it, or rather, I paint all the connections I can see for it. Of course there's a physical aspect that I want to stress, but first what comes to me is just this vague image; I can actually see it on the sizing, and I try to take this image and to focus it on that canvas—but what I put on that canvas must be flawless, perfectly a translation of that image and what it evokes in me—what I want to invoke in other people—I mean the literal types, those who just want a picture they can look at but it's nothing else to them. . . . Don't you see that it's a way of reaching out to those people? It's a way of reaching out, a way of trying to forge a common way of seeing things—it's much less lonely. I feel that—for the space of time I'm painting—I'm in connection with . . . with . . . How could I *live* without painting? And yet—it requires such drive, this intensity that rips me to shreds! And how do I stand the pain, the, the tension, the sheer exhaustion without at least a drink to relax? I get up there to this *force*—wound in and strained out of shape—and how do I relax? How do I do it—how does anyone do it—how do you do it, if you don't drink?

C: Hunh. Beats the livin' hell out of me.

Jane: For the true alcoholic, everything represents a bona fide excuse for drinking. Just don't paint. . . .

. . . just don't breathe.

When I was in school I felt this way, like everybody else was trying to get by, and I was trying to *become*.

I suppose I haven't given up hope, but God knows why.

H.R.

P.S. Yes, I did get Ed's letter. His English is still awful.

Brother mine: Dec. 12, 1976
                                                 11:00 AM

I think I am adjusting to this place. At least I know everybody. Which brings up the question of what I will be when I am
perfectly adjusted to this place—to an artificial environment—
more like an orchid, or more like a plastic plant?

Today is Fred's birthday and tomorrow Hedda is leaving,
so we had this lovely party at which Fred gave a speech. It went:
I am not a young man. In fact there are them would say I am
getting on, I suppose. I have had a lot of these here birthdays,
but this one is the very first birthday that I will be able to
remember. I mean that probably I will remember it. I mean I
don't remember when I was a little boy because it's been too
long. But I don't remember my wedding either—I mean my last
wedding day—and I was 43 years old. I just remember that nice
little gal of mine, I just remember her looking at me and saying,
Well, I guess *you* had a good time anyway. But you know, I don't
believe I did.

He stood there in that damn silly baseball cap and rattled
off his milder offenses and I sat there staring at Hedda and
thinking of you.

You and your goddamn natural moderation. Not only your
not romancing, or drinking to excess, or picking up some flag-
waving crazy political cause, but that slight sniff of disinclination
you offer when somebody else does. I think you are balanced
differently from us. I think an evening with a genuine enthusiasm and you'd go straight off the roof.

Hedda is leaving and it occurs to me that this will leave my
room with an empty bed. Hedda is this intense little dumpy little
frump who wears these rhinestone-cluster hairnets to bed;
something about her makes you think of a nice little pettable
animal wearing pancake makeup. The first—no, second night I
was here (the first blurs out), she took one look at me in the next
bed and said, "It's a *shame* for a Christian woman to be housed

with a common woman *of the streets!*" I think I thought the whole thing was hilarious. God knows I needed a laugh.

Right now there are an even dozen petite beige cases neatly packed and sitting on her bed. This morning after breakfast I came in and she was arranged upon her perfectly made bed with her suitcases around her, hands folded, face perfectly composed, staring blankly out the window at the oxygen.

And I thought, What if perfect roasts and unstreaked glasses aren't enough?

And she told me: *It's not that I'm frightened; no. It's just that before I knew what I could look forward to. If things got bad . . . if things were good . . . and now; well, what do I do right now?*

But I have lots of things to look forward to, don't I? I can sit around and watch everyone be *moderate* all around me.

It sounds *lovely.*

H. Roderiguez

4:30 PM

Me again.

I'm feeling kind of shaky—wish you were here. I have a few minutes before supper so I'm writing again, your aura helps me down.

In Group we were discussing children, futures, things that we most wanted—I was getting bored, back into that staring state where I see myself toddling across the table, slipping beneath the window and out onto the roof, and somebody mentioned the *loneliness in misunderstanding.*

Do you realize how seldom I cry?

I started thinking about the night I met Ed; it was at a party given by the staff of the Chicago Museum of Modern Art (you were about thirteen when I was working there) and there was a thirties theme with a live band. A woman was singing that song—I think it was done by Billie Holiday—

> More than you know
> More than I'd show
> Man of my heart, I love you so! . . .

More than I'd show,
More than you'll ever know.

Ed was introduced to me and said, "So you are the one who did the Lake series at the little gallery. It was very sentimental."

Perhaps you remember this was a set of stills on the rapid death of the Lakes—the fish, the birds. I was stung, and I was drunk, so I snapped back something nasty and succinct. It wasn't until later I found out how badly he spoke English, that he'd meant "sensitive" and somehow lost the word, and he was so shocked, so hurt, with those black eyes like a beautiful dog's—

That's the pattern of my life.

I fell all over myself.

Do you know, that's why I married him. I should never have married *anyone*.

Words *are* the "source of misunderstandings." I'd rather paint. And then I can drink, and then I can go back to jail or straight stark staring mad.

I would like to understand about our marriage. I would like to try to understand what happened. But anything I say will be lost in all this neverending jargon. If I mention divorce, if I mention *art,* I'm interrupted with *What does that mean to you?* when that's exactly what I am trying to figure out. I can only be concise on canvas. The other day Bill said in Group, "I have never been able to figure out why other people lived and what they lived for." I wanted to shout *That's it exactly*—and Jane said, "Let's get that down to a more personal, practical plane."

What sort of courage does it take to face such blandness? If I can get her to shut up, I'm going to ask.

Wish me luck, little brother.

Love to all
Helen

P.S. Tomorrow I could mail these, but having read them over I've decided to hell with it.

Jack: Dec. 13, 1976

I'd like to ask you a serious question, the kind you don't ask your little brother: How in the world did you get so . . . wise?

You have come, time and again, through the whirlwinds of emotion without one fair hair out of place.

I remember one time when I walked all the way to your grade school to get you—*and there I was, beneficent older sibling come to herd her precious brother from first grade*—and you looked so forlorn with your head shaved like an onion—*and I was feeling so big and fifteen and protective, and we got home and* I had lost my key. We couldn't get in. I felt I had failed the universe—you and Mom. And you blinked those unblinking eyes of yours and said, "Here. I got a key from Mom—I was afraid you might lose yours."

I think that's where you shed your cute-patina.

Yes. Well, I have reached the conclusion that I'm not like you. I think I had some wot of it around the time I started borrowing your money (and-good-advice) but that is over now for good. If I were to ask you anything, it would be something like: Well, Wise One, here I am 37 and unattached and card-carrying crazy and there you are married and mild and congenitally bourgeois. Won't you trip out some good advice—sans loan—and tell me what to do?

The other day I watched somebody leave, marching behind her two grown sons who were loaded down with luggage, watched her get into the car without looking back and without looking ahead. I'm not going to look like that. I won't be cured of expectations. While she was feeling nothing, I was hurting for her and for them and for *me*—for losing a friend that I never even *had*. And I don't want to be sentimental, mushy, shallowly entranceable—or a piece of rock like Hedda. *Or* like Jane—whatever that is. What we need around here is social euthanasia.

You remember the state I was in when I arrived. When they dragged me in.

Well, the numbness in my fingers is brain damage. Per the nurse. And there's liver and heart and kidney damage, and doubtless several other kinds, of which I hope to stay forever blissfully unaware. I don't have anyone else to thank for doing this to me—thankfully. Revenge is so fatiguing. So much for my solution to the problem of adaptation.

And for theirs.

Maybe I never tried to think my solutions completely through—but now I'm thinking.

I think that all my life I have fallen into things—especially the ways I care for people—and I'm sick and tired of it; and now I feel I've been opened up like the great womb of the world, pried open with a stick and all the tender tissues poked and *fumigated . . .* it's not voluntary, this waking-up, and I know I'm scarring *shut.*

Yesterday this drunk lady—shaking and crying, I'm impatient; I sit there listening and nodding and wishing she'd just shove her damn self-pitying wretched whining. How she had four kids and buried two; that her husband came home from jail a fiend from hell who raped and beat her; how her dad had gelded himself in a drunken fit, to stop the kids—and then she says *You understand?* And I just listen, and oh-and-ah, and say, *That's all right* which it manifestly isn't. And she says she's got uterine cancer, they think, and how godawful scared she is. And I say, *I can relate to that.*

Relate? Like HELL!

I don't know what *any* of that is like, and believe me, *I don't want to.*

Before, my shield and my backbone both were booze. And now? What is it now? If this is the way my pieces go back together I don't want them. I should have said, *My God that is one of the most grotesque things I have ever heard.* That's what I should have said, but why didn't I say it?

Do I get to be *Sane Jane* and not *Drunk Aunt Helen?* And open up a future painting houses? I can't both *live* and *feel*—

But.

I can rid this rotten world of at least one facile little liar—I can erase these lines around me they've been helping me to draw so insincerely. Of course, this all may be a *stage;* they're very big on *stages* here. Maybe I come through the Mellow-fog into a bright new dawn of Reason. I'll make a deal with you, Jackie—if I come through this veneer stage, if I'm not a Janelike mouth-piece for the Mellow Generation, I'll write . . . another letter—and mail you all of these.

In any case: For God's sake, wish me luck.

Helen Hanson Roderiguez

HEROES

My sister Katje comes in with our mail and the news that the lady-across-the-street is upset, which in itself is not unusual, but this time there's a reason. They've been burglarized.

("Robbed," says Mrs. Van Metre.)

We really must go say something to her, now that the police have left. That's one of the things you have to do for your neighbors.

Mr. Van Metre likes my nephew, but the Mrs. doesn't think much of any of us: myself, my sister Katje, or her son. But since she needs to talk, she'll talk to me: "This used to be such a nice neighborhood," she says.

Five of us are standing just off the erratically clipped strip of greenery that lines my sister's property: the roomer, from the house left of ours; the Silent Man, from our right; Mrs. Van Metre, from directly across the street; and Lenny Shigano, to their right. The people to the left of Mrs. Van Metre's house have moved, and that house is for sale. And I don't see her old gentleman anywhere, and that worries me.

"This is so hard," she says.

They came home this morning after a quick trip to the ocean (she just has to see the ocean sometimes), and she walked into the kitchen, and there was this *hole*—did we remember her kitchen? They just remodeled—

She is shorter than I am, plumper than I am, more venerable than I will ever be; and after forty years in Seattle she still sounds like Harrisburg, Pennsylvania. She usually keeps her hands in her duster, but they're fluttering out, red-nibbed anxious nuances of her dread.

—And at the very same time her husband walked into the bathroom, and at the very same time he says, *Why, what happened to the window,* she is saying: *Why, Leo, we have been robbed.* It wasn't robbery, however, it was burglary.

All of us except for the man who rents the room have been ripped off in the past six months. There is a method: During the day *they* break a window that can't be seen from the street and walk small, fenceable things right out the front door. No one ever sees them, but they're pros (say the police), and fortunately no one has been home when they've come in. They case our block—knew the Shiganos had football tickets on Sunday, which is the only day Lenny's mother ever leaves the house.

Thieves took everything, even the old lady's porcelain bowls that had been hidden throughout Detention in a berry field (the farmer was a good man, she told Lenny).

Leo, says the Mrs., is not taking this at all well; *they* took some pacemaker batteries and all the medicine in the house, and Leo's had two pills already and it's only noon. . . .

Something interrupted the thieves, say the police. They could be back again—quite a few things left (drills, television) worth stealing. This frightens the lady and she meets our eyes in turn. "This used to be such a nice neighborhood," she repeats, and begins to cry.

The Roomer thrusts his handkerchief out, and begins to swear emphatically. How he'd like to get his hands on the sons of bitches.

It's easy to imagine him heroic—jumping too quickly, not

thinking to save his own neck. It's interesting that he's from New York, like Kitty Genovese.

"This used to be such a nice neighborhood," she mourns.

It may be an unworthy thought, but I wonder if she is thinking of us?

Seattle is one of the last places in this country where there are people left who think renting is a form of vagrancy—people like Mrs. Van M.; she doesn't even know we're not renting. Like the burglary, renters, real or imaginary, are evidence of life-coming-apart. And then there's our lack of young men. . . .

She doesn't like our puppy. He's too enthusiastic. She doesn't approve of our compost heap, and she's not at all sure about our garden. We don't grow the right things, nor do we grow things right.

She once pointed out a brassica shoot, naming it cabbage. It was broccoli. Then she tried the next one, which was brussels sprouts. She tried cauliflower, turnips and kohlrabi, thinking I was sadly misinformed—all of them had obovate, serrated leaves. We like brassicas of all denominations, but it was too early to see the small variations in the seedlings. I could hardly see the difference, and I had planted them.

I pointed out the cabbage, next to the spinach. She knew the spinach.

She took a hard look at the spindly things and asked if I knew my nephew ate oxalis. She had seen Arman nibbling some of the flowers in her yard. I say something like *Oh, that must be because he can't have orange juice;* and she looks exactly as if I had said we tethered him out in her yard to graze. He's five and he likes the sour taste but has allergies. I assure her that we'll keep him out of her flowerbeds.

It is nearly four: time to pick up my nephew.

"I just can't believe it," she says. "We've lived here thirty years and nothing like this has ever happened to us. . . ."

She remembers when this land was cherry orchards. She thinks it's only a matter of months since it's all simply changed. Like a law for which she somehow missed the vote.

★ ★ ★

She wouldn't want me to contradict her, but Seattle is just another ugly little city. When I first arrived, back in '79, I stayed with my sister and Suliman on Capitol Hill, and it did seem safer than San Francisco. And one summer evening we were at the kitchen table, eating cherries and peaches and drinking wine, and Suli was telling us about his mother in Dahkla, how she would not eat fruit. How everything had to come from an indoor market, canned, and one scalded the top. She was very *European*. He was laughing when two men kicked in the screen door; Suli was an Arab, therefore rich. That was robbery, not burglary. Suli lost teeth. Which would not matter to Mrs. Van M. very much.

Her husband's heart—suddenly her eyes open wide, fearful—which reminds me of something helpful: prescription numbers. Call the pharmacy. Replace everything; the pharmacy will know. . . .

Prescriptions. Her mind moves fitfully (think of them fingering her possessions, rifling through her letters. . . .)

She doesn't wish my help, but she thanks me anyway.

I have to go, I explain. I have to go get Arman at the swimming pool. She nods.

Behind me, she is saying again "This used to be the nicest neighborhood you ever saw," and I wonder if her eyes are on my back.

Katje works Saturdays, so it has become my job to move Arman from swimming class up to gymnastics class on Saturdays. His gym class meets on the top floor and naturally the pool is in the basement. He won't remember (his mother says) what to do because he has only been coming two weeks. Counting today. He has to remember to take a shower and find his clothes and how many flights of stairs to climb, and each floor has its fascinations. Like the aerobics class on the middle floor.

His swimming class is nearly over and I have to look hard for him at first. He is off by himself near a float rope, and by his cocked-up chin I can tell he is singing to himself. Arman's such a dreamy little boy.

I find myself wanting to believe that he remembers Suli. He is so much like him: the same beautiful hands and eyes and a collarbone so sharp and deep it seems like a fitted yoke. Same bright imagination.

Before he could swim (before Kat could get him in the pool) Arman made up a long talk about when *he* was a man who worked very hard at swimming and it was real hard but he really *didn't* drown, and became a famous something, and won a lot of stuff. Then he climbed down the ladder, a big-eyed human sacrifice. He invents himself an instant before he lives himself—like his father.

Suli would be alive today if he had told himself a different story; say, about an atheist Muslim who married a Yankee wife and didn't go home again; but he saw himself as the dutiful son. He would start to talk of staying here, and he'd make some kind of verbal left turn and be telling us stories of home and kin; and he did want to break the news himself: his marrying Katje, having a son, in a country his parents would never visit; a wife and child who would remain U.S. citizens.

He saw himself as good, reasonable, romantic—dashing, perhaps. Suli was an anthropologist, neither informed about politics, nor interested.

I am told that the boy the Sécurité was after looked enough like Suli to be his brother. We know about the coat, so I think what actually happened was the young man approached Suli in the terminal, possibly in the washroom, pale and in trouble. Actually he was bleeding into his coat.

That would have happened to Suli. In this country, many kinds of people—lost children, beggars—came up to him on the street, looked straight in his eyes and talked to him. His face was entirely open. A hero's face.

Soldiers found the bloody coat in Suli's carry-on luggage and he either could not or would not help them. They never found their guerrilla, so Suli never had a chance.

I watch the instructors working and I wonder if I imagine that they are paying more attention to the girls than the boys. Or the boy, for in his class, there's just Arman. Apparently other five-year-old boys can swim. He is just five—awfully young to be failed already, but perhaps if he had a father . . .

(His father would have thrown back his head and roared. Suli couldn't swim to save his life.)

Now in the ladies' locker room and he speeds to his locker—skins out of his yellow trunks, his pink heels flash against the ochre of his body and he's hopping frantically up and down while he figures out the faucets in the showers—gang-type, rather weak streams in a tiled vault. Now he slides into the far right corner, the shower slapping his squeezed-shut face and flattening out his hair, and a small mob of little girls comes swarming in around him, most of them naked or stripping quickly. He cowers, hiding in the corner.

We didn't think.

He sidles around the girls, not touching, ducks around a mother and dashes for me, shielding himself with the locker door, teeth chattering.

He drops his shorts in the growing puddle under him; I grab his socks. The puddle is cold; he hates cold water. "Wasn't the water warm?" I say, and he says it was, but his lips are blue. I think he won't admit he can't figure out the faucets.

Rubbing the folds of towel against his bony little frame is reassuring. The gristle-resistance promises he'll last. That boys are tough.

"I swum across the pool," he announces as I tuck away his dripping trunks and underwear. I smile and squeeze his arm, though it's a lie. I guess I agree to the lie because we both wish it were true.

I am starting supper but look up quickly when I think I hear children's voices, even though there hasn't been any racial trouble since we moved out of Ballard; but my nephew is just screaming because he likes to. He's that kind. Other children haven't bothered him here (and *What's not attended is soonest mended*, says Katje; and I do keep out of it, but I always listen, because this isn't the South in the thirties, and I do think there are things I could do, like call him in. Or go out and offer everybody cold distracting ice cream, or another newspaper psychologist thing that works when you Think Good Thoughts).

But maybe there isn't anything I could do to help and he has to make his own way, even now.

And maybe if there is no issue it is because there are no children. This is a neighborhood of singles and working couples, and retirees convinced the younger ones rent.

Katje bought this house with the insurance money. And the reason she did was to have a place to live. Almost no one would rent anything in a safe area to her, because there was a period of time in this idiot place when it was as if in Seattle children were *in bad taste: Wait till they come back in style. Go somewhere else.*

Originally this was money she had been going to use to take Arman to see Suli's parents; he had stressed the importance of a son to his parents. His parents had had no other surviving children; but though they accepted her registered letters, it was not until ten months after the first one that Katje finally received a reply.

In the elegant envelope were three things: a cashier's check for Arman, a Polaroid of Suli on the bloody tarmac, and instructions in his mother's French copperplate: *This is my sone whom you forced by hand of his ever own goodness. You take him from us two times. God condemn you.*

The check was for $3,365 and fifteen cents, American.

Outside more than one child is shouting, and police lights silently play across the garage next door.

Arman is across the street next to the police car with some neighbors and two kids from the next block; I touch his shoulder and he shrugs me off—too old for touch. . . .

"They weren't robbed again?" I ask (but I don't mean robbed). "These guys are detectives," Lenny explains. "This is going to scare my mom to death. When my mom first moved in here, people would have thought you were cracked if you locked up the place. Now look at this. Two sets of cops in one day."

How right he is, chimes a woman I don't know. "It used to be a real nice place," she says. "Your kids could leave their bicycles out. Now look. Houses broken into. You know that old man over on Fifty-fourth with the paper route? He was held up by two kids."

She glares at Arman, and says to the Roomer: "It's changed

so fast, you don't have your neighbors anymore. Transients don't have any investment in the area, they don't keep it up, and they increase the population, there's no parking, nobody knows each other—"

We deserve this chaos, but she herself has done things right.

"In daylight," she says. "And we didn't even know about it. Can you imagine—"

I introduce myself and Arman.

"What a good-looking boy. Is his mother foreign?" And then Arman screams. "Look!" He turns to me. "Look! He's sick!"

Van Metre is weeping, stepping carefully down the steps between two policemen. Mr. Van M. who took him to the baseball game.

"God, oh yeah," says the Roomer. "The son's service pistol. They got his older kid's service pistol. It was all they had left. They don't get along with the ex-wife, I guess. Van Metre was saying how about an hour ago he remembered to go look in the basement, and— Well, they got the service pistol. That's a—"

"I would kill them!" explodes Arman.

"—bitch," adds Lenny mechanically.

We stop. Stare. It strikes us: He means the thieves. The other kids have told him about the thieves.

"Well, we don't have to worry with this guy around," booms the Roomer, reaching out.

Arman dodges.

The man's fond gesture bends, tucks into his pocket.

Safely alone, Arman stares at Van Metre. He stands like a little dark falcon, whispering "I would kill those men," and drops his voice to nothing, but those are bold and reckless and generous things he is promising Mr. Van Metre. Revenge, reward, renown. "When I was a policeman . . ." he begins.

A hero. Don't be a hero.

Not just yet.

SEE YOU IN THE MOVIES

Early traffic was whooshing past and everything was going just swell, except they were just the bittiest bit off schedule. They might arrive late. Ginny looked to the rearview mirror at her children. Katie Lee was about lost in the blankets, her fluffy hair the exact honey color of the stuffed giraffe and two of the teddies. Johnny Allen's red head nearly matched his father's sleeping bag—from that musty, buggy hunting gear of Phil's. And no need to think of Phil any more on *this* trip.

Things were *under control*—except of course John Allen's sucking on his thumb, which strictly speaking, at that exact instant, Ginny was not obliged to notice.

"Hon?" She nudged Barb. "Barb, honey, I don't suppose you want to drive, would you, hon?" Barb's salt-and-pepper head rolled gently. Ginny generally preferred that Barb be butch.

"My God, we're moving." Barb yawned. "What time is it?" Barb was a freckle-faced broad-shouldered thing with kissable lips and a butch streak that was cute in a little round person.

Ginny leaned down for a peck, weaving the van all over the road. Which woke Barb.

"You," said Barb, "are the Morning Type—" The way Mama would have said "round-heeled." "When did we leave Harrisburg?"

"Practically eight!" said Ginny, the morning type indeed. It wasn't eight. "I thought we'd start in looking for some nice little place to eat!"

"But we've been driving since—" Barb stopped herself. She was even-tempered, nothing at all like Phil. "How far did you say this cabin was?"

"Not very . . ." sang Ginny, and launched into humming "There's a Coconut Grove," which she was very fond of humming sometimes.

She was just the littlest bit cross, although they were making fair time and should be at the lake by noon. A weekend at the old summer place, perfect surroundings and arm-in-arm; a picnic before they unpacked. A psychic reminder to Phil of what he had lost . . . The kids on the beach and everything lovely—unless they slowed down. If they slowed down, the lighting would be all wrong.

"An o-o-open be-e-each," she soothed for the thousandth time. "There's the loveliest little shore birds . . . and these little hawks. I think it's just about the only piece of Pennsylvania still undeveloped. And so-o-o sought after. Phil could just see it as time-share condos, but *nobody's* going to get that place while Mama's alive."

Phil was present only as a sleeping bag—he still stored it in the garage, so it wasn't like she didn't have any right—she hadn't asked him for a thing. The van didn't count.

Suddenly, Barb swan-dove over the seat—

A baby-sized denim behind was shining plainly in the mirror; a Volkswagen was passing on their left, with a ski rack full of baskets. Barb had hold of Johnny Allen—he'd tried to snag himself a basket right over Ginny's shoulder, right through Ginny's window.

She jerked round. Barb, in transit back, snatched the wheel, bringing them out of a swerve. Ginny hauled the rest of John Allen back in. She wanted to smack him.

"You get in here," said Ginny to John Allen, "and you keep your head, your hands and your body in here or we'll all turn right around and go straight back to Harrisburg, do you hear me?"

"It's too far," he whined. "We *can't* go back this morning, it's too—"

"Want me to drive?" asked Barb.

"Whatever made you think you could have that gentleman's baskets for, when you hadn't even asked him! He probably sells them. He probably feeds his whole family selling those poor little baskets, and here you go and try to cheat him out of his— I have told you and I have told you that you leave your fingers off of other people's things—"

His eyes were suitably alarmed, so she didn't smack him. "Well, I know you didn't mean it. And *what* on earth is— Honey!" This to Barb. "Honey, why didn't you get a better hold of him? He could have fallen or got himself caught, or— Besides. That car was much too close; it could have clipped us—"

"More like bought at Bonwit's" Barb off-handed.

"Say *who?*"

But Barb was muttering at the window or the traffic. Up ahead, a bright sign read COUNTRY KITCHEN FARMS—BREAKFAST 24 HOURS. FAMILY ORIENTED DINING. Good. Ginny stood on the brake and slewed them across a crowded lane toward the almost-passed exit and into a parking lot. Barb went sideways; John Allen, the more experienced, hung on better. Little Katie Lee began to wail.

"They're hungry," chirped Ginny. "Now we're going to have a real nice breakfast, but we've got to hurry! We've got to be right at the lake by noon!"

"Are we there yet?" moaned John Allen.

Ginny power-rolled up her window and bounced cheerfully out of the van. "Every little body out!" She hauled a back door open and beamed at the kids, who didn't. "We'll be at the beach by picnic time! Do you have to go to the potty?" Johnny Allen shook his head. Then thought better of it, climbed out his door, and nodded.

Barb was looking a little frayed at the ends. "Barb honey . . ." Ginny turned to face her, for a Private Talk. "I'll steer Johnny Allen, and you and Katie go freshen up and we'll all meet up inside, all right?"

"I want to see the trucks! I want to sit by the window!" said John Allen.

"I don't have to go with her!" wailed Katie Lee.

The parking lot was crowded, and every single window had its trucks.

"I want to see them jack up one of them eighteen-wheelers—brrrrrraaammmmmm . . ."

"Now, honey," she said to Katie. "You just mind Barb and go over there to the ladies' room, and then we'll all meet up and have the nicest—"

"I don't have to do what *she* says," said Katie Lee. John Allen leaned back like his father and said, "She doesn't, you know."

"Then you come with Mama and John Allen can just be a big man and take himself. Barb can show you which door is the—"

"I know which one!" he said.

"Should I go get a table?" said Barb, inscrutable.

"Sweetie," Ginny said. "They're a little high-strung, they're a little hungry—"

"We may have to wait," said Barb. "There's quite a line—"

"Ma, can I have pancakes? Ma, can we have a table by the window—"

He was repeating himself, so Ginny turned round, expecting to see little Katie, but it happened she didn't. "Katie?" she said.

John Allen pointed. "I want to see all the big rigs. We gotta get a table by the *win*dow—"

"Honey, you run on and go to the potty, and come right straight back." There was an elderly gentleman standing at the screened restaurant door, talking to what appeared to be a waitress. "Ask that gentleman over there at the door where the men's potty is." John Allen skidded off, tripping and recovering himself again. More graceful than his father, at any rate.

Barb stood, hugging herself, close to frowning.

"You're just naturally good with kids," Ginny said encouragingly. "I guess that's because of the kind of work you do, but you just intuitively know when little ones are getting high-strung."

Barb was unreadable.

"I guess working with childlike adults, honey; well, in some ways I think it's just the same. You make yourself heard, and all of you have to back each other up on discipline. You just say what you think is right, and I back you up, and you do the same with me. You say no, and we both stick to it. It's like I told you, in three weeks you've done more with my kids than Phil ever will—unless John Allen gets himself a prize and Phil comes out to get his picture in the press. Don't worry about a little naughtiness. They're only testing you. Katie Lee's just trying to get your goat."

"Get my—?"

"It's an expression," snapped Ginny.

John Allen popped up under Ginny's arm. "I forgot my *truck*. Katie's locked the door, and I *can't* get my *truck*."

"Locked the—" Ginny leaned her tall frame down and peered in. There was her pretty little girl with two fingers in her mouth, behind the steering wheel. She tried the door. Yes, locked. Ginny felt in her pocket. There in the ignition were the keys. "Open the door, honey," she sang sweetly.

"Just unlock the door," said Barb.

"I can't!" snapped Ginny, pointing to the keys.

"Tell her what to do, then." Barb made a circular gesture in the direction of the door. "Get her to flip the lock up. She flipped it *down*."

"I want my truck," grieved John Allen.

The mechanism was one of those foreign things designed to frustrate burglars. The latch was below the base of the window, had to be tripped forward and then slightly upward into a slot.

"Push down on it," Ginny said evenly, pointing down. After a moment of sucking on her hand, Katie pushed and pulled on the unseeable latch with small, clumsy fingers. "I can't, she cried, her face beginning to crinkle for a wail. "We need a knife!" decided Ginny. "Honey," she said to John Allen. "You go ask that nice waitress for a flat butter knife."

"You can't open a latch like that from the side. Not with a knife. See? There isn't any way to reach the blade down to the lock. The lock is below the window, it's too far away, and besides, it curves up."

Damn, thought Ginny bloodily. "A hammer, then. There's probably a hammer we can borrow, or maybe just a big old rock—"

"This is in Phil's name, isn't it? You can't risk vandalizing his car! Think, don't you have another key somewhere? In your purse, say—right, of course, it's in the car—but maybe somewhere that—"

"Daddy puts one in a box!" said John Allen. "Daddy puts the box under—"

"John Allen," Ginny exclaimed. "Take this dollar bill and go in there and get yourself some of those chocolate mints—"

"Hey, can I get jujubes?"

"And you stay right there and wait by the candy case for Mama. *Do* you hear me?"

He had heard.

They had to do some fancy maneuvering but the magnetic keybox was fortunately *under* the engine block, in a line from the crest. "All right, babylove," crooned Ginny, lifting Katie. "Now let's all get us some nice breakfast—"

"I want jujubes too," said Katie as they quick-walked her off.

At John Allen's age they could only remember so much. The candy would probably help him forget to tell Phil. . . .

"We'll get you some nice raisins, Katiebabe," she said. "You hate jujubes."

No, they *weren't* there yet. She probably shouldn't have had Barb turn onto 36 so soon—they should have stayed on the interstate till they were closer to the lake, anyway. They seemed to be lost in a maze of little roads, largely unmarked, frequently blocked by horse-drawn buggies.

Breakfast hadn't quite been delightful. They hadn't been placed near a window; John Allen, cuddling his truck, had sat kicking the table and sinking down in his chair to where you could only see the misanthropic top eighth of his eyes. Katie Lee had chanted I *don't* have *to,* I *don't* have *to,* in a pathetic *sotto voce,* which after a while became *I want Daddy* as she took the tops off the little jellies on the table and smeared the goo on her chair.

Johnny Allen had filled up on candy, and Katie would only eat half a piece of pale toast to accompany little sugar packets poured into her milk, her water, and her juice. And Barb's egg. Ginny left a perfectly enormous tip, and when she couldn't help but look back at the damage, she saw that Barb had left a bigger bill on top.

"Is that a *Amish?*" yelled John Allen.

"Don't point—" began Ginny.

"Yes," said Barb, canting them all left to see past the little one-horse cart. They were going up a hill. There was no way of knowing what was coming, because they were stuck behind this primitive conveyance. A little boy on the back of the cart was making horrid faces at their van.

"That's not nice," said Katie primly. "That's not nice, is it, Mama?"

"No," said Ginny, brightly, looking up from the map. They shouldn't be going south, and this was south, wasn't it? "This road may be going the wrong way," she announced to Barb.

"Imagine that," said Barb.

"Are we the-e-e-re yet, Ma?" wailed Johnny.

"What is that river's name?" asked Katie, but nobody knew. A song, thought Ginny; we need a river song, now. And started right in singing about a river. . . .

"Is this the Columbia?" whined Katie.

"This might be the Susquehanna, I think. I guess it has to be, because all the other rivers are so much smaller. Unless this is the Allegheny . . ."

"You think *every*thing is the Susquehanna, Ma," said John Allen.

"The Susquehanna is all over the state," she said serenely, deciding she should include Barb in family talk. "The Monongahela is somewhere," she coaxed, "But the Columbia is in Oregon. Or— Barb, is the Columbia in Washington . . . ?"

"Want a Life Saver?" Barb said, reaching back over the seat.

Both of them jumped.

"They could choke," Ginny said. "And besides, it's between meals. Their uncle," she added, *"is a dentist.* I said, Honey, is the Columbia in Oregon or Washington?"

"Is what?"

"The *Columbia.* The Columbia *River.* Is it in—"

"I think it's in . . . Oregon. And Washington. And I think maybe Idaho, too? I think it starts—"

"Or in North Dakota. And you know, it's not that far across that little northern strip of Idaho, and it could go through Montana. What do you think?"

"You're thinking of the Mississippi," said Barb. "But that goes south and north."

"I think probably Montana, and—"

"Wyoming, Texas, Ohio, Pennsylvania and always remember the *Maine.* Only the Mississippi crosses that many states. Okay?"

"Do you think this is the Susquehanna?" Ginny coached.

"I do, I do, I do think it's the Susquehanna," snapped Barb.

"The kids are bothering you, aren't they?" whispered Ginny.

"The *kids?"* stage-whispered Barb.

"Mo-non-ga-he-la," John Allen said, testing the word. Then said it again. It was the kind of sound that kids are fond of making, and Katie joined him. Ginny turned her attention to timing again.

The vacation was being seriously slowed by the certainty of fifth-rate roads. Maybe Barb wouldn't mind speeding up just a little bitty bit, so they could make some time anyway. Ginny would have done it herself, but did not dare drive fast anymore. Phil had claimed they might even put her in jail the next time, and he was a lawyer.

Barb was glaring at the cart ahead as if she had gone plumb out of her mind, as if she were going to snatch the little Amish boy baldheaded. Oh—the kids. Still chanting.

"All right." Ginny clapped her hands—once, twice. "That's enough—"

"Mo-non-ga-he-la," intoned the back seat.

Barb spoke up: "What would your father do," she said, "if he told you to shut up and you *didn't* do it?"

"He would, he would *knock me flat!*" yelled John Allen.

"He would—take *me* by the little toe, and start *peeling,*" exclaimed Katie.

"It's just an expression," Ginny interjected. "Just one of those *things* you *say—*" Like "I just love kids." "I know, let's *all* sing a river song!" Anything not the Monongahela. Might as well go back to the song that had started it all. "Roll, On, Columbia Roll On—Roll On Columbia Roll On!"

This got them upright and singing lustily, so sing-along songs seemed like a good idea. "Come on and sing," she said to Barb. "Come on, Tiger. Sing a little old bitty bit." Her left hand insinuated itself into Barb's tight back pocket. "We won't *crit*icize. . . ."

On cue for once, Katie declared: "If *she* won't sing, *I* won't sing!"

"See, honey?" said Ginny. "See what you've done? We'll all sing songs together—just like in the movies!"

"I can't carry a tune in a bucket," said Barb, fixed on the road.

"A *basket,*" sniffed John Allen. "You *can't* carry a *tune* in a *basket.*"

Ginny opened her mouth—

"How do you know I can't carry a tune in a basket, Bub? I said *I* can't carry a tune in a *bucket—*"

"John Allen," said Ginny, "I don't like you correcting your—"

"—Harrisburgers carry tunes in *baskets,* but Yablonskis from New Rochelle carry tunes in buckets, and streetcars, and fedoras."

"*—elders.*"

"Why is a tune in a *basket?*" Katie demanded.

John Allen chorused "What does 'fedora' mean?"

"Not so *loud,*" said Ginny, and began to sing: "Whoopie ti yi oh—"

In fact, Barb had a marvelous voice, a trained voice, when she joined them for the chorus. Pretty ostentatious. "Git along little—"

"Doggie—" sang Katie.

"It's 'dogie,' stupid!" said John Allen.

"Don't call her stupid!" snapped Ginny, and Katie began to wail.

They were about to lose the cart to a rightward road and enter what looked like an open mining shaft. "You've made your *baby sister* cry!" Ginny exclaimed.

"Naturally. You practically told her to," said Barb.

"How long is this tunnel?" yelled John Allen, plumping himself over the seat.

"Where," said Ginny to Barb, "did *that* remark come from?"

"Tropical Samoa," said Barb, "site of the ever-expanding Columbia River . . . Eighteen hundred miles," she added. "And don't yell in my ear."

At the next pit stop (this time they needed gas), although they had not yet recovered their time, the rest was welcome. So was the pop. Ginny had a guilty theory that soda pop kept children from being sick—or kept them at least from yelping about it.

There was a convenience store and one of those horrid roadside menageries, largely featuring marine forms. Amazing to have marine things this far from the coast. There were large and small cheap tanks loaded with murky greasy water and . . . *things.*

Even Johnny Allen seemed amazed. Barb held him up so that he could look at the crabs and lobsters from above while he criticized their glass surroundings. Katie, having been taken to the ladies' room and having drunk half a Sprite, crawled back into the blankets and fell asleep.

The tanks were not the only show at the tourist attraction. An incredible selection of expensive dolls stood in the office, above the chips. Ginny was glad her baby was staying asleep.

John Allen, ever the curious one, the star-bright inquisitive one, was staring at a ponderous tank, asking if the gross, slimy "manarays" were *monsters.* And how do they breathe?

At length a red-faced attendant with a feed bucket strolled around from the back of the tank and loomed over John Allen.

"That's a mo-ray eel," he puffed. "Like a 'lectric eel. You seen one of them?"

"Yes," John Allen said. "And this isn't real e-lectric. It's only like a snake."

"Real smart little boy," said the man heavily, and grimaced. As Ginny stood, she was three inches higher in flats.

"My dad says places like these are just sucker bait."

"Does he," said the man, and Barb laughed fakely.

"Must bring a real lot of sunshine in your life," the man said heavily.

He finished throwing food in the tank ("He's doing that for the fish," said John Allen) and turned to leave. As the man was thumping up the few stairs to the service-station office, wiping his neck with what looked like a dipstick rag, Ginny finally found her ON switch: "Both my children are a great source of joy to me," she announced.

"Pleased to hear it—" The rest of his sentence was lost as he closed the door.

"Take it easy, honey," said Barb, and pulled her back.

Easing behind the tank, John Allen on its other side, Barb kissed her full and pleasantly and she wanted to kiss for several additional minutes.

Ginny took the wheel, and they were under way—Ginny insisting on a finger kiss or two because there were kids. On their way to the place she'd spent her honeymoon with *him*. She would reclaim it; it would be fine. And it is the nature of driving in cars to feel as if life is fairly all right.

During one of their trial separations before Katie was two, she had gone to all the Neighbors Talk programs at the local grade school, and there she met Barb. Talking about developmentally disabled adults and their abilities. One look, one good look at that pleasant face and frank stance and Ginny said to herself, *I have met a Lesbian.* She had always wondered about herself, and now she knew. And part of her had already known.

At the time, Phil was always dropping by in his newest car or with a selection of girls to pick up John Allen. And sometimes Katie. Ginny was jealous only of his arrogance.

Six months, she met Barb again at Meadowbrook Shopping

Plaza and ended up charging $1,462 including sporting equip-ment, following Barb around the mall.

Barb had been buying for a group home. Phil didn't press charges. It came out of the alimony and Ginny had to give the Gold Card back.

Sometimes she wanted to call Phil and tell him about his successor. How would *he* feel that a woman had displaced *him?*

At the moment she was noticing the countryside again, beginning to slow the van. The trees came down to the road here. And there were pine trees. She hoped she could remember the exact point where you turned. . . . She slowed the van a little. Whoops, seventy-five. A little more.

"Anyway," she continued, "it sure didn't bother Phil, and I didn't know any better. When we were married, my mother kept saying *no* lady really likes it, they're just animals and that's sort of a woman's work, you know—then they go punch a clock and you can go take yourself to the beauty shop—"

"Know why my dad says they have *live lobsters* in a tank in a restaurant where you eat, like, fish?"

"John Allen, adults are talking—"

"But you know why they keep them alive and cook them in a big pot *right there, where you see it* and you eat them and stuff?"

"Lobsters—" Ginny stopped. "Johnny Allen, did your daddy take you to the *Commodore Hilton?*"

"—So people can watch 'em *die,*" he said cruelly.

"John Allen—Johnny Allen, they don't really die. It's not like they *feel* anything—they're just like *in*sects—"

"Insects die," he said.

"No they don't. No, I mean they're not alive anyway, not like we are. They just jig around a little—"

"She talks nature into pseudo-animation," Barb said.

"Why do I get the feeling that somebody in this car is being critical of somebody else?"

"That's *you,*" explained John Allen.

"And who was it who said we ought to get away and test the relationship?" said Ginny.

"It was the big one by Dad's office—"

"I said we needed to know each other better; I said we could leave the kids with their dad and—"

"Ma! We're supposed to be with Daddy this weekend. Aren't we? We didn't go *last* week—"

"Tell me he's wrong."

"It's Annie's place too. Annie sleeps with Daddy."

"Don't tell me you're running out on a lawyer with visitation rights!"

"Now don't stir him up," hissed Ginny, touching the berm a little.

"Is Daddy going to be up at the lake?"

"I can't believe it. A man who abandoned his own children, taking up with those— And you side with him—"

"She means Dad," said John Allen. "Daddy says you'd try to tell God what to do, but nobody tells God what to do, do they?"

"I, always, enjoy, hearing, about your, father," syruped Ginny. "A gentleman, generous, in his, wisdom."

"Ma?"

"It's perfectly clear why I took the chance. It's your one week of vacation, your one chance to relax and enjoy us, get to be a part of us as a family—it was supposed to affirm my conviction that I was supposed to be with women. That I made the right choice, that the only thing actually wrong with my marriage was the—"

"Mama?"

"—wrong sex. It was right with women, we didn't have to mark out our needs like different roads on the same map and negotiate over—"

"A cartographer, that's what you are—dragging us down some path you alone can draw."

"I told myself a woman would *not* belittle the way I think, would *not* criticize the way I raise my children—she would know what I felt—I thought a woman would understand!"

"You certainly tell yourself a good deal. Don't you ever sit down and listen to yourself?"

"Mom?"

"Not now!"

"Yes, not now!" snapped Barb.

"Don't you raise your voice to him!"

"What am I *supposed* to do with him? I'm supposed to give him limits but I can't tell him I'm past *mine?*"

Both suddenly seemed to hear him. He was crying.

Guiltily, Ginny turned. "Johnny Allen, honey, what is it? What's the matter? Did Mama hurt your feelings?"

Sobbing, he outbreathed: "No-o-ot re-a-ll-y . . ."

"Well, what's the matter then?" Doing eighty again. She started to ease the pedal.

"How come," gulped John Allen, "Katie got to stay at that neat gas station and I had to stay in the car?"

Ginny made a left-hand U-turn over the grass of the dividing strip and jetted back. No one said boo.

Face smeared with dirt and tears, Katie was with her one hand gripping the thick pink fingers of the red-faced owner, and with the other a brand-new Baby Huggy; and looking frail and shocked. The fat man was fairly sweating nerves. They stood framed in front of the Pennzoil display, to the left of the station door.

The baby was safe. Tear-wracked and she didn't like that greasy man, but she was safe. How she had gotten back out of the car, Ginny couldn't imagine. But they had been otherwise occupied. . . .

She could *see* the headlines now. Great for selling papers: SIMMONS COUNTY LESBIAN DIVORCEE STEALS, DUMPS CHILD AT whatsit MARATHON STATION. " 'I rest my case,' says Dad." Phil's brother didn't write for that rag for nothing.

Parking parentlike by the restrooms, Ginny climbed out and, absently aware that John Allen had dived for his door, said "Grab him" over her shoulder and slammed the door.

The man was standing stiffly, no longer worried now that he saw her. He was accusing her with his high chin, backthrown shoulders, formidable breadth of body, with his might-made-rightness. He was going to throw his weight around, and loud. Maybe he had already called the police. And *how* much would that blessed doll cost? If the baby had held it any closer it would have merged with her flesh. Her poor lonely baby girl—

Ginny eased back, looked into the car. John Allen had his

fist wrapped around the door handle; she opened the door and leaned down. "John Allen, you stay in this car and keep your body entirely inside it and don't say a *word* that any soul can hear outside this car. You make a peep or make me any madder than I already am and we are going to find out that Daddy is not the only one who will blister your behind!"

His mouth popped open—his eyes went wide and he shut it.

It was probably empty as such threats go. Probably.

She marched for the owner, with each stride steeling herself more furiously: *I should never have said such a thing; he'll repeat it at a custody hearing, I just know it.* By the time she reached the man—who had kept his eyes fixed on her—his shoulders had started to round.

She was in form.

"I see you have my daughter," she snapped. She focused on Katie, weepy, tired, dirty-faced. "Oh, sweetheart," she exclaimed. She refocused on the man: "I don't know what has been going through your degenerate mind, but don't lay another hand on this child. If she's in any way harmed . . ." She let it drop. "Darling, let Mama see you. Sweetheart-baby, has this man been being mean to you?"

"No-o-o . . ."

"How did he get you out of that car? I know you wouldn't just get out of that car when you were plainly told not to. . . . She seems to be in one piece," said Ginny, and turned to glare at the owner, who had started to fade away.

The doll, it seemed, was free.

After a while, they were all safe back on the road.

"That," said Barb, "was incredible. You ought to get a job in the State Department."

"Do you really think so?" Ginny beamed.

"Yes," said Barb, looking cross. "Well, it's one thirty-four. Time to think *lunch*—right, Bub?"

"Yeah, and the dinosaurs!"

"What are you doing? Barb, you can't pull off here, this isn't what we planned. We can't eat our lunch till the cabin. Don't you remember?"

"John Allen and I have decided to see the dinosaur display, since we've been seeing the billboards since Peterberg. Besides, I'm hungry, if you're not. Dinosaurs make me hungry."

"Yeah!" said Johnny.

"Well we simply can't do it! We just lost time and we aren't scheduled to stop until we—"

"We'll just have high tea. We'll have high tea at the cabin. Real romantic."

"That's them! That's them! See that sign?"

They were passing a large sign that said: SEE THE AL-LOSAURUS! BRING ALL THE KIDS! "That's plastic! That's not a dinosaur!" snapped Ginny.

"I'm hungry," said Katie Lee.

"Now you've put it in her head! See here. Now you listen here. It was my planning this vacation and you said to me, you go ahead and plan this trip and—"

"Good planning doesn't keep folks from eating lunch. For that matter," said Barb with increasing firmness, "planning is not the same thing as running everybody's business."

"Yeah," said Johnny, and retreated all the way to the back.

She had tried so hard. After all they'd been through. After what Phil would say. And the papers could have said, too. And everything.

"You should see the look on your face," Barb said archly.

There came a tiny giggle from the back.

"I hope," said Ginny, a little flustered, "I hope you're satisfied, making me look foolish in front of my own children—"

"But, love, it will be all right. We'll get to the cabin, and we'll have a great—um—picnic supper and the kids will make sand castles—"

"I suppose."

"Lovely." Barb was nodding. "Honey, just like a—a fairy tale—"

"Just like in the movies." Ginny sniffed.

And she was *planning*.

ACCESSORIES EXTRA

My five-year-old banged down the phone in the other room and I stopped myself from calling "Put it down right" (cord to the right, the right-handed way) and went back to the catsup. (Left-handed kids are smarter, I keep reading.) Should we use the onion-garlic kind or the 57 kind? Laurie wouldn't notice there was an onion taste if she didn't see the little white bits.

"Did you have a nice conversation?" I called, but she was shoving back the swinging door to join me in the kitchen.

"Yes," she said positively. She climbed up onto a stool and began to watch me. "It was pretty much like the six o'clock man."

I was thinking I could just use powdered milk. I said, "Who?"

"Bong, bong, bong . . ." She gave a credible imitation of a gong. " 'We have an important message for you. Please *hold* for your important *message*. . . .' " This child is like a parrot. Or a phonograph.

"I didn't realize the calls were that regular," I said. "I mean that punctual."

" 'Bang bong BONG,' " she began, with vigor.

The calls, thanks to the law, come between eight A.M. and eight P.M., weekdays only.

"Hand me the pepper, please. With the green top."

She reached for the jar and examined the contents. "It isn't black," she said. "It has white speckles in it."

"I never said it was black," I said. I had a large green bowl and a small aluminum bowl, hamburger in the green one.

"B-L-A-C-K. Doesn't that spell 'black'?" she reasoned. She has a dark, curly head with heavy thoughts. I think she sifts information from the air. "What's that?"

"Supper," I said. A surprise. I never make meatballs.

"I don't want a hamburger with that in it."

"I'll find somebody who does." I poured in the oatmeal. Her last visit, Laurie had loved Joanne's cooking. Especially the meatballs. That cooking was all she had talked about for a week. That and the tropical fish. "Who was that on the phone?"

"The Revolving Lady."

"You should have called me."

"You *said* I could talk to the robots. . . . You're putting crackers in it. Why are you putting crackers in it?"

"You said it was a woman, Laurie. We need to either hang up or I have to talk when it's real people. We don't need to make them any madder."

"Oh," she said airily. "She was a robot one. I mean, first it was a robot, then it was a lady. 'There-will-be-a-brief-silence. Bing!' " Laurie dah-dah'd a few bars of "I'll Be Home for Christmas," and began precisely, in a nasal-lady voice: " 'It's-about-your-revolving-charge.   The-season-is-here-when-we-may-overlook-our— Oh ick. You're putting *milk* in it. Why are you putting *milk* in it?"

"You mean, after the electronic voice it was a woman's voice? A taped message?"

" 'Please-hold-for-the-following-taped-message—' "

"Was it a tape or a lady?"

"I think it was a taped lady." Laurie was losing interest. "I said 'Hello?' 'Hello?' *three* times, and she goes, 'It's-about-your-revolving-charge. The-season-is-here—' What are you going to do with that? Ugh. The milk is *pink.* "

"You *like* pink milk," I said firmly. I had to roll the things in cooked rice and set them in a pan. And make the sauce.

"Oh," she said, exasperated. "That's a different kind and you know it. . . . Mom? That kind has a strawberry taste in it. Mom?"

"What?"

"Do you know where I went after kiddiegarten today? I went over to Sneddigars'. And you know what? They have a new kitten. It's a boy kitten. Kevin let me hold him. And you know what his name is? It's Tom Kitten. Just like we read in the book. He's so cute! He purred in my lap. Mom—"

"The landlord says *no.*"

"He's all black with gray stripes."

"He'll be Tom Kitten for six months, and then he'll be Mrs. Cat."

Laurie cocked her head, quizzical.

"All kittens are female until proven otherwise. Laurie, most people can't tell the difference. Little boy cats look too much like little girl cats. People get a kitten, and they don't know if it's a boy or—"

"This one's a boy."

"You can't be sure," I said doggedly.

"He has test-icles," she said. "Kevin's brother Brian showed me he has test-icles. He doesn't exactly have a pe-nis though."

I gathered that the parts referred to were the kitten's, but I made a mental note to talk to Kevin's mother.

"Could we have a kitten if I lived with Joanne and Dad?"

I shut my mouth.

"Oh, they're like doughnuts, the holes I mean," she said. She meant the meatballs. I was pressing in all these green-pepper bits, making jazzy little patterns. "Is that meatballs?"

"That's to make sure they cook evenly," I said, opening the oven.

"Joanne's had red things. Um, pi*men*tos—"

"That comes *later.* You put it on." I closed the oven. *"Later."*

"Are you mad at me?"

"No."

"Are you sure?"

I was putting back the spices, putting up the oatmeal, washing off my hands. ". . . I'm sure," I said. The cabinet was clean. I had to get the little bowl back out to make the sauce. Basil, pimentos . . .

"You like dogs better than kittens, don't you, Mom? Daddy says you know so many dogs. I wish I had one. Mom, Kevin wanted to know if I could go with them to see *Kidnapped* at the Children's Theater. They have a real parrot and he says it's neat. . . . Can I?"

" '*May* I,' " I corrected.

"You've got your money face on. Mom?"

"Yes?"

"Are you mad?"

"Why should I be mad?"

"I don't know. Mom?"

"What?"

"Does Daddy like cats?"

"I don't know. There's every evidence in the world that Daddy likes dogs—" I shut myself up.

"I bet Joanne likes cats. I bet Joanne likes kittens. You know what?"

I was going through the cabinet. Basil . . .

"I bet Joanne would like you. If we lived with them, I bet we could have a kitten. Daddy and Joanne have got lots of room. Joanne likes animals. They've already got fish, but they're not cute or anything. You can't play with them—they don't go out, I mean."

"We have a lot in common."

"Oh, that woman called again when you were in the bathroom. Tony. She says to call her. She hates kids, doesn't she, Mom?"

The phone was ringing, and Laurie slid off her stool. "You want me to answer that?" she said.

"I said I'd get you some tropical fish."

"You want me to call you if it's a real person? Even Daddy?"

I'd forgotten the pimentos. I didn't have any damn pimentos in the house. I didn't have any cash. *Not if it's Tony, not if it's*

Daddy, not even if it's the Sears lady. You handle them better than I do anyway.

"Mom?" she was patiently calling. "Hey, Mom? It's a *person* again."

SOMEONE TO WATCH OVER ME

I

It wasn't a dream, exactly, but some unfocused dread that had shaken Liz out of her sleep, that waked her after a hard set of rounds and the kids' arguments in the evening, and her own frantic calls for a plumber—because if the water in the basement kept rising, it would put out the pilot light.

So it wasn't a dream that woke her up, and besides, she didn't dream very much. It had to be that, just like when they were little, there was something going wrong about her kids.

Elizabeth Cecilia Heneghan found herself on her feet, stumbling into her kids' rooms, dimly aware that her heart rate was up and her body was wide awake.

There was a quiet shape in Cassie's bed, her older girl's bed; so she turned and walked into Allissa's room, which was festooned with bears and bunnies and posters of glamorous stars. There was a shape on the upper bunk that resembled Lissa. And without having dreamed she would ever have done it, Liz went to that bunk and threw back the covers.

Her kids were beautiful asleep. They were beautiful kids

and she had silently adored them (asleep especially) for thirteen and eleven years respectively, and yet without hesitation she had walked up to an allegedly sleeping Allissa and had thrown off the covers . . . to find that under the blankets were bunnies. Pillows. Pajamas . . .

Cassie's subterfuge was more sophisticated: She had rolled up blankets and pillows, and that sad-looking quilt fish (Liz was not much of a hand at sewing). The look was more real. The effort more shocking.

It was 2:45 A.M. on a miserable New England November night. There was nothing Liz could do about where they had gone. It wasn't as if they had been kidnapped, not as if you called the police. A few hours ago she had collapsed thankfully into bed, the girls still fussing back and forth but pretty close to fading . . . Now they could be anywhere. Maybe even New York City. Except that Eddie had never actually wanted his kids; he'd only wanted to take what he knew Liz was desperate to have.

Liz went into the bathroom and took the lid off the tank, banged open the stool, dusted Scrubduty on the sink and its back and the bathtub; threw up once and flushed, poured bleach into the toilet and began to scrub, to excoriate the vomit, the wordless anguish.

This year had promised so much; it had seemed like a godsend to be able to move in here, into a place like a home of their own. The kids were excited. Subsidized housing. The grant for Liz to go to school and really begin to make something of her life. Really have a life to give her kids. But it was true that she wasn't home as much now. . . .

There was the floor to wash, that gunk that seems to edge every surface in the bathroom—

Liz was in the kitchen cleaning the oven at 3:59 A.M. when she heard a key grate, hesitate, and grind unsteadily in the door that faced the street, Fifty-fifth Place, a thoroughfare much too busy. The door creaked fully open and suddenly Liz realized how she must look. Hiding from her kids with a greasy oven mitt on her hand; thinking, *What am I going to do now, what do I say?*

Liz folded the greasy glove, tucked it into the dish-towel drawer, and was just walking into the living room when it occurred to her to breathe. Lissa was slack against the unbolted door; Cassie was lying slewed across the couch. The room stank like—

Whiskey. Tastable in the air between them: whiskey. The sweet acridity seemed to freeze her thoughts. Lissa's baby face was a Christmas-wreath green. Liz felt herself pick her key up off the TV set. Cassie, the sophisticated pretty one, looked stupid.

"Wherever you've been," said Liz—she sounded like she was reciting, "I don't care where you've been, but we're going to go right back." Then she was gripping Cassie's shoulder enough to hurt, enough to maim, and steering both girls back out into the sharp almost-winter air.

Their street frightened her, but she never admitted it. What was the use? Men and boys at all hours; *noises.* Her kids on those streets.

She was aware they were passing their car and were heading on down the street when Cassie, her hair half down from barrettes, began a drunken, frightened sobbing. "I'm sorry, Liz!" she said. "Hones' to God."

Liz couldn't stand to see her humiliated and wouldn't look at her.

Lissa was sniveling. "It wasn't my idea and— Oh, I think I'm going to be sick! Mom, Mama, I'm, I'm real sick—"

Liz said automatically: "Not here." Kids played in every filthy patch of snow around here. "Aim in the gutter."

And the smell of vomit and too-good whiskey shocked her again. The straining. Her kids had always smelled like sweet babies. Lissa was very sick. Very sick before had only underscored her innocence.

Liz wasn't exactly thinking. It was more like someone else's words were parading through her head. Maybe her mother's. *Shouldn't have left the main city. Should have left them with* (with whom?) *while she was in school. Or why* not *a Catholic school? It hadn't killed her or kept her from coming out—*

"Mom, you can't go in there!" urged Cassie. They had apparently arrived—only two blocks away. Their own neighborhood.

There were two or three boys smoking joints on the steps of

this row house, a place almost exactly like their own, and it was obvious the party wasn't over. Along the sidewalk, the street light was out; open windows leaked a driving beat and shadows were slumping rhythmically behind gold curtains. Light made long blue angles across the dirty snow.

"Hey Mama," said a kid on the stoop. "You want a real good time? Oh," he interrupted himself. "Hey Cassie."

Blood was in her temples and her throat. Liz had let her grip on Cassie go and was recognizing as she shoved through the door, that this was where Cassie's friend Tonya Sovic lived. Tonya was fourteen.

And there was Tonya. And that drunken slut with her hand on that drunken kid's crotch must be her—mother.

Afterward, neighbors said they could hear Elizabeth Cecilia Heneghan a city block around. She didn't have a good voice for dramatics—her voice got shrill—but by the time she was in that woman's face—and she was shorter, Liz was shorter than everybody—she had built up to a banshee scream, words to the effect that if that woman ever allowed her two kids in that house again she was calling the police, driving her car up the steps, blowing the place up and knocking the shit out of Mrs. Sovic. And the fact that several of these promises were mutually exclusive did not slacken her.

A large thug loomed over Liz to grab her arm, and, circling her elbow deftly around his hand, she eluded him, parade-turned, and stalked back down to the street and steered her kids the two blocks home. They were both sick, horribly, wretchedly sick, outside; and when they stood up again, it came to her that they were both going to be taller than she. But then, almost everybody was.

Liz finally reached class at eleven, theory of nursing; a class that didn't concern her very much.

She had been scheduled for some early rounds at seven and pathophysiology at nine; but reality had managed to get in the way. What had happened the night before. She had to deal with discipline, facts, pronouncements; and they had got through that.

She had had to sit down with her kids (they didn't want to

get up; they wouldn't eat Cocoa Puffs; "Oh ugh barf," said Cassie). Actually, what Liz had first had to do was make phone calls. And then lay down the law, as soon as she had figured it out: which was that the old lady from across the street, Mrs. Jackson, was going to be coming over after school was out, and she'd be there every evening until Liz got home.

(And they'd rolled their eyes. . . .)

She did have to agree to get a color television, but things were basically back to normal. Mrs. Jackson had to have a color TV; and maybe Liz would win a TV. You never could tell.

And so Liz, her classmates seething with unappreciated virtue, finally dropped into a chair during the third nursing class of her day at eight minutes past eleven. Norris, the instructor, kept trying to catch her eye (all disapproval; from this Liz guessed that it was Norris who had directed early rounds). Asked a direct question about a drug interaction, Liz pertly rattled off the answer and relaxing, followed with a smile. The smile was from relief, at the resumption of classes and routine, at the fact that her kids were in school and all right with the world; but that wasn't the way Norris took it.

During afternoon rounds she stopped at the nurses' station on her floor and called home, greeting the sullen Cassie with a cool "How are you feeling?" *You sound like a cold bitch,* she warned herself. *One of these days you'll sound just like your mother.*

"It's all over school," Cassie said. "I got chased out of the lunch room. They called me a baby. They said I was a suck-up and chased me out."

"*Who* chased you?" said Liz.

"That's your signal," said the charge nurse, leaning over the desk. She meant the lighted numbers on the overhead board. "The Green Team goes to the procedure room."

"Let me speak to Lissa," Liz said blankly, staring at the nurse. She had one of those painted, pretty faces, a TV nurse.

"Mom?" came Lissa's voice. "I threw up at lunch. I was sick all day."

"That's what you get," said Liz. *You sound like your mother.*

"I wish you wouldn't make personal calls from the ward,"

said the charge nurse. "Please hang up. Green Team to the procedure room."

They'd be fine, Liz told herself, fast-walking; those kids would do just fine. High-spirited kids always got in some kind of a mess. Look at herself—knocked up at seventeen . . . She had loved school actually, hidden from the world in that school; at least it had got her out of the house. And she'd graduated anyway. Making her the most educated woman in her family. And the marriage, the girls. Getting rid of Eddie . . . a whiner, but sometimes crazy; and now look. The homemaker grant, the jobs. So much hope and hard work; finding love and Things Would Be All Right. Those kids were good.

At 4:23 the Green Team, the greenest of the student nurses, was learning to move the very large Johnny Krauss—a city lineman who had fallen from a cherry-picker and was now a quad—move him like a loose-jointed tackling dummy into a reasonable series of necessary physical positions. Relieving stress, conserving skin integrity, probably preserving his mind. He seemed to like the company. He was pleasant.

"This is a condom catheter," began Andrews, the instructor, in her deviated-septum voice. Some of the kiddie-agers giggled, and Johnny's brows made a dignified arch, as if he'd crossed his arms. "Shaped like a condom, it fits like a condom and it's joined at the tip to the urine bag that will go under *here* . . ." Underneath one of the side rails.

And Andrews droned on.

Krauss was used to being used for instruction—at this moment by a number of very young girls and two young men and Liz. This was better than lying alone with a set of extremely quiet roommates, and he winked at Liz, as one grownup to another.

The most educated person in her family. Dad had wanted to be something besides a millhand, he said; but it had been his mother who talked up the books. Wanted so much to be a somebody, maybe a nurse; and here was Liz, in a college class. The most educated person in her family since time began. . . . Her kids would be all right; they

*were really stubborn. They set their minds on something and it was
remarkable the way they always got it—*

"—Mrs. Heneghan?"

Liz had been staring down over the snow-blown parking
lot. She moved her stare.

"Since you don't seem to require any further instruction on
this, would you please demonstrate the condom catheter? Let's
not keep Mr. Krauss waiting."

Johnny smiled, encouraging, and Liz smiled back. She
could have fitted that kind of thing on limp spaghetti.

As soon as she touched this man she liked, she forgot, as she
generally did, that the others were anywhere around. In beginning to touch him, she found his stomach was unusually dis-
tended. "Do you think you need to pee now?" she asked. "Well,
ma'am, I wouldn't know," he grinned. "It hasn't said a thing
to me in months."

She really liked him.

Liz stopped touching him and scrubbed quickly, slipped
into rubber gloves and, rattling off an explanation that the man
himself couldn't have needed, she unrolled the rubber catheter
onto his penis. He was lightly erect at her touch, which helped
considerably, and she taped it to him securely without sticking
his hair. She had done this for many months as a hospital aide.

She caught some students looking mortified; probably, she
thought, because he was stiff. Yet they were straight. Which was
another difference . . .

"Now position him," said the instructor.

There was tension between this instructor and Liz. This
class and Liz. This community-college nursing school and Liz.
It was her age, her welfare status, her boyish shortness; it was
how silly she looked in the blue pinnie over striped skirt-and-
blouse student-nurse outfit. She had bony legs. She was sharp-
nosed, sharp-jawed, leading with her chin when determined.
Her brothers had used to say that she looked like a terrier dog.

The thin striped skirt rode up the back of her legs as she
leaned to grasp him. All her life she had despised herself in a
dress. On the other hand, she was strong like an ant, and she
lifted and pulled Krauss slightly off his buttocks.

★ ★ ★

In putting it back together later, she decided it was the combination of bodily tensions he'd been put through, the sudden release of pressure when she lifted him off his behind, and the heavy use of laxatives on his particular kind of ward, which caused the eruption.

All over the bed, which she changed; the floor and walls, which she washed; on the instructors' papers, and all over Liz.

Downstairs in the locker room she changed into gym shorts and a T-shirt that said WEST SIDE RAMS and put on her old blue jacket, because that combination was all she had in the locker. She rolled her uniform up and stashed it in a plastic bag, which she pitched into the trunk of the car. It was in the twenties outside and it smelled like the inevitable Boston snow, more snow; and in the shorts, her bare legs looked exotic. Not the way to walk into that housing project, where everybody stared at you anyway.

After a little fuming she decided to laugh.

"Mom," Cassie stage-whispered, "do you *have* to *dress* like *that?*"

"What's that?" Liz pointed at a mess of paper on the kitchen table. "And where's Mrs. Jackson?"

"She had to go home and cook," contributed Lissa.

"Well it was *house food* money, and this is our *dinner*," started Cassie. "And we got it to come with pineapple the way *you* like—"

"I don't like pineapple. Doris likes pineapple. I don't *like* pineapple—" Liz was repeating herself. "For half the same price we could have cooked a—"

"—six-course meal," mimicked Cassie.

"It was a bargain, Mom," said Lissa. "It was a two-for-one sale, and I said, Could we just get the free one? Mom? And he said that was just advertising, but I said wasn't that false advertising? And, Mom? He said we had to *buy* the one and then we could get one—"

"You could at *least* say thank you we got everything *ready!* Didn't we? And we got *two* pizzas!"

"She interrupted," spat Lissa. "Mom, she is *always inter-rupting me*—"

Cass responded fairly predictably, and it occurred to Liz that she had been brooding about them off and on all day only to come home and feel completely irrelevant. She hated pineapple. And they hadn't got any onions. On the other hand, you had to be glad it was food.

"Where is Mrs. Jackson?"

"She said you're late," said Lissa. "She says she has to go start supper for her grandkids. How come you weren't here by six?"

"Tell her she can bring them over, except I don't know if we've got anything they like—"

"I'll figure it out," said Cassie. "I'll take care of it. Oh, Mom! Doris is back from New York!"

"That was *my* news, creep," said Lissa.

Doris, Liz thought. *Could you believe the luck? When I need her most, that shows you things are okay.* Mechanically she said, "How's the baby?" but Lissa wouldn't stand for nonchalance. "Oh Mom, you're pleased to *death* about it. You know you are!"

"*God,* you're such a cold fish," said Cassie. "Oh, Doris says she—"

"—she might leave Charlie at her sister's house. But she's staying here tonight. She'll be in—"

"*Now* who's interrupting?"

Charlie was such a sweet bright baby. Affectionate and smart, with his mother's eyes.

"Anyway, maybe she won't," contributed Lissa. "I think he's so cute! But he screams too loud—"

"Ew—Liz!" demanded Cassie. "What have you got in that sack? God, you stink!"

As Cassie was stuffing the pizza wrappings into the garbage, Liz reminded them that they were both still grounded for the next two weeks; they seemed astonished. Last night, it seemed, had been so long ago. They had nearly managed to get her convinced that the whole thing hadn't happened.

How would she pay the old lady, she wondered, scrubbing the plastic dishes in the sink. That is, pay her enough. There was gas money . . . no. Shoe money, but Cassie really needed more up-to-date shoes; treat money—movies, soft drinks—no. Well, if she just bleached them a little she could get a little more use out of her old uniforms, but the bleach made the tiny holes around the cuffs come out big holes. She wasn't the only one in the project who washed clothes in the bathtub, but the way the kids took it, it was like she smoked a corncob pipe on the stoop.

She'd take the new-uniform fund for a while, and something would eventually show up. The old ones would work a little longer—they were ugly, and like most ugly clothes, deathless.

By eleven—still no Doris, still no kid—Liz gave it up and hit the sack. She had a quiz first thing in the morning.

It was an intensely pleasurable sensation. The breath on her cheek glacially flavored with Boston air, and there could have been words, though Liz only absorbed their affect. But the ice-tipped fingers on her bed-warm neck definitely woke Liz up, and propelled her into a bear hug. Doris's face and hands and arms were Boston-cold. Liz nuzzled in under the Gore-Tex coat, and there was her sweet warm woman. . . .

It was one A.M., and Doris was hilarious; snow glistened in her fluffy hair as she kissed gin into Liz's mouth. Liz wrapped her arms around the bulky coat and pressed her cheek against the sweet round face . . . a mosaic of chill and warmth; it surprised her how much she really needed those arms. It didn't matter how much Doris needed to fly away as long as she always flew back again. Nothing was perfect. Least of all in love. And Doris laughed into her ear. "Guess what, it's snowing again—"

Doris! Here! Warm and smooth and laughing—Liz carried bright exclamation points in the back of her head.

The test the next morning, she might as well have slept through. But everybody was safe and most things paid for; and that's about the best anyone can hope for.

Mrs. Jackson called the ward the next afternoon, and Liz answered her overhead page to find that at least there was a different nurse in charge. This one acted as if student calls were no concern of hers, and in any case were an everyday occurrence. Liz was thankful.

"They's a phone call for you, Mrs. Hennig," said Mrs. Jackson.

Mrs. Jackson was an ageless and dignified woman—defiantly erect and Deep South black, which shamed her family. She was good with kids, but many things made her nervous.

"What kind of a phone call, Mrs. Jackson?" In the background blabbed an announcer for a game show.

"It was that school. I come in at two thirty, like we said, and they was a call came for you." This arrangement was for those days when Lissa came home early. "They are wanting you to call them back about . . ." The lady ruminated. "About Cassie," she said conclusively.

Liz looked sharply at the charge nurse. Still no interest in the call. Deliberately she turned her back and continued. However liberal this charge nurse was, you just couldn't stay on the phone. "Yes?" Liz said, encouraging.

"They say she isn't coming to the school."

"She's not— She's what? Is she there now? Did she go to school this morning?"

"As far as I know, she did. Except that *they* were saying that she didn't."

"Did she get on the school bus?"

"Mrs. Hennig, now how would I know that?"

"I just thought maybe you looked outside and . . . No, of course not. You wouldn't see if . . . I'm sorry."

"I see my grandchildren get on the bus this morning." The lady was wounded.

"Is, is Doris there?"

"I don't know where she is, Mrs. Hennig, but the baby is here. He is such a sweet child—and he is sound asleep."

"Thank you. Thanks for calling me," Liz babbled. "Call me anytime you think you have any reason to, okay?"

Well, she had to call, and she couldn't be stuck to a ward phone, so she took off down the hall and down the stairs to find a phone that was somewhat private. On the main floor, all three of the phones in front were in use, so she continued down the stairs to the basement. Three malevolent-looking youths were hanging around one set of phones but she found a pay phone in back, outside one of the employee dressing rooms, and dropped 25 percent of her earthly wealth in the phone.

"Mmm, this is Elizabeth Heneghan, Cassandra Hunt's mother," she told the answerer crisply. *Stop chewing your lip,* she told herself. *It's childish.*

"To whom do you wish to speak?"

"Ahh, somebody called from this office about—"

"With whom do you wish to speak?"

"My daughter. Somebody called me about my daughter Cassie. Cassandra Hunt—"

"And she is in what grade? And what section?"

Liz thought instantly of tracking, wondered if her kid was being dumbed out of school. "She's thirteen and in the eighth—"

"Just a minute."

"She's thirteen—"

"Just let me look in the computer." Clicking sounds. "And is she listed under your name or under—"

"Hunt. Her name is Hunt."

Was that silent disapproval over there?

"Eighth . . . I think you want Mr. Balemann. She would be part of his section." The phone clicked over and the electronic air was flooded with glitziness.

How long would she have to hold? Liz looked around uneasily, but the youths at the other phone were occupied. She had been off the ward ten minutes. The shit would hit the fan when she got back.

"Balemann here."

"Hello, I'd like to know if—"

"Who'm I speaking to?"

"This is, I'm sorry, I'm Elizabeth Heneghan, Cassie Hunt's mother. I understand you were trying to—"

"Hold on please." *Unchained Melody.*

"Are you through with the phone, yet?" Outside the booth was a sour-faced woman, dressed in blue-and-whites like the nurse's aides.

"No, not yet. Look, I'm talking to my kid's school, and I'm on hold—"

"Ms. Heneghan? Yes, we tried to reach you earlier at a time during which you had listed yourself as available on our P2 form—"

"That's my old schedule, but you see, it changes—"

"I only have a fifteen-minute break," said the aide, stubborn. "Would you mind could I make a call—"

The voice rolled on "—has been expelled from school?"

"Are you almost through?"

"No! I mean, no, I didn't know she was . . . expelled from school! What for? I mean, what has she done that's so terrible that you have to—"

". . . school," he overrode her.

"I beg your—"

"—missed three days of classes unexcused. She missed classes two weeks ago, then was making some progress with her counselor, and now she has missed the last two days. Unexcused absences are—"

"She skips school, so you throw her *out* of school?"

"Are you through yet?"

"No," she snapped. "Get out and get a phone from somebody else! —Why are you doing this? Couldn't you call me first? Why are you doing this? She's a really good kid, a smart kid. She gets good grades and— All kids skip school, don't they? Why make such a deal out of it and make it harder for her to catch up when she gets back in? It's been a hard year for her. This is a new school. She's a good kid, she likes school, she gets good grades. . . ."

Liz was supposed to have signed and dated a note from the counseling office about Cassie, a note which, apparently, she had never received. Apparently someone else had signed it. Apparently someone whose signature didn't match the signatures they had on file . . .

One thing you could say about Eddie, his magic member had got her out of her mother's house—endless belittlement, endless cleaning up after the phalanx of boys that had followed her. Boyish, she had always looked boyish; her mother had been sure she wouldn't marry, that her eldest (and the only daughter) was a heaven-sent maid.

Mother was completely obsessed by her wish that Liz not have sex and get away; but there was Eddie from down the street, a girlish blond with no shoulders or beard and lots of marijuana. It wasn't hard to lie under him at first, it was exciting and a jolt to realize how sensitive those parts could be. And how evil it was. How defiant she was. She had been so horrified at the mess and filth and touchlessness of her own and her parents' and her brothers' bodies that she had honestly not known about it. No playing doctor, no midnight vice. And then pregnancy (and the meanness of others). And then the baby, perfect and tiny, a little bit premature, that was Cassie. The first consuming love Liz had ever had.

And after she was completely and thoroughly tired of Eddie (and had seen those Lesbian books) there had been Allissa. So sweet and so affectionate. She had adored her kids, adored them. But that didn't necessarily tell her what to do.

Monday she called in, got the receptionist for the nursing program and took off class time to have breakfast out with Cassie; they would have breakfast out, they would go to see the counselor, sign all the forms; it would be all right. Cassie had always been the level-headed one; the kid who figured all the angles and smoothed the wrinkles out.

"You won't like her," Cassie said flatly. Apparently, she had seen this counselor before.

Yet maybe, Balemann had said, the counselor could Fix Things. "You're taking this too personally," Liz explained. "But this is business. She's a bureaucrat. They pay her to do a job. You can bargain with people like that because her job is to bargain. She doesn't personally care about you; she couldn't if she wanted to. She has too many kids to deal with. You see what I mean? You just jump through whatever hoops she gives you to jump through, and then you just don't ever give her the chance to bother you again."

"Liz, you don't get it. You'll hate her," Cassie said.

* * *

Liz thought they should start the day off hopefully. They had to maneuver from the very best frame of mind, so they had to start with the very best possible breakfast. Liz turned the wagon in at Chez Alexandre. When you can't afford a thing, you should go for the best. What did Cassie want? Toast and a donut. All Liz wanted herself was coffee, but she ordered coffee, juice, milk, eggs, toast, a rasher of bacon. Maybe she could feed it to her daughter. That had worked remarkably well with both daughters before.

"You won't like her," pronounced Cassie.

"Look. It doesn't matter if I like her. It doesn't matter if she doesn't like me. It doesn't matter to me if she's Hitler's little sister. It's just her job. She can't get involved; I mean she doesn't personally give a damn what the school wants, or what anybody else wants. It's just a job. You can always negotiate with a person like that. You just do your job by letting them do their job. Do you see what I mean?"

"She's not like that," said Cassie, cutting the donut into peanut-sized pieces, into sequin-sized and bacteria-sized pieces. "She's gonna hate you."

"How do you know that?"

"I just know. You don't get along with anybody, Liz."

Liz let that wash, wondering what provoked it, and suddenly Cassie exploded: "You can't trust her. She says you can talk to her and then . . ."

Oh, a betrayal. After a moment, Liz looked up from her impossible eggs to find Cassie, fists balled, silently in tears. With the varicolored rock-star makeup beginning to leak with her tears, she looked younger, eminently hurtable. Liz tried to think of something to say, something safe. But there was still the strain of that recent night, which had left them with some new unbroachable barrier. What could you say so they'd feel like part of a team again? Liz couldn't think of anything to say.

The ceilings were low. The entire building was sort of squat and flat. But it impressed Liz how much she hated being in a high school again (no: This was a junior high). It was wonderful how she hated all her memories. In the outside world she remembered only the good parts: geometry, memorizing poems. Smoking in the girls' room, blowing smoke rings.

Liz quick-walked on with her hospital hustle, feeling for once competent and professional in her uniform. Most of the kids were apparently in classes. Cassie, in wraparound shades, had her coolest who-are-all-these-people glare, and though nearly as tall as Liz, was shrinking progressively somehow within the red ski jacket she had thought was so cool last winter.

Here in the hall were the trophies, awards, rules and announcements, the endless fine-tooth separations of children in schools. The lockers. For some reason, when she had first brought Cassie there, she had felt worlds more, well, indulgent toward all this.

And sitting endlessly in the anteroom to the counseling office, Liz had the time to conclude that in her uniform she looked like a twit.

The scenes that followed kept returning to her and stinging like hornets; came to her on the ward, driving home, doing something repetitive. When she was nearly asleep. Trying to relax, to massage and make love. Doris said to *Take your time,* she *understood,* but perhaps she didn't . . .

The counselor person was a self-satisfied little makeup artist, who looked pissed off that Elizabeth was competitively thin. Liz heard herself start: friendly, positive, we're-all-of-course-on-the-same-side. And the phrases began erupting from that lipstick.

"So she can get back into school—" Liz began.

Adult concerns . . . impressionable young adults.

"Well, of *course* she's at an impressionable age. I mean in part, isn't that what this conference is about? Look, Cassie knows you can't just not go to school. She knows you've got to face the music, too, but somebody has to tell us what we can—"

—burdened with sordid environments that—

"What did you say?"

—of dysfunctional families—

"What are you talking about, dysfunctional? That's a misuse of a psychiatric term. We may be different, but we function just fine. We make birthday cakes, we pay our taxes, there is nothing more or less dysfunctional about this family than in the average working-class—"

—*stress of a highly unusual constellation, don't you?*

"We . . . ah . . . I shared that with her. I mean, I talk about my life with my kids. I believe in telling the kids what's going on, that's what they need to know. My folks didn't do that, if you see what I mean—"

—*great burden of difference.*

"I'm always honest with my kids. Aren't you honest with your kids? Anyway, why are we talking about my business? We're here to talk about my kid," she said mechanically. "How does she get back in school?"

Cassie began to cry.

—*dysfunctional Lesbian family*—

"Now you listen. The way you talk—you make it sound like Lesbian equals dysfunctional. I'll tell you what dysfunctional is. It's when your mother tapes your hands together so you can't touch yourself when you sleep—"

—*many signs of dysfunction*—

The kid had signed an agreement on sharing information. "Let me see that," Liz said. She read it. It gave full rights to the school, no guarantees. "She didn't know what she was signing," snapped Liz. "You tricked her. You tricked my kid into signing statements against—against herself. Against her family."

And after this, they went to Mr. Balemann: *In addition to the additional truancy.*

Liz stared. "Additional? But you said she'd missed three times. I know she came to school today—she's here. What do you—"

—*misinformed,* he interrupted. *She was talking to Miss Adams back in October. This is the first time we have seen her in this school since Monday noon when she was involved in an altercation in the school cafeteria*—

"I told you, Mom." Cassie had begun to sob again, mascara in large swaths down her cheekbones. "I can't go back anyway. If I go back again I'll get beaten up again. . . ."

"Say, can't you protect her? She's a little kid. Can't you

protect her from this, these whatever-they-ares, that want to beat up my kid?"

—*overdramatization of the problem. And if we wanted to, we couldn't be everywhere at once. On the other hand, if Cassie is uncomfortable, when she returns, she could eat with the cafeteria monitors—*

"Mom, I can't do that! Nobody will talk to me—"

—*for the duration of the suspension—*

"Wait. Why suspension? Why? She can't make the work up if you suspend her. It's almost exam time, she could fail some of her classes. She's always been a good student. You're taking too much away—"

As they walked back down the hall, it seemed like doors banged shut all around them.

II

It was thinking about being spring outside. Liz was drifting out of pathophysiology, and fogged under the weight of the CO_2-bicarb cycle (respiratory rate, hyperoxygenation, hypooxygenation, alkalosis, acidosis), when she felt a light touch on her upper arm. It was the prof. "We need to talk," said Dr. Fieldhaus primly. She was dean of the nursing school, the kind you could imagine wearing white gloves to butcher pigs. The other students widened their eyes as Liz passed them; and then, safe in groups, stared after the two, smug with clique virtue.

The transition felt strange. One moment Liz was in the sort of clever awe that comes with hard thinking, with studying something genuinely new—grappling with and grasping the intricacies of life and death—and the next it was like high school again, with the principal.

The nursing office was on the same floor of the same ratty building, past almost every human being who was connected with the nursing school. Liz froze her expression. For a few minutes she stood in the plastic and mood-color office with the secretaries, who Knew Everything but played elaborately dumb, and then Fieldhaus came back to get her. Liz followed her into her inner office and within a few moments they were joined by Dr. Norris and Mrs. Andrews. And a recorder. It was hardly needed though, since the secretaries would be listening like bats.

"You seem to have been ill a good deal this semester," began the dean.

Had she missed that many quizzes, that much rotation? How could she blow something like this, something she wanted and needed so much?

The dean was just repeating words. She was Doing Her Job. Andrews had that self-satisfied look that says, *These are all just words. We wash out the dogshit like you.*

Liz said something about her kids having trouble. That things would settle down. The dean looked polite, but the others were really going for her throat.

An almost fatal rage crashed over her. They knew nothing about her life; they cared nothing about her life. They didn't deserve any explanation. Nobody did—if she could pass the tests anyway, whose business was it?

Except it was their business. So much of nursing is what you learn on the ward.

She felt for that thick barricade that had served her so well, took a firm grasp on it; she shoved past her emotional dam so that she could grovel.

On the way out to the hospital her mind registered nothing. She didn't even feel the emotion she had just been through; it was like she had locked it in a box someplace and lost the combination. To the basement to change; up to the ward to sign in; downstairs to pick up some cigarettes. Her mind was blank until she saw a main-floor phone, and she dropped in a coin. And Doris answered. *Honey, just talk to me.*

She said: "Hi—uh—?"

"Liz? Is that you?"

"Hi. How's everything. How, how is Charlie?"

"Fine. He's been fine all day. He's taking a nap. Are you all right?"

"Yeah," Liz said unevenly. "Sure."

*   *   *

Johnny Krauss was trying to be his usual pleasant self, and that was painful. "I'm sorry I got you all messed up the other day," he rasped. He breathed noisily; his lungs were full of junk. "I've been washing clothes since I was born," Liz said cheerfully. "And that was just one more load." She was messing with the turnable bell on her stethoscope.

He was sick now. He was still the tackling dummy, but now he was sick; she ought to be professional enough to listen in and learn how the fluid sounded. Learn what this sort of pneumonia sounded like. He was swollen all over and hot to the touch.

Liz pressed the stethoscope beneath his left nipple, then above it; she walked around to his other side, pressing the cold steel against his back. He couldn't feel it. . . . "Whisper ninety-nine," she said mechanically. It sounded as if he was shouting the words from every place she touched.

Quads, they had been taught, usually died like this. With pneumonia, heart failure, a urinary-tract infection.

"Mr. Krauss!" It was Andrews—efficient, clean, impersonal. "Are you keeping our student busy?"

"Trying to!" he laughed, and started to cough.

"Orthopnea," Liz reported. "Tachypnea, stridor, rales, pectoriloquy." Liz wanted to ask what they could really do for him. Shoot him maybe. She wanted to say, He's going to drown in bed. After surviving what he survived, giving up his body, after that hole in his throat. But she would have heard *You're too involved with your patients,* and *This is just the beginning. Wait till they're really your patients.*

Liz did various reasonable things with him and followed the instructor into the hallway. Andrews wore her imperviousness, standing with her clipboard, obviously looking for some screwup. She had that patent superiority of "I can look sympathetic and be a million miles away. Baking a cake in my head while this guy expires. And so must you." Liz thought: *She smiles, but she cares for detail, appearances and everything but people. Just like my mother except for the fact that she smiles.*

Liz went back to Johnny's room and poked her head in: "You keep it together," she told him. "See you tomorrow."

★   ★   ★

She heard three codes called on that floor the rest of that shift. All three of them were on Johnny's side of the ward.

III

Over the next few weeks she passed her exams. She got a color TV set from Doris's sister, and Mrs. Jackson had absolutely fallen in love with Charlie. But there was no similar magic around for Cassie. No matter what Liz did, no matter what she could think of, Cassie wouldn't go back to school. What was Liz going to do, call a cop? Commit her to one of those queer-hating youth homes? Give her to Eddie? If she'd had the heart; if she'd had the energy, she might have tried to beat her. But she knew from direct experience just how poorly that worked.

Doris just looked sympathetic, and handed the baby to Liz, and he hugged her neck like Cassie had once, like Cassie.

All you could say was, Cassie had got herself a job—that was something (even baby-sitting was something) in an area where most adults went out on the stoop and *sat*. Cassie had managed to lie her way into a job, because she liked kids.

It was February 21: Cassie turned fourteen. She baby-sat now, and was hoping to work at a day-care center in March. In day care. As a baby-maid. A hundred years of Foxes and McDaviers and Heneghans as fish packer, spud digger, ladies' maid, hooker, wet nurse, and this. She could have had a chance to go somewhere, so much easier. Style had always been so important to Cassie.

If you watched TV, you'd have thought kids today wouldn't touch a shlock job, and especially without much money, and that brought up other concerns, and—Cassie. She had even been a very fastidious baby. . . .

That fucking school.

At least she had a job. Didn't watch soaps all day.

The garbage can had been knocked all over the street again, so Liz parked, wrestled the can upright, and because she didn't like dragging it through the house, staggered down two houses and through a small alley and around to the back, fixed the can, climbed the short flight of back stairs and entered the back door. Which hadn't been locked. Damn, she thought, unwinding her scarf. Where did these kids think they lived, the garden of Eden? Damn, damn, damn . . .

The pot was still warm, and she was lifting the coffee off the burner when she heard the voice, clear as day. What with the thin walls, the kitchen door that didn't catch, Liz first heard the words without the meaning. Then the meaning, and after she registered that, finally, the voice.

"*. . . She never will, I mean . . . uptight Catholic lady . . . colder than a witch's tit and she just does not get . . . Other day, she asks me what is nose candy. Nose candy. And she's going to give you advice?*

"*. . . Do what you're going to do, baby—what do you think she is going to do about it? There's two of you!*"

Liz could hear the electric clock, thundering over the stove.

"*. . . Once said she whipped your ass, you ran out in the highway, and you know what she does? She cries for half an hour. . . .*

"*. . . What do you think she will do to you, kick you out?*"

If only the voice were somebody else's. Some other kid. Or Mrs. Jackson.

"*. . . your life. You want to do anything you want, it's your life. You want to go out, you just go. You tell this little old lady Jackson—*"

At first it was as if Liz hadn't understood the language. And then it was like that time so many years ago with Cassie in the street. As if she had seen a snake on her kids. A scorpion.

Liz shoved the door back and stomped into the living room. The baby was pleased, and raised his hands to be lifted; she hardly saw him. Keys went one way and coat another as her voice was rising: "Out—get out—"

Doris, her back toward Liz, was the last to turn and when she did, she was doing her *Hey baby, everything is cool* smile.

"Out," Liz was saying. She moved mechanically, in the back of her head acknowledging that Doris, sweet-faced no more, topped her and outweighed her by eighty-some pounds. And that there was a reason why her nose always ran. Liz grabbed the sleeping bag she had given Doris as a Christmas present, yanked open the door and hurled it down to the street. With the spare boots. The baby's bag. And shoe after shoe . . .

Charlie, looking confused, still held up his arms.

"We have to say bye-bye, sweet-boy," she said. His face began to crumple and she bent to him, squeezed him in a rocking motion and kissed Charlie on the forehead. Walking to the door, she was aware of the astonished look on Lissa's face and the furious look on Cassie's. "Bye, sweetheart," she said mechanically, not to Doris; and kissed him on the top of the head. She handed him over to Doris, who stood expressionless, holding him like a sack.

"Have a real nice forever," sneered Liz's once-sweet lover. "And don't hold your breath for me this time, babe."

Liz slammed the door and the window cracked all the way across.

IV

For the first time since adolescence, Liz couldn't sleep. Her mind was on Charlie: Who had him now? Did they let him cry too long. And on Cassie. Was there something she ought to be saying or doing or being to her? Cassie missed Doris. And probably Charlie, and definitely, school. (Had Doris urged her to quit? Liz could never forgive that. She couldn't have. Of course, Doris probably had.)

On the other hand, Lissa would probably not act the same way; she was timid and pleasing, the type who sucked up to authority. It was really sad how Liz disliked that trait, but now she could see the use of it after Cassie and all her directionless fury, her misery, her isolation.

How could she get Cassie back again as a friend? And maybe she should have kept Charlie. Where was he now?

In the afternoon she had picked up Cassie from the Bunny-town Day Care; this was a barnlike old house with a purple-wood-fenced yard; most of the exposed purple wood or packed dirt surfaces were pitted by rain and snow and white-streaked with pigeon droppings. There were so few toys.

Emerging from its wide Dutch door, the exhausted Cassie looked harder, but not any older. Her makeup had often been garish before, but now it was clownlike. And that wasn't all. She was wearing some new leather style that Liz couldn't have afforded and a grim attitude only barely softened by the kids.

Tired and whiny kids stood around the yard, next to the fence, overdressed in coats and scarves; most of the staff was tired and teenaged and pregnant, except for Cassie. She still looked a little like a schoolchild, except for her eyes—which fixed on Liz and then flitted away.

Cassie flounced out to the car, got in, slammed the door without looking at Liz, and waved to a tall, overdressed man on the sidewalk. The man yelled something.

Liz pulled the car into traffic.

A short distance farther, traffic ground to a halt. It was only fourteen blocks home, something Cassie usually walked, and now Liz was sorry to have picked her up. There was some sort of accident blocks ahead, and the wagon could overheat. It generally did. She turned when she came to Eleventh Avenue.

Forced off Placer Avenue by four lanes merging into two, Liz found herself emerging from an alley unexpectedly close, almost into the front yard of the Jefferson Junior High School, next to the lot she'd parked in back in August. Next to the school she and Cassie had retreated from. It was late but some girl-women were muscling busily out—heavy makeup, gesticulating widely, grasping and hugging and dangling their books and coats. Girl-women. Able to be children for how many years, *by hiring a Cassie Hunt.*

"Now what?" snapped Cassie. "Liz, what is *with* you? You never cried for *me*, but you cry every time we pass this fucking school—"

"Please don't do this!" Liz sobbed. "Please, please Cassie—you're fourteen and you're already in a dead-end job, you're never going to climb out of this if you don't do it while you still can—please, please don't throw everything away like this—"

"Mom, stop it! Everybody's watching!"

There was an opening in traffic and Liz turned right. It was left she had needed, but she turned.

"You *are* a cold bitch!" Cassie hissed. "Doris was right. No, you don't have to worry about being stuck with me. I'm not stupid. I'll find a guy and get the hell out of here. Damn, you are crazy," she almost whispered. "You never feel anything at all. You just act!"

It was harder and harder to sleep sometimes, with finals coming up. But finals weren't really the problem.

Liz encircled the pillow with her arms, her cheek against its cool fabric. What if it were Doris—or even Eddie? Someone to talk to; just, for God's sake, someone to talk to. To tell me I'm doing okay with any part of my life. Someone to cling to. Someone to watch over me.